# SALSA NOCTURNA

ALSO BY DANIEL JOSE OLDER

**Bone Street Rumba Series**
*Half-Resurrection Blues\**
*Midnight Taxi Tango\**
*Battle Hill Bolero*
*Salsa Nocturna\**

**Young Adult Novels**
*Shadowshaper\**
*Shadowhouse Fall* (forthcoming)

**Anthologies**
*Long Hidden: Speculative Fiction from the Margins of History* (edited with Rose Fox)

*available as a JABberwocky eBook

# SALSA NOCTURNA

## A BONE STREET RUMBA COLLECTION

# DANIEL JOSÉ OLDER

Published by JABberwocky Literary Agency, Inc.

This paperback edition published by JABberwocky Literary Agency, Inc. www. awfulagent.com/ebooks

Lyrics From "The Mothafuckin' Riot" by King Impervious from the album "Red Handed Royalty" produced by Desmond Pocket. Copyright © Brooklyn Boogie Records, 2013. Used with permission.

Lyrics from "Katarsis" by Juan Santiago performed by Culebra from the album "Como mi ritmo no hay dios." Copyright © Way Down Underground Music Collective. Used with permission.

Publication History:

"Graveyard Waltz" was previously published in *The Freezine of Fantasy and Science Fiction* in 2009.

"The Collector" was previously published in The ShadowCast Audio Anthology in 2010, and in *The Freezine of Fantasy and Science Fiction* in 2010.

"Protected Entity" was previously published in *Crossed Genres Magazine* in 2010.

"Salsa Nocturna" was previously published in *Strange Horizons* in 2010.

"Tenderfoot" was previously published in *The Innsmouth Free Press* in 2011.

"Phantom Overload" was previously published in *Subversion: Science Fiction & Fantasy Tales of Challenging the Norm* by Crossed Genres Publications in 2011.

"Victory Music" was previously published in [PANK] in 2015.

Original edition edited by Kay T. Holt.

Bone Street Rumba Map by Cortney Skinner.

Interior design by Estelle Leora Malmed

Cover art by John Fisk

ISBN 978-1-625672-41-4

# TABLE OF CONTENTS

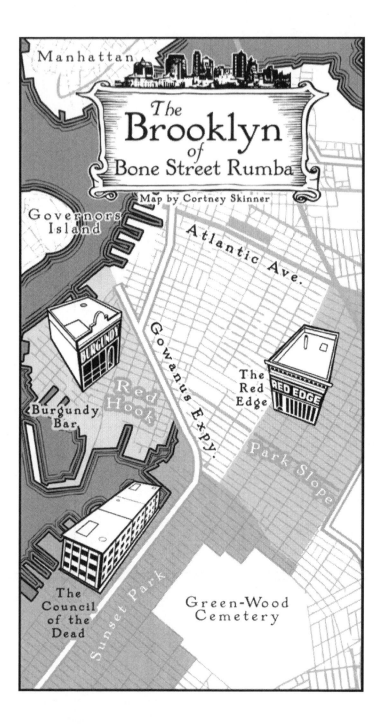

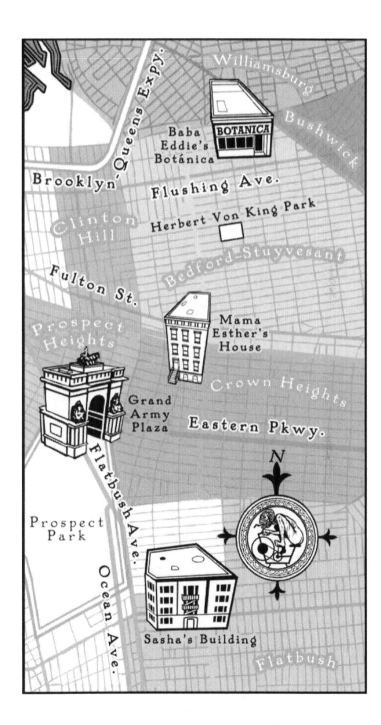

*For Dora, Marc and Malka*

Cantan
De memorias y tragedias
Valses y demonologías dispersas
Cantan para evitar
El escozor de lo que pudiera haber sido, hubiera podido
ser, si sólo
Y construir un nuevo lenguaje del quizás
Cañones de posibilidad  se abren con cada nota
Cada molécula un chance
Una esperanza o sueño apagado
Lenguas meneándose y dientes rechinando
Ojos mojados y agudos
Para detener la duda

Cantan los Muertos
Y el mundo se rompe abierto
Y desangra otro día

They sing
Of memories, tragedies,
Waltzes and scattered demonologies
They sing to ward off
The sting of might have been, could have been, if only
And build a brand new language of maybe
Canyons of possibility open with each note
Every molecule a chance,
A hope or extinguished dream
Wagging tongues and gnashing teeth,
Eyes moist and sharp,
To keep the doubt at bay
They sing, the Dead
And the world cracks open
And bleeds another day

From the song *Katarsis*
by Culebra

# INTRODUCTION TO THE ORIGINAL EDITION

In the hyperbolic world of jacket review copy, and self-congratulatory "blurb speak," we are often told that so-and-so—who once parked cars and saved starving children, who climbed Mt. Kilimanjaro with two of said children on his or her back while penning their first novel at the age of ten—is a "writer to watch" and an "up-and-coming superstar" in the world of literature and letters. Most of the time we read these descriptions and blink back a knowing smile, then flip to the author's pages (or the author's photo), wondering if the writer will live up to the advanced hokum and ballyhoo; however, in this case, all the hype is true. Really.

From the very first workshop at the now dearly missed Frederick Douglass Creative Arts Center in Manhattan, I knew—indeed, we all knew—that Daniel José Older had a magical way of writing the world. Daniel had a distinctive imagination and voice that spoke of wondrous journeys. Somewhere, somehow during his very busy and full life, this writer had parked his butt in a chair, rolled up his sleeves, and done some good work. The music, the wisdom, his compassion, and humor came through in every line of his draft of a short story called "Salsa Nocturna" at that time. It wasn't a perfect, flawless work—what newborn vision is?—but it was a vibrant, living thing that offered that "sense of wonder" readers enjoy and discuss beyond the page. We loved meeting "Gordo" and his family in a reimagined version of the city we all thought we knew. Daniel's music was a startling, strange brew of remixed New York City street songs from Harlem to Brooklyn, and like the best salsa music, it blended ancient Afro-Cuban rhythms and a wicked grasp of how a people's disparate histories can impact present and future lives in surprising ways. Who else could offer us ghostly refugee camps and gentrification in the middle of the 'hood, negrita noir and neocolonialism in the afterlife equipped with bureaucracy and spiritual red tape? Daniel imagined this, troubling the waters, and all while penning a Lovecraftian love song to New York City.

That evening we left workshop with the magic of Daniel's prose still flowing through our heads. Laughter, mixed in with a little darkness and a lot of light, is what characterized his first work. The idea that people, ordinary people are far more powerful, courageous, and brighter than they think they are is a general theme in all his pieces, and that is the wisdom that has stayed with me. The general consensus of those gathered at that very memorable first workshop session on the second floor of the NAACP building on 96th and Broadway, is that we wanted more, far more of Daniel José Older's stories. His work invited us to enter a unique world that made everyday, ordinary living seem that much more remarkable.

Much respect to this very talented writer and to all those spirited hearts and minds who supported this debut collection of short stories you're holding in your hands. Making good mojo in any art can be a tricky business, an intricate dance. Daniel José Older has captured the eclectic rhythm of New York City and reimagined it with his own special salsa.

Sheree Renée Thomas
Memphis, Tennessee
2012

Author of *Sleeping Under the Tree of Life* (Aqueduct Press, Seattle 2016) and  *Shotgun Lullabies: Stories & Poems* ("Conversation Pieces Series," Vol. 28, Aqueduct Press, Seattle 2011)

Editor of *Dark Matter: A Century of Speculative Fiction from the African Diaspora* (Warner, 2000)—Winner of the 2001 World Fantasy Award and a New York Times Notable Book of the Year and Editor of *Dark Matter: Reading the Bones* (Warner Aspect, 2004)—Winner of the 2005 World Fantasy Award

# AUTHOR'S PREFACE

It was just past eleven p.m. on December 31, 2008—that dizzy in-between time when we're not quite here but not yet there—and white kids crowded the trendy streets of Haight-Ashbury. I was in San Francisco with my family but they'd all stayed in for the night and left me to wander my old stomping grounds—I'd spent a few months here after high school, first as a bike messenger, then a waiter at Mel's Drive-In. I had stories on my mind.

I'd always been a big reader, but that year I felt like I'd rediscovered literature. I devoured all of Octavia Butler's works, Junot Díaz's *The Brief Wondrous Life of Oscar Wao*, and, in one sleepless night that felt like it somehow flew past, Walter Mosley's short story collection *Six Easy Pieces.* The literary chemical reaction of all that brilliance plus Stephen King's *On Writing* and bingewatching Cowboy Bebop set a fire inside me. Up to that point, I'd put most of my creative energy into music, although stories had always lingered at the heart of it. But something was different now. Octavia and Walter and Junot were speaking a language I'd heard all around me on the street but never read on the page, certainly not in the context of stories about aliens, detectives, or supernerds. This was a new mythology; it was permission. I'd always known I could get lost in a book; now I knew I could be found in one too.

I dipped into a brightly lit headshop for a pack of cigars and a pocket sized rum. Lit a smoke and walked back out into the street, weaving through the crowds. An old homeless guy sparechanged; some twenty-year old rich kids sparechanged. Somewhere not too far away, the darkness of the panhandle and Golden Gate Park churned and beckoned. What mysteries did it hide? What magic? What stories would come from this night?

I didn't know what being a writer meant, but I knew I loved writing. I'd always loved writing. I knew that telling stories was as essential to who I was as my own name, that stories sought me out, took shape in the air around me, poured forth when summoned.

A tall, wasted, and impeccably dressed cat with tightly wrapped locks stretching down his back addressed the festive street: *Whaddup douchebags and douchebaguettes?* A few passing revelers chuckled, but most ignored him. A blond lady rolled her eyes as if she was being hit on for like the four hundredth time tonight. *Why so serious?* He yelled into the sky. *This is the year, people! The time, she has come! People, get ready!* We made quick friends and partyhopped for a few hours. The new year entered with a few drunken yells and random objects thrown into the air. The night slid past with no major event, no fight or crisis, no sudden love affair or break up.

I came home, moved into a new place on Lexington Ave in Bed-Stuy, set up an office in the basement. I had been working graveyard shifts on the ambulance, coming home, blogging about the various disasters and doldrums of the night before. It was easy: I just wrote what happened; took a handful of minutes and the results flowed smoothly and encapsulated a tiny piece of what it's like to work at the messy crossroads of life and death. I thought: what if I just made some shit up? Then it'd be fiction, not a blog. And some little dam inside me broke. *Just tell the fucking story*, became my motto. I stopped overthinking and started writing the book that would one day become *Shadowshaper*.

During the next year, as I was amassing the first dozen of what would eventually be some forty rejections letters from agents, I took a class with Sheree Renée Thomas at the now-defunct Frederick Douglass Creative Arts Center on the Upper West Side. There, I started writing the stories that would one day become this collection. One of the first ones began like this: "It's just past eleven p.m. on December thirty-first—that dizzy in-between time when we're not quite here but not yet there—and hip young white kids crowd the trendy streets of Haight-Ashbury." Eventually, that went on to become the first chapter of *Half-Resurrection Blues*, and the Haight became Park Slope and Sunset became Prospect and that mystery hiding in the woods became an entrada, a secret entrance to the Underworld. And the Bone Street Rumba began.

Sheree midwifed that world into existence, nurtured my writing with love and precision while more rejections piled up and the publishing world started looking like that misty impossible-to-scale cliff in the Princess Bride. I kept writing. Gradually, a few small and midsized publications took my work. When I approached *Crossed Genres,* who had published two of my stories, about serializing some of the longer ones, they said, "What about a book?" Under the editorial guidance of the excellent Kay Holt, *Salsa Nocturna* grew from a bunch of stories into a coherent narrative. It was Kay, during a phonecall I will never forget, who pointed out that the book was a damn sausage party, and I got my shit together and wrote Krys and CiCi's stories, "Magdalena" and "The Passing," and then the characters took hold, as Kia Summers would later do, and started popping up again and again.

Besides the two additional stories, "Victory Music" and "Date Night", and this introduction, this new edition includes some small updates to the original texts. When I first wrote these stories, Carlos *was* the only inbetweener anyone had ever heard about. He hadn't met Sasha or the Survivors yet, he hadn't fallen in love. Except, of course, he had, I just didn't know it yet. So in the interest of series continuity and making shit work, I've made a couple changes here and there.

The fun part about writing an interconnected collection was watching the arcs and structure emerge on its own. There's no sense that any one arc needs to see itself to completion over the course of the book, so many disparate threads become their own unusual fabric. It is an ensemble production, the portrait of a community. In *Salsa*, without realizing it, I created two somewhat related worlds: one centered around Carlos, and one centered around Gordo. As with real-life communities, everyone knows someone who knows someone else who knows that guy, so all paths seem destined to lead into each other at one moment or another. Worlds collide; communities break down and re-form into brand new communities.

In my head, the sprawling map of the Brooklyn I know and love stretched for miles and miles amidst the complex tangles of power and history. Writing the world of the Bone Street Rumba meant deploying these characters into the world and letting the world do the talking. Narrative is melody, I tell my students, and worldbuilding is harmony. The stacked notes of literature, context-work allows us room to draw on all those messy intersections and imbalances that make places come to life. When I was a kid I loved those cartoon birds-eye-view maps of cities, where different sites of interest (and paying businesses) would stand out and decorative elements like balloons and trolley cars hinted at so many stories lurking beneath the surface.

We all have personal cartographies of the places we've lived; memories crowd the crossroads like ghosts: here's the corner where we stood in the rain; there's the club we played that gig and then walked the streets all night. My own maps include the many shootings, stabbings, heart attacks, and drunken disaster calls I worked over the years, plus the many walks I took with friends or alone, and that night on the brink of a brand new year, two time zones away when I roamed the streets of the Haight with a pack of cigars and pocket rum, imagining the world that would one day be the Bone Street Rumba.

Daniel José Older
Brooklyn, NY
August, 2016

# TENDERFOOT

I remember Delton Jennings. Bumped into him pretty regularly on my late night sojourns and the guy was nice enough, if you could get past the rambling and hygiene issues. But this flattened mass of flesh, blood-crusted hair and organs? They put a name tag where they guessed the foot would've been and called it a day.

The one thing that is impossible not to notice is the smell. It's not the pee-plus-beer-plus-a quarter century of body odor combo that Delton usually rocked. It's something more animal-like. As if he'd been wrestling in a zoo and lost.

I concentrate hard, watching the air around him for those little shining satellites that tell me what's going on with folks, but nothing comes. He's already been dead at least six hours and rotting in this morgue for three, so whatever memories his corpse carried could easily have fluttered away. But then, slowly, a few flashes return. It's the sound of leaves rustling; something huge moving through the underbrush. Terror courses through me—I assume it was Delton's, 'cause I don't frighten easily. I hear a high pitched shrieking—something not human. Light bursts out of the darkness and the inside of my head turns summersaults. Then everything goes black.

I'm dizzy when I open my eyes. It's not that I'd been

expecting Little Bo Peep, but dealing with this giant screeching monstrosity seems a little out of my pay grade. My creepy, translucent bosses at the Council of the Dead are gonna need to hear about all this, but there's a few more leads to check up on first.

* * *

I like to get a strong Puerto Rican coffee after I visit the morgue. It's the perfect palate cleanser for all that creepy sterility. I sip the extra-strong, extra-sweet brew out of a little paper cup as I walk up Nostrand Ave towards Eastern Parkway. I'm sure the ghostly dickheads upstairs have selected my half-dead-half-alive ass to do this job for some nefarious reason. Whatever it may be is fine by me—I have some forgetting to get busy doing, and a creepy job is the perfect distraction.

The rain keeps starting and stopping like an anxious lover who doesn't know if he should spend the night. The sky has been clouded over all day but the true evening darkness is just beginning to settle in. I finish my coffee and walk into the sloping park that's nestled between the Botanical Gardens and the library.

Brett Colson crouches like a scruffy gargoyle in his regular perch on a bench halfway up the slope. He's talking to himself, but waves at me genially as I approach.

"Bad business with Delton," I say.

It takes Brett some effort to pull away from whatever conversation he was busy with before I showed up. "Bad indeed," he finally manages.

"You see him before it happened?"

"Carlos, me and Delton been running these streets together for damn near twenty years. I seen Delton every day."

"So what's the deal?"

"I dunno, man." Brett fists up his face in disgust. "D

disappeared one night last week, showed up again reeking like he was rolling around with some circus animals. Couldn't get the smell off him."

The smell came *before* he got stomped. I have some recalculating to do. "Didn't say where he went?"

"Didn't remember. But that's not so odd for Delton. Thing is though, he actually got hisself cleaned and everything at the shelter on Fulton and still couldn't get that reek of shit and death offa him. We woulda teased him 'bout it but it was all kinda creepy. Now I'm glad we didn't."

"Damn."

"Did you know D had a dentistry degree?"

"I didn't know that."

"Yessir, went to school and everything. Had a wife and kids once upon a time too. His degree'd up ass still landed next to mine on this here park bench."

"Look how she swings."

Brett pours a swig of his bottle onto the grass and takes one himself. I wonder if Delton will turn up in the afterlife, maybe even end up back here, and keep his old drinking buddy company. You never know.

\* \* \*

Like drunk teenagers with too much toilet paper, cops have strewn that ridiculous yellow tape haphazardly across the upper park area. I find that if I act like a real dick and scowl a lot, I don't even have to flash the fake badge that the Council of the Dead gave me—the street grunts just assume I'm some high up brass they've never met and do whatever I tell them. But I'm not in a mood to take chances, so I exaggerate my grimace, lean hard on my wooden cane and flip out the silver shield. With a few arbitrary curses thrown in for good measure the two uniforms guarding the crime scene fall right into line.

You can tell the new guys 'cause they have a lot to prove. It's written all over their faces. This one's named O'Malley and he's masking how mortified he is with an exaggerated brotherhood of cops chumminess. "What's going on, Sir?" he chuckles like we're old college buddies. "Didn't know the brass wanted in on this one."

"We don't," I say curtly. I don't like forced friendliness, especially when I'm in character. "Just swinging through for a looksee. Where's the kill spot?"

O'Malley makes a I'll-take-him-you-stay-here sign to his partner, who just rolls his eyes. I follow the kid up a winding path into the darkening underbrush. "You shoulda seen the body, man," he yammers. "It was like someone ironed him." I'm too busy trying to weed out all the new-guy excitement this guy's projecting so I can focus on the crime scene. So far though, it's just your basic city park deal: The slow pulsing of plant life arching towards the sky, a flurry of insects and the scattered frenzy of midsized mammals scurrying for trash. Oh yes: And the unforgettable aura of homelessness—that pungent, lived-in clothes desolation.

"Here we go, boss." O'Malley waves his light over a dark stain on the path. "This is where the bum got done." I scowl at him and walk up close to where Delton's blood is slowly absorbing into the cement. Forensics teams and the urban wilderness have swallowed up most of the useful details. A few candy wrappers and beer bottles lay scattered around, remnants of Delton's last supper no doubt, and a little further away there's a used condom and an old hat. None of this is particularly helpful. I take a step into the total darkness of the underbrush. It's here I realize that there's something else odd about the park tonight. It'd been bothering me since I stepped in but I couldn't put my finger on it, like a humming you don't notice until it stops. There's no ghosts here. Usually any city park hosts a whole cross section of spirits. This park's particularly alive with the dead; you can see 'em fluttering in their strange circles like glow bugs anytime after sunset. Well, I can anyway. But tonight, it's like an empty school house. A silence so deep it curls up inside my ears.

Then, all at once, I'm inundated by a rush of thick, pungent wind. The trees around me tremble and send up a mournful shushing. Back on the path, O'Malley shifts his weight uneasily from one foot to the other. The leaves convulse more frantically. I hear the snapping of branches. Something huge is moving very quickly towards us.

I smell it before I see it; that same old-feces-circus-tent stench from the body. O'Malley yells and I duck as three gunshots ring out behind me. There's a flurry of motion—the huge, fast thing lets out its deafening shriek and thunders towards us. It's only a fuzzy flicker—tall as a two story building, long matted hair and all shiny transparent like a jellyfish. It bursts out of the trees and knocks me on my ass.

For the first year after my death, I got the heebie-jeebies each time I rolled up on some runaway spook. In time, I got used to it, and I haven't felt much of anything for quite a while. This situation, on the other hand, has reached some place deep inside of me and crushed all that cool-headed resolve. *Find out what's going on*, the Council message had said. Okay, I found out: There's a huge hairy freak show in the park. Done. I hear that inhuman shriek mixed with the wet crunching sound that's probably the end of Officer O'Malley. I don't look back, don't think. I just run. I don't stop running 'til I reach my friend Victor's spot in Crow Hill. I ring the bell until I collapse in a heap on his doorstep and only then do I realize I'm bleeding.

* * *

"Really, babe? Penicillin? You gotta be fucking kidding me."

"You can't crush up some aloe, love muffin, and make this all go away, okay? That gash is deep as shit."

"Oh, is that all I do? Crush up some aloe? Victor, I swear to god, if Carlos wasn't here bleeding all over my couch, I would stab you in the neck."

It's comforting really, the gentle love-hate routine that Victor and his girl Jenny banter back and forth over me. I wake up smiling, in spite of the dull throbbing in my flank. The brand new thing called terror is a faraway echo.

"He's awake. Put the kettle on, Vic."

"You're the tea-master general, you put the kettle on."

"Victor..." There's a serious threat in Jenny's voice. It might be the threat of no ass for a month, but whatever it is, it works. When I open my eyes, it's Jenny's calm, slender face that's looking down at me. She's one of these new age urban herbalist types, straight out of Minnesota or Ohio or somewhere, by way of some fancy liberal arts school. In spite of it all, she's grown on me. Victor's a paramedic with the FDNY. The combination makes for some fiery dinner-time showdowns about the best way to manage a broken bone but the make-up sex is sensational, from what I can hear one room over.

"You're gonna be alright, Carlos," Jenny says. "I'll keep Victor busy making tea so he can't get to you with any of those synthetic death medications."

"Actually, synthetic death medication sounds like it might really hit the spot right now," I say. When I sit up it sends splintering pain down my right side.

"Lay down," Jenny scowls. "And shut up. I'll let you know when dinner's ready."

\* \* \*

Dinner is fake chicken mixed with something green called kale but I eat it anyway.

"You gonna tell us what happened?" Victor asks. By the way he gets a little rounder each time I visit, I'm guessing he still sneaks in a few pernil sandwiches during those long nights on the ambulance.

"Probably not," I say.

"Really, you should go to a hospital, man. That wound is nasty."

"You know damn well I can't do that." We have this argument almost every time I show up at their door with some otherworldly injury. My heart barely beats at all. My complexion is a dull brownish gray. Medically speaking, I'm all but dead—a partially resurrected, gimp-legged half-wraith. Treatment at a hospital would mean answering far more questions than I care to. Much easier to just come here, where I only say what I need to and get some form of dinner on top of it.

"What's up with the elephants?" Jenny asks. I look at her with raised eyebrows. "Elephants. You wouldn't shut up about them when you were writhing around on our couch." She flails her arms in the air and affects some version of a Spanish accent. 'Oh, the elephants! Estop the elephants! Oh!"

"Okay," I say. "I got it. I have no idea what you're talking about." But my mind is racing. Is that what I saw flashing out of the underbrush?

"That's what did this to you?" Victor gapes. "I've never had an elephant injury before."

"No," I say. "It was...hairy." The frenzied memories aren't leaving me with much information to go with. "It was huge and hairy and stank. That's all I got."

"The Hindus believe that elephants used to be able to fly," Victor informs me. "Until one of them fell out of tree onto a great meditating sage and he cursed away their wings."

"Whoopee," Jenny says. "I know how to Google too."

Victor grunts.

"Elephants," I say, retreating deeper and deeper into my mind. "Elephants." I look up at Jenny and Victor. "Can I use your phone?"

* * *

When the regular old fully dead Council agents want to get in touch with headquarters, they just use that special afterlife telepathy shit and it's done. My half-and-half ass has to use the phone. I receive all their irritating updates and directives perfectly clearly—comes through like a radio blasting inside my head, but for whatever reason, it doesn't work the other way. They rigged up a phone line and answering machine somewhere in that vast, misty warehouse they've taken over in Sunset Park. I call the number, leave my message and wait for the reply to blare through my skull.

"It's Delacruz," I say (as if anyone else calls them on that line). "Updating on the Delton Jennings park murder. Checking on a possible link to a phantom pachyderm." I feel stupid saying that, but it sounds better than 'ghost elephant.' "Check and advise on any recent circus or zoo fires. Also: An Officer O'Malley with the NYPD was injured or killed earlier while I was at the scene. Advise on status. That's all." Is that all? Is it ever all? I hate updating. I hang up and sit on the bloodstained couch to wait.

The reply takes a little longer than usual. When it does come, it rustles me from a troubled nap. *Council of the Dead to Agent Delacruz.* A dull ache begins to spread across my forehead. *Your orders are to detain but not destroy the subject. Do not, under any circumstances, damage the ghost pachyderm.*

I hate my job.

*Capture it and bring it to headquarters. That is all.*

I don't know if I can all the way die or not, but I have a

feeling I'm about to find out. Just the thought of going anywhere near the park sends a shudder through me.

"I'm out," I say, poking my head into the kitchen.

"You're not even better yet!" Victor says.

It's true; my flank still burns every time I move. I shrug and then scowl in pain.

"See?" Jenny says. "Just lay back down on the couch for a few hours."

I shake my head. "Thanks for dinner."

"You're a pain in the ass."

\* \* \*

Since they can't be trusted with full missions, kids who turn up in the afterlife end up wandering around the city aimlessly, running errands or causing mischief. It's a bleak existence. You can usually catch them floating around the industrial south Brooklyn wastelands, not far from Council headquarters. That's where they congregate, like tiny shiny bored teenagers, wasting infinities of time and waiting for some spook to send them on an errand in exchange for toys or candy.

"You there," I say as I wave down a passing ghost child. "You like cowboys?" The kid wanders over glumly, eyeing me. I produce some small plastic figures from my coat pockets. I usually carry a handful of cheap doodads around for just this purpose. The kid's unimpressed.

"Not really," he says. He looks to be about five, maybe an underdeveloped six.

"Breath mints?" I say, digging deeper in my pockets.

"Uh-uh." The kid shakes his head.

"Dice? Rubix Cube?"

"Nope."

"Look I need a message delivered. What you want for it?"

"Try ten bucks."

"Smartass."

"Or a gear shift."

I raise one eyebrow.

"Like from a car. Leave the wiring on, please. Who the message go to?"

I give him a folded up piece of paper. "Agent Riley Washington, COD."

"Ooh, an agent? Must be important. Why don't you throw in a fan belt to make sure it doesn't get to the wrong person?"

"Why don't you do what you're told so I don't go find some other wee dead thing that'll do it for free? What are you building anyway?"

"Nonya."

"What's a nonya?"

"Nonya damn business, man. Go get my shit and Riley will get his."

This is why I don't like kids. I scowl down at little man and head off to find an old car to break into.

* * *

When something sinister seems to be brewing at the Council of the Dead, Riley is the dude I politic with. They usually partner him up with me on assignments, and he's the closest thing to a friend I've got in the Underworld. Also—he has an uncanny ability to wreak havoc on authority figures and an entire network of like-minded phantoms scattered throughout the Council that he goes to for information.

He materializes next to me at the Burgundy Bar. The Burgundy Bar is a rundown saloon in Red Hook owned by a one-eyed drunk named Quiñones. It's mostly a bunch of dazed alcoholics in there, so no one pays much mind when I sit at the bar carrying on a full conversation over drinks with someone that ain't there. Long as Quiñones gets his little package of twenties at the end of each month, courtesy of the COD, he's perfectly happy ignoring whatever hints of supernatural activity sputter up at our after-hours spot.

"What'd you find out?" I mutter at the gently glowing apparition beside me.

The drunks can't see or hear Riley, and he enjoys taking full advantage of the situation. "Found out you stepped into another dead people clusterfuck," he says loudly. "Get me a Henney."

I nod at Quinones. "A Hennessy for my friend." He winks at me like I'm some happy idiot and busies himself with my order.

"It wasn't an elephant," Riley says. He loves knowing shit I don't.

"What the fuck was it then?"

"I got a guy coming, Dr. Calloway. He's gonna fill us in on some shit."

"What's the word on O'Malley?"

"The cop that got squashed?" Riley lets out a belly laugh.

"He got *squashed*-squashed?" I say. "Or just kinda squashed?"

"No, he gonna make it," Riley chuckles. "But the thing got his shooting arm. Looked like God took a spatula to it. Just flat and splayed out. Like Wile E. Fucking Coyote."

"Wow."

"They had to take it off. He's got early retirement, line of duty compensation, and now your freakazoid park killing is big news. Press all over it. Major Crimes Division investigating. A hot mess."

A sparkly, bearded form fizzles into existence in the barstool next to Riley. "Carlos, meet the good Doctor Calloway." The ghost nods and looks around nervously. "Doc, thanks for joining us today. You will note, no afterlifers besides us two are present and everyone else is drunk as fuck and can't see you. You can speak freely."

Calloway nods again. His fingers fiddle endlessly on the bar. "What's the what?" I say.

"The what," Doctor Calloway says, "is that the Council of the Dead is engaged in the systematic categorization of all things phantom."

"This we knew," I say. "Get to it."

"Which includes building a secret zoological theme park for the afterlife."

"A ghost zoo?" I say.

"Essentially," agrees the doctor. "For the purposes of both study and entertainment. And they are particularly interested in tracking down specimens that haven't previously been analyzed."

"Eh?"

"Meaning, things that were around before we had the ability or technology to really find much out."

"Extinct shit," Riley explains.

"It's all very sinister, really," Calloway says. "Like a prehistoric Noah's ark."

"Charming," I say. "So my friend in the park?"

"*Mammuthus primigenius,*" says the doctor.

"You tangled with a wooly motherfucking mammoth," Riley translates.

I order three shots of rum. "It seems," the doctor continues, "that certain species continue to move in migratory cycles even centuries after they are extinct. The COD charted a pattern of savage disasters—unexplained building collapses, mysteriously crushed vehicles."

"Flat dudes," Riley adds.

"All bearing the unmistakable stench common to longdead pachyderms, left like footprints behind the stampede. The Council calculated a few routes and determined when the herd would be passing through our fine city."

I down all three shots in quick succession. "Go on."

"Their team of forensic zoologists, of which I am occasionally a participant, proposed that the ancient pachyderm may share a common behavioral trait with the modern elephant: An almost fanatical protective drive in relationship to their young."

Riley's looking ornery about me hogging all the shots so I order two more and give him one. "Using a method too complicated to get into right now, they secured a sample of baby mammoth dung."

"Then they kidnapped a vagrant that no one would miss," I put in, "and covered him in it."

"Precisely!" exclaims Calloway, looking a little too impressed with the whole thing. "Turns out, mammoths were very attuned to scent. They could tell what kind of mammoth it was that produced the feces, how old, whether it was an ill mammoth or healthy one, all kinds of information."

"Fascinating," Riley says.

"Fascinating indeed," the doctor nods.

"So a ghost momma mammoth returns to the park after the herd passes through," I say. "She's thinking she'll find a stray ghost baby mammoth there and take him along."

"Instead she finds Delton Jennings," says Riley, "and makes a bum pancake."

"But why's she still there?" I ask.

"Once she was inside," Calloway explains, "the COD put the area on a kind of spiritual lock down. She is trapped within the boundaries of the park."

I slam my hand on the bar, perhaps a little harder than is really necessary. "That's why there were no ghosts in the park! She scared them all out." A few drunks look over at me with their shut-the-fuck-up faces and I settle down.

"Only trouble is, they had to put down such heavy barriers to hold her, now nothing dead can get in or out. It's a no-go zone for ghosts. If they take them down to go in, she'll make a break for it before they can subdue her."

"Leave it to the Council to come up with a plan so brilliant that it doesn't work," Riley chuckles.

"That's where I come in," I say. "*Detain but don't destroy the subject.* Send the halfie in to catch the momma, cut open the damn boundary from the inside and lure her right into their little Underworld entranceway in Prospect Park. Fuckers got me doing their dirty work again."

"That's your job," Riley reminds me.

I grunt. "Where's the rest of the herd?"

"Oh," Calloway throws his translucent arms up in the air. "They're long gone, stampeded out across the Atlantic Ocean a few days ago."

"Great." I finish my drink, grab my walking stick and head for the door.

"Where you off to?" Riley calls after me.

"Gotta sleep off this rum and figure out what the fuck to do."

\* \* \*

I wake up the next afternoon to the sound of Victor and Jenny's grunting, passionate reconciliation. It's almost as comforting as their bickering—a sweaty, breathless reminder of life amidst all this death. Outside, the sky flirts with the beginnings of night. I'm trying not to think about my date with the giant prehistoric ghost in the park, but it's not working. I'm not comfortable being on the same planet with that thing, not to mention subduing it. And I like even less the thought of turning it over to the Council's probing curiosity. But Riley's right: It is my job. I let myself out quietly, without disturbing the festivities and head to the Puerto Rican spot for my coffee.

The park is mostly shadows. A few sad lamps let off eerie glows; pathetic little constellations that reach out into the woods. Now that I'm expecting it, the lack of anything supernatural at all is jarring, a scream of white noise. How do the living bear it? I wrap my fingers around the walking stick which conceals my ghost-killing blade. It is my only comfort right now, and I pray that I won't have to use it.

The police grunts are gone but, as if to prove their utter disregard for the rest of the world, they've left behind a little makeshift cop memorial to O'Malley's arm. It features a few corny snapshots of him, a candle and some empty liquor bottles. If I hadn't promised myself that I'd walk as slowly and calmly as possible, I would scatter it into the weeds. I make each move matter; inch forward at an agonizing pace. The momma will come, but she won't come angry. I find my spot, a few feet from Delton's grisly stain, and wait.

\* \* \*

I wake up from pleasant dreams of a beautiful dark skinned Puerto Rican woman who only wants to stare into my eyes, and find I'm looking directly into a tower of ghostly fur. Momma mammoth has arrived. She's standing about five feet away, studying me. I close my eyes again; make a concentrated effort to suppress the urge to run and vomit at the same time. I breathe deeply until my heart rate returns to the melancholic six beats a minute that I'm used to. I open my eyes again and she's still there. She raises her furry trunk towards me. I let it explore my whole body. The trunk makes little snorts as it probes my cane, then proceeds up to my face. It's wet and smells foul like Delton did. But I am alive. She's not trampling me, yet. Perhaps the rage has subsided some.

Slowly, I raise my hand out, palm to the sky. The snout snorfles its way through my fingers and then retreats back to its owner, apparently satisfied. "I'm going to take you out of here," I say very slowly. "I'm going to break the barrier." She just stares at me, her humongous body rising and falling like a furry tide. "To find your herd." Maybe I'm imagining things, but she appears to perk up a little. Her breath quickens. Of course, she was alive millions of years before anyone thought to say 'herd,' but a halfie can hope.

I take a step backwards, beckoning with my hands. "C'mon," I say in the friendliest voice I can muster. "Come to the edge. I'll take you to freedom." It's hard to say that word, knowing that where I really have to take her is quite the opposite of freedom, but I'm trying to push that out of my head for now. Getting all sappy doesn't make this job any easier. "C'mon, Mama."

I think what really gets me is her first step forward. I keep cooing, "C'mon, Mamma, come to freedom," but by the time we've reached a full stride towards the edge of the park, tears are streaming down my face. I will never be able to explain why. We keep walking along, a strange night procession through the park; me crying and cooing, waving my hands in little circles towards myself and the ghost mammoth lumbering along cautiously.

When we reach the stone wall around the park I try to collect myself. I wipe my eyes with my sleeves like some chick on a talk show and take a few deep breaths so I can stop making those damn little hiccupy sobs. "I'm sorry," I say to the mammoth. "It's been a rough week." She's glaring furiously at the Council's force field. Surely, she has already made more than a few unpleasant attempts to escape.

I pull my spirit-killing blade out of its walking stick sheath and the she-mammoth lets out that ear-shattering shriek and rears up. Her legs kick the air a few inches from my face. I take two steps back and slash behind me with the blade, trying to feel out the damn force field. I'm cutting air. She lands and I swear New York must be registering a minor earthquake. Her tusks are aimed right at me, two great translucent curved swords reaching out to run me through. She stomps forward.

I slash some more, and finally feel that satisfying pressure against the blade that means I've found my mark. The force field gives way, ripping open around us. The great ancient matron stops mid-charge and regards the air that was once her prison wall. A crowd of relieved phantom park critters trickles back in through the new tear. The mammoth watches them scuttle past and then she looks at me. I make a show of sheathing my blade and step over the wall so she sees it's alright.

"See?" I say. "It's safe now. C'mon. Come over. You're free. You're going home." Damnit—the word home chokes me up again but I recover quickly. She's huffing and puffing as she reaches her trunk cautiously towards the wall. When nothing happens she takes a step forward. Then another. "C'mon, ma, c'mon," I say. She lumbers out and then we're standing on Eastern Parkway at four o'clock in the morning, me and my new friend the momma mammoth.

I'm trying to figure out how we're gonna make it to Prospect Park when I feel her warm trunk wrap tightly around my waist. Panic sweeps across me like floodwaters. I can't breathe. I can't move. I can't even see straight. The whole world turns upside down and then I'm deposited gently onto her mountainous back, looking down on the street. I catch my breath and right myself, reaching one leg down along either side of her body. If God or whoever brought me back to life just so I could live this moment, it was worth it. I take two firm fistfuls of ghostly fur and the momma mammoth jolts into a run. Without regard for which streets are populated or who might see us, she barrels headlong down the parkway.

The Council of the Dead has a very strict rule: Do not involve humans. Don't fuck with their lives, don't appear to them if you're a ghost, don't let on that you can see ghosts if you're not one. In short: Leave the greatest mystery of the afterlife a damn mystery. But the Council of the Dead also kidnapped Delton

Jennings, covered him in mammoth shit and sent him off to be trampled. So if tonight a few nocturnal stragglers are startled to see a dapper and ecstatic gray-skinned Puerto Rican fly past with tears in his eyes, I could really give a damn.

The wind ripples fiercely around me, cleansing me of all doubt and indecision. What is left is pure exhilaration. We gallop down the Parkway, cut a left across Grand Army Plaza and burst like a furry ghost rocket into Prospect Park. We rush towards the turnoff that would lead to the waiting arms of the Council and their infinite imprisonment. I could urge the mammoth that way. She trusts me now. Instead, I smile as we thunder past.

The Park is alive around us. The morning birds twitter a high pitched symphony and the city forest ghosts erupt into a flurry of activity as we pass. We break out of the wilderness and speed down Ocean Parkway at a steady ass-breaking cantor, through Midwood, Gravesend and over the Belt Parkway. Ahead is the infinite Atlantic darkness. I take a deep breath of ocean air and laugh out loud. Some doofy joggers pass and try to ignore me, the crazy laughing man floating in the corners of their eyes.

When we hit sand, she's walking. Her body heaves up and down beneath me. I pat her gratefully. Then I grab hold of some fur, dangle down along her wooly flank and drop onto the beach. Side by side, we stroll to the edge of the water. I imagine a whole army of ghost mammoths, thundering out across the waves somewhere, but all I see is darkness and a few stars. I don't have to tell her to go on now; after a brief pause, momma mammoth launches herself out onto the water. I plant my ass in the sand, light a cigar, and watch her flickering glow disappear into the night. There will be hell to pay in the morning—eyebrows raised, forms to fill out, suspicious interrogations. But all that is tomorrow. Tonight, for the first time since I died, I feel alive.

# SALSA NOCTURNA

People say that all geniuses die in the gutter, and I've made my peace with that, but this is ridiculous. Anyway, it's a boiler room, but let me start at the beginning: The whole gigging around at late night bars and social clubs really began drying up right around the time the great white flight did a great white about face. Mosta my main night spots shut down or started serving cappuccino instead of El Presidente. Two of my guys moved to PA. Things were looking kinda grim, to be honest with you. I mean, me—I knew it'd work out in the long run—it's not that I'm an optimist, I just know certain things—but meanwhile, the short run was kicking my ass. Kicking all our asses, really.

So when my son's girl Janey came to me about this gig at the overnight center, I had to pay her some mind. Janey's a special kid, I gotta say. I couldn't ask for a better woman for Ernesto either. She keeps him in line, reminds him, I think, where he is from, that he's more than that fancy suit he puts on every morning. And she makes us all laugh with that mouth of hers too. Anyway, she comes to me one morning while I'm taking my morning medicina with my café con leche and bacon, eggs and papas fritas. I always take my high blood pressure pills with a side of bacon or sausage, you know, for balance.

"Gordo", she says. My name is Ernesto, just like my son, but everyone calls me Gordo. It's not 'cause I'm fat. Okay, it's 'cause I'm fat. "Gordo," she says, "I want you to come interview at this place I work on Lorimer." You see what she did? She made it look like I would be doing her the favor. Smart girl, Janey.

I eyed her coolly and put some more bacon in me. "They need someone to watch the kids at night and later on, maybe you can teach music in the mornings."

"Kids?" I said. "What makes you think I want to have anything to do with kids?"

\* \* \*

There's two kinds of people that really are drawn to me: Kids and dead people. Oh yeah, and crackheads on the street but that hardly counts because they obviously have an agenda. Kids seek me out like I'm made of candy. They find me and then they attach themselves to me and they don't let go. Maybe it's because I don't really buy into that whole, 'Aren't they cute?' shit. I just take 'em as they come. If I walk onto a playground, and I swear to you I'm never the instigator, it's like some memo goes out: Drop whatever game you're playing and come chase the fat guy. Family events and holidays? Forget it. I don't really mind because I hate small talk, and if there's one thing about kids, they give it to you straight: "Tío Gordo, why you so big?"

And I get real serious looking. "Because I eat so many children," I say.

Then they run off screaming and, usually, I give chase until I start wheezing.

It beats *How's the music business?* and *Oh, really? How interesting!* Because really and truly, I don't care how everyone's little seed is doing at CUNY or whatever.

I'm not bragging but even teenagers like me. They don't

admit it most of the time, but I can tell. They're just like overgrown, hairy five year olds anyway. Also, notoriously poor small talkers.

\* \* \*

Janey told me exactly how it would go down and exactly what to say. She's been doing this whole thing for a while now, so she speaks whitelady-ese like a pro. She had this Nancy lady down pat too, from the extra-extra smile to the cautious handshake to the little sing-song apologies dangling off every phrase. Everything went just like she said it would. The words felt awkward in my mouth, like pieces of food that're too big to chew, and I thought that Nancy was on to me right up until she says, "That sounds terrific, Mr. Cortinas."

"You can call me Gordo," I say.

\* \* \*

It's called a non-profit but everyone at the office is obviously making a killing. The kids are called *minority* and *emotionally challenged*, but there's a lot more of them and they show a lot more emotions than the staff. It's a care facility, but the windows are barred. The list goes on and on, but still, I like my job. The building's one of these old gothic numbers on the not-yet-gentrified end of Lorimer. Used to be an opera house or something, so it's still got all that good, run-down music hall juju working for it. I show up at 9 p.m. on the dot, because Janey said my sloppy Cuban time won't cut it here so just pretend I'm supposed to be there at 8 and I'll be alright. And it works.

They set up a little desk for me by a window on the fifth floor. Outside I can see the yard and past that a little park. I find that if I smoke my Malagueñas in the middle of the hallway, the smell lingers like an aloof one-night stand 'til the morning and I get a stern/apologetic talking to from Nancy and then a curse-out from Janey. So, I smoke out the window.

It's a good thing that most of the kids are already sleeping by the time I arrive, because even as it is I can feel my presence course through the building like an electrical current. I can't help it. Occasionally a little booger will get up to make a number 1 or number 2 and not want to go back to bed. I make like I'm gonna slap 'em and they scatter back to their rooms. Soon they'll be on to me though.

* * *

A little after midnight, the muertos show up. They're always in their Sunday best, dressed to the nines, as they say, in pinstriped suits and fancy dresses. Some of them even have those crazy Spanish flamenco skirts on. They wear expensive hats and white gloves. While the children sleep, the muertos gather around my little desk on the fifth floor foyer and carry on. Mostly they dance, but a few of them bring instruments: Old wooden guitars and basses, tambores, trumpets. Some of them show up with strange ones that I've never seen before—African, I think—and then I have to figure out how to transpose whatever-it-is into the piano/horn section arrangement I'm used to.

Look, their music is close enough to what I'd write anyway, so either they're some part of my subconscious or it's a huge supernatural coincidence—really, what are the chances? So either way I don't feel bad jotting down the songs. Besides, I started bringing my own little toy store carry-along keyboard and accompanying them. 'Course I keep the volume low so as not to wake up the little ones.

There's a jangle to the music of the dead. I mean that certain something that's so happy and so sad at the same time.

The notes almost make a perfect harmony but don't. Then they do but quickly crash into dissonance. They simmer in that sweet in-between, rhythm section rattling along all the while. Chords collapse chaotically into each other, and just when you think it's gonna spill into total nonsense, it stands back up and comes through sweet as a lullaby on your mami's lips. Songs that'll make people tap their feet and drink melancholically but not realize the twisting genius lurking within until generations later. That's the kind of music I make, and the dead do too. We make it together.

\* \* \*

But tonight, the muertos didn't show up. They never scared me. If anything they kept me company in those wee hours. But this? This silence, made me shiver and feel both like I was being watched by a thousand unfriendly eyes and all alone in the world. I looked down that empty hallway. Tried to imagine my brand-new-long-lost friends making their shadowy way up towards me, but it remained empty.

Just to have something to do, I made the rounds. Each troubled young lump in its curled up spot. Some nights when I don't feel like doing my music, I read their files. Their twisted little sagas unwind through evaluation forms and concerned emails. Julio plays with himself at meal times. Devon isn't allowed near mirrors on the anniversary of his rape. Tiffany hides knives in case the faceless men come back for her. But night after night, they circle into themselves like those little curl-up bugs and drift off into sleep.

One bed, though, was empty. The cut out construction paper letters on the door spelled MARCOS. A little Ecuadorian kid, if I recall correctly. Untold horrors. Rarely speaks. The muertos being gone was bad in a supernatural, my immortal soul kind of way and Marcos being gone was bad in a frowning Nancy in the morning, lose my job kind of way, and I wasn't really sure which was worse. I turned and walked very quickly back down the hallway. First I spot-checked all the rooms I'd already passed just in case little man was crouching in one of the corners unnoticed. But I knew he wasn't. I knew wherever Marcos was, there would be a whole lot of swaying shrouds with him. Remember, I told you sometimes I just know stuff? This was one of those things. Besides, I don't believe in coincidence. Not when kids and the dead are involved.

When I got to the end of the hallway, I stood still and just panted and sweated for a minute. That's when I heard the noise coming from one of the floors below. It was barely there, a ghost of a sound really, and kept fading and coming back. Like the little twinkling of a music box, far, far away.

\* \* \*

To the untrained eye, I appear bumbling. You can see my blood vessels strain tight to support my girth. These hands are ungainly and callused. For a man who makes such heart-wrenching, subtle melodies, I am not delicate. But if you were to watch me in slow-mo, you would then understand that, really, I am a panther. A slow, overweight panther, perhaps, but still, there is a fluidity to me—a certain poise. I flowed, gigantic and cat-like, down the five flights of stairs to the lobby, pausing at each landing to catch my breath and check for signs of stroke or heart attack. Infarto, in Spanish, so that in addition to perhaps dying you have the added discomfort of it sounding like you were laid low by a stinky shot of gas.

The lobby is covered in posters that are supposed to make the children feel better about having been abused and discarded. Baby animals snuggle amidst watercolor nature drawings. It's a little creepy. The noise was still coming from somewhere down below, definitely the basement. I wasn't thrilled about this, was hoping the muertos had simply gathered in the lobby (perhaps to enjoy the inspirational artwork) but can't say I was surprised either. I opened the old wooden door that leads down the last flight of stairs and took a deep breath. Each step registered my presence unenthusiastically. At the bottom, I reached into the darkness 'til my hand swatted a dangling chain. The bulb was dim. It cast uneven light on a cluttered universe of broken furniture, file cabinets and forgotten papier-mâché projects.

I followed the noise through the shadows. I could now make it out definitively to be a melody; a lonely, minor key melody, beautiful like a girl with one eye standing outside a graveyard. I rounded a corner and then held perfectly still. Before me hovered all my friends, the muertos, with their backs turned to me. I tried to see past them but they were crowded together so densely it was impossible. Ever so quietly, I crept forward among them, their chilly undead shadows sending tiny earthquakes down my spine.

The muertos were gathered around a doorway. I entered and found myself in this dank boiler room. At the far end, little Marcos sat calmly in a niche of dusty pipes and wiring. He held my carry-along in his lap. His eyes were closed and his fingers glided up and down the keys. Between myself and Marcos, about thirty muertecitos bobbed up and down, their undivided attention on the boy. You know, I never think much about those who die as children, what their wandering souls must deal with. Who watches over them, checks on those small, curly-bug lumps at night? The ghost children were transfixed; I could feel their love for this boy and his music as surely as I felt the pulse pounding in my head.

And, to be quite honest with you, at first I too found myself lost in the swirling cascade of notes coming from my little keyboard. It is rare that I feel humbled, rarer still by a ten year old, but I'm not above admitting it. The song filled the heavy boiler room air, so familiar and so brand-new. It was a mambo, but laced with the saddest melody I've ever heard—some unholy union of Mozart, Coltrane and Perez Prado that seemed to speak of many drunken nights and whispered promises. It tore into me, devoured me and pieced me back together a brand new man.

* * *

But now the song has ended, breaking the quiet reverie we had all fallen into and ripping open a great painful vacancy where it once had been. I'm strong, and not the addictive type, so I shake my head and welcome myself back to the strange silence. But the muerte

citos are not so quick to move on. A furious rustling ripples through their ranks, and the small, illuminated shadows nudge towards Marcos. The boy finally looks up and turns to me, eyes wide. He starts to play the song again, but he's afraid now. His heart's not in it and the ghostlings can tell. They continue their urgent sway, a tough crowd, and begin to edge closer to him.

I carry a few saints with me and I find more often than not, they do their part. They tend to really come through when my more basic human instincts, like caution, fail. This is definitely one of those times. I surge (cat-like) through the crowd of wily young ghosts. Their cool tendrils cling to me like cobwebs but I keep moving. I scoop up little man and his living body feels so warm against me compared to all that death. He's still clutching the keyboard. Eyes squeezed shut. His little heart sends a pitter-patter pulse out like an SOS.

I decide if I pause to consider the situation around me, I may come to my senses, which would definitely mean an icy, uncomfortable death for myself and Marcos. So I make like a running back—fake left, swerve right (slowly, achingly, but gracefully) and then just plow down the middle. They're more ready for me this time, and angrier. The air is thick with their anger; any minute the wrong molecule might collide and blow the whole place up. Also, I didn't gain quite the momentum I'd hoped to. I can feel all that stillness reach far inside me, penetrate my most sacred places, throw webs across my inner shrines, detain my saints. I realize I might not make it.

But there is more music to write. I won't be around to see my legacy honored properly, but I have a few more compositions in me before I can sleep. Also, I enjoy my family and Saturday nights playing dominos with the band after rehearsal and my morning café con leche, bacon, eggs, papas fritas and sometimes sausage. Young Ernesto who's not so young and whatever crazy creation him and Janey will come up with in their late night house-rocking—there are still things I would like to see. Also, this little fellow in my arms seems like he may have a long, satisfying career ahead of him. A little lonely perhaps, but musical genius can be an all-consuming friend until you know how to tame her. I have room under my wing here, I realize as I plow through this wee succubus riot, and many things to tell young Marcos. Practical things—things they don't teach you about in books or grad school.

Is trundle a word? It should be. I trundle through those creatures, tearing their sloppy ice tentacles from my body. The door comes up on me quicker than I thought it would, catches me a little off guard, and I'm so juiced-up thinking of all the beautiful and sad truths I will tell Marcos when we survive that I just knock it out of my way. I don't stop to see how the mama and papa muertos feel about the situation; I move through them quick.

At the corner I glance back. An intervention of some kind seems to be taking place. The muertos have encircled their young. I can only suppose what must be happening, but I'd like to believe it's a solid scolding, an ass beating like the one I would've gotten from Papi (God rest his troubled soul) if I'd trapped one of my younger brothers in the basement and made like I was gonna end him.

* * *

When we reach the c'mon-get-happy lobby, I notice that dawn is edging out onto the streets. Marcos's song must've been longer than I realized. I put the boy down, mostly because I'm losing feeling in the lower half of my body and my shirt is caked in sweat. Wrap my fat hand around the banister and slowly, languidly, huff and puff up the stairs behind him. I pause on the landing, listen to the quick, echoing tak-tak-tak of his footfalls bound up the next three flights. He will be curled in his bed by the time I reach the second floor, asleep by sunrise. At six, the morning crew will come in, smiles first, and I will chuckle with them nonchalantly about the long, uneventful night.

Tomorrow evening, as I show my new student a few tricks to keep his chops up, my friends will return. In their Sunday best, they will slither as always from the shadows of the fifth floor hallway. And this time, they will bring their young along with them.

# DATE NIGHT

A phonecall breaks the spell; I'm equal parts shattered and relieved. The music swings along like a graceful monster—something from another world but something I've always somehow ached to hear—and Charlotte's hand stays pressed against my thigh, but the whole room recedes some as I register which phone it is that's ringing.

"Reza?" Charlotte's hoarse, hushed voice reaches me through the thunder of drums and horns.

My face crinkles at the screen, a sudden bright beacon in the dim club. *Sasha.* There's no reason for her to be calling my work number.

"Sasha from the lighthouse? With the twins?" Charlotte unabashedly peering over my shoulder. I don't mind; it's brought her warm body even closer to mine. I nod. The music simmers than builds. "You're not gonna—?"

I pocket the phone, pull Charlotte closer to me then bring my face up to hers.

It's our third date, first kiss. First kiss with Charlotte; first kiss since Angie. This new Reza is slow. Once on the prowl, all sizzling fingertips and the raw mastery of timing, it took me almost sixty years to finally grow old and when it happened it happened overnight.

Charlotte tastes like pineapple juice and spearmint gum

and some musky body oil with the slightest hint of chronic from a joint she smoked earlier. No hint of the musty library she works in—she is fresh. I probably taste like this rum & Coke and mouthwash. At first, my wavering imagination circles the club, wondering which faces gawk, which corners of whose eyes catch us, who can't be bothered. The saxophone brings me back. It's that huge one, the baritone. The woman playing it unleashes a series of ferocious raspy blurts and the whole band stops and then falls back in around her as Charlotte's lips become the whole world. I pull her closer. My hand slides down her cheek; wandering fingertips insinuate all the things I will one day do to her body; they chance a suggestion: *maybe tonight*, and then we both sit back and she glares at me with a slight smile and one eyebrow raised.

"Well," she says, sipping her juice.

"Well indeed," I mutter, the old Reza teasing at the edge of my skin, threatening to emerge. We could leave now, reach my place within an hour and be naked by midnight. The sax hollers again; the band hums to a halt; silence descends between the guttural howls. I can almost taste her. My pocket vibrates.

*Sasha.*

"What?" Charlotte says when I roll my eyes.

I shake my head as my face lights up again with that blue haze. It's a text this time: *911911911911911191911911*

* * *

"I'll drive," Charlotte says. It's a warm Manhattan night. The streets glisten with a recent downpour and Soho bustles with well-dressed revelers.

"The hell you will." It comes out rougher than I mean it to. Immediately I want to swallow the words back up inside me. Who is this woman with regret and an uncertain step? Three dates and a kiss and already I've lost myself.

But Charlotte just smiles and wiggles her eyebrows. "You been drinking." She holds her hand out for the keys.

"You can't come," I say, feeling like a stubborn child.

"The hell I can't."

"It's probably going to be..." Words fail. Knowing Sasha, knowing me, it could be any flavor of horrific from ghost to gangster. Part of me is relieved: the familiar deep focus of urgency is like a deep sigh compared to this...*this*. But Charlotte is right: I'm in no condition to drive and there's no time to take the damn late night train or wait for one of my guys to come get me. "I drive for a living." A pathetic last ditch effort; she knows she's won.

"I'm sure that's what you do." She winks, taking the keys from me and sliding smoothly into the front seat of my Crown Vic. Slick.

\* \* \*

"Just get here." Sasha's voice betrays no desperation, but that's Sasha: impossibly poised and somehow deeply genuine. "The spot's on Lorimer. Gonna text the address. Come in through the side entrance by the dumpsters. I'll explain the rest in person. And Reza?"

"Hm?"

"Come heavy."

She hangs up.

*Heavy.* The trunk has enough fire-power to take on an invading army. It lays concealed beneath several false layers of felt and plastic. Even on this relatively off-duty type night, a Mauser hugs tightly to my ankle and one of my Glocks hangs under my left arm. I'm always heavy, and Sasha knows this, which means come extra-heavy, which means some real bad shit is in the works. I grimace at the smudged lights of the Williamsburg Bridge as they dash past. Charlotte is making good time. I might be impressed.

She turns down the salsa blaring on the radio. "You're not just a driver."

She knows damn well I'm not. It's been implicit and understood since we met, her voice guiding me along the Long Island backroads as Sasha and I headed out to stop a deranged half-dead guy holed up in an old lighthouse. Implicit and understood and unspoken. And that's how I liked it.

"You're right," I say, still watching the lights. "I'm a *chauffeur.*"

She chuckles. "Okay, Reza, but the moment in which you're going to have to explain more is rapidly approaching."

I grunt. She's right.

"Twelve minutes, according to my GPS."

"You're gonna drop me off," I say. "This isn't safe, whatever it is."

"Reza." My name a small song on her lips, a dusty blues, the clipped howl of that baritone sax. I shake my head, still a little tilted from that rum.

"Doctor?"

"I've had a good time tonight, so far." Her eyes are on the road ahead. My eyes are on the dashboard, but all I see is her. "You give good date, even though you like to pretend it's all whatever."

"I don't—" I start, but she's right and anyway she's not done.

"And I hope we do it again, as a matter of fact. And I haven't said that after a date in a long time now. You're a good kisser, Reza, and I can tell you give bomb head."

I won't smile I won't smile I won't smile. I shrug.

"But I don't fuck with secrets and lies. Not when it comes to people I care about. And even though I barely know you, Miss Villalobos, there's something about you. Something that tastes like tomorrow. And people I care about are the only people that have a shot at tasting this glory, which I happen to know you want a taste of."

My head wavers in a noncommital side-to-side samba, but my chest catches fire. *Of course*, I want it, my God. Dr. Charlotte Ann-Marie Robateau Tennessee moves through the world like a warm breeze through palms. She got that smile. Those hips and that ass been calling my name since I first saw 'em shuffling around behind the research desk at the Harlem Public Library. I said her name over and over as I fell asleep that night, memorized it like a speech so I could say it back to her the next time we met, in full and with unfiltered flow. Dr. Charlotte Ann-Marie Robateau Tennessee. It even rhymes, goddamnit. Of course I want my tongue inside her.

I must've let out a little grunt, because Charlotte laughs and shakes her head as we pull off the bridge and into the labyrinthine criss-cross of Williamsburg. "If you try to protect me from whatever it is your life is really about, it won't even just backfire, it'll explode. And I'll be gone. So—"

Because at this strange, dizzy moment, I am hers and I will do anything to stay hers, I blurt out three words I've simply never said before: "I'm a killer."

We slide along a steady flow of traffic under the rumbling J train. I close my eyes, let this new silence set in, resign to whatever will come.

"Well that wasn't so hard, was it," Dr. Charlotte Ann-Marie Robateau Tennessee finally says, her voice almost a whisper.

"You can't even imagine," I manage.

A text comes in from Sasha: *wherever you are, hurry.*

\* \* \*

Happy brown kids frolic on the painted storefront windows of the Braden-Belzer Center for Community

Development. It sits between an all-night nail salon and a fruit stand on Lorimer. We follow a narrow alley towards the back, my duffle bag full of the requested heaviness bounces against my spine as I maneuver between the brick wall and rusted fence. Past the dumpsters, up a small flight of stairs, through a glass door, into a brightly lit rec room with more painted brown kids chasing rainbows and butterflies amidst melodramatic posters of grinning revolutionaries and generic colloquialisms. Sasha waits for us with her arms crossed over her chest, braids pulled back in a tight bun, face unreadable. Beside her, a very stressed out white guy scratches something on a notepad, and a woman who could be Sasha's sister throws us a brief glance before glaring back at a door on the far side of the room. She's got a metal baseball bat on one shoulder, poised to strike.

"Everyone, this is Reza," Sasha says. "She handles…stuff."

"Great!" the white guy sighs. He's scrawny and wears a lumberjack shirt and jeans shorts. Only the thinning flap of blond hair suggests that he might be significantly older than fifteen. "That's what Janey said about you, but here we are. Can *she* handle *this* stuff?"

Sasha's scowl is so tiny, I'm pretty sure I'm the only one to catch it. "Reza, this is Josh Tremont, and that's my friend Janey by the door. They work here."

I nod at them. Josh is trying to project some ethereal white dude in control vibe but only managing to look exceptionally freaked out. Janey's keeping it cool but that grim set of her jaw says she's ready to make her first kill if need be. "This is my associate, Dr. Tennessee," I tell them.

"Oh good, a doctor," Josh says, I think unironically. Charlotte's degree is in library studies, but she just smiles and plays along. It takes physical effort not to swoon.

I look at Sasha. "What seems to be the problem?"

"Janey," Sasha says.

Janey opens her mouth but then the whole room shakes as something huge crashes into the door on the far wall. She takes a step back, readying the bat.

"The hell is that?" Charlotte whispers.

"Janey here still hasn't fully told us," Josh says, taking a few steps away from the door. "Some kind of class art project, you said? Whatever it is, it's big and pissed."

"It was a teambuilding exercise," Janey growls. "Just went a little off the rails."

Josh rubs his hands through the blond strands trying to cover his forehead. "Whatever—at this point, we just need to get it handled. By protocol, as the supervisor on scene right now I'm supposed to call the co—"

"No!" Janey, Sasha, and I yell at the same time. "No damn cops," Sasha finished.

He puts both hands up. "Okay! I get it! I wasn't going to, I was just saying that's what I'm supposed to do. Obviously, that's not an option, fine, I'm willing to—"Another huge thud shakes the room. Josh shakes his head, eyes closed. "—I am *willing* to try to figure out another way. I don't want the cops here either believe me, but look, we have to do *something.*"

"You shouldn't even be here, Josh," Janey says. "If you hadn't been working overtime without telling anybody your Cover-Your-Ass obsessed ass wouldn't have to have known about any of this and you could've been sipping PBRs at your favorite fake dive bar in peace right now."

Josh frowns. "Well, that was unnecessary."

"It's a monster of some kind," Sasha says. "Made of clay and earth mostly."

"And it's fucking huge," Janey adds.

"And it's fucking huge," Sasha agrees.

"So I gathered," Charlotte says. I raise an eyebrow her way but she shakes her head: she's staying.

"Can it be killed?" I ask.

"That would be the million dollar question," Josh says. Everyone stares at him. He cringes. "Sorry, that came out more sarcastic than I meant it to. I apologize."

"Janey used some Panamanian magic to bring it to life," Sasha says. "But she's not exactly an expert, just some shit she picked up from her grandma so…"

Janey rolls her eyes. "The point—" *SLAM!!* "—is that I didn't know it was gonna work in the first place, otherwise I wouldn'ta goddamn done it."

"Well, now you know," Sasha says.

"Isn't this your department?" I ask. Sasha's not just in touch with the dead, she's half-dead herself: a long complicated story she hasn't bothered filling me in on and I haven't bothered asking about. I don't see ghosts. I don't fuck with ghosts. I don't even dabble. I'm good.

"Feel like it kinda fits in the inbetween," Sasha says. "Being that it's a physical thing and all."

"Bah." I set down my duffle bag of goodies and cast a sideways glance at Josh, who's back to scribbling away on those papers. "He can be trusted?"

Sasha shrugs. "Don't think so, but what choice do we have? He's here."

"Indeed I am," Josh says, miffed.

She looks at me. "What's the move?"

This time, a sharp crack sounds when whatever-it-is smashes into the door. I shake my head, crouch and unzip the duffle bag. "We kill it."

"What?" Josh and Janey say together. An unlikely alliance, and you can tell they're both taken aback too.

"We can't," Josh says. "I mean we literally don't even know if we can, right? And besides, we created it, or Janey did, and the kids, and yeah it might be dangerous but…but…"

I pass Sasha an AK and sling one over my shoulder, suppress my smile as Josh's eyes grow wide. "You called me to handle a problem, this is how I do that." The clip makes a satisfying click as it slides into place and just like that the last threads of that rum-tinged fog fall away and everything glistens. I glance back at Charlotte—she stands by the door, a slight smile on her lips as her eyes take me in. "Guess you were right about that moment rapidly approaching. You wanna leave?"

She just shakes her pretty head.

As Sasha goes through the motions I taught her to get comfortable with the weapon, Josh places himself between us and the door. "There *has* to be another way! I-I don't consent to the taking of a life, even a strange new life that may want to kill us."

"Consent isn't yours to give," I say. A few flash grenades go in my pockets along with another clip.

"If you go all Scarface up in here with those big guns," Janey says, "cops'll be here in about ten seconds and then what?"

I stand beside Sasha facing the door. "Three minutes and fifteen seconds."

"What?" Josh demands.

"Average response time to a shots fired call in Williamsburg. I know, trust me."

"I do," Janey says, eyebrows raised.

"So unless you have a better idea—"

"We talk to it," Josh blurts out.

Now even Janey steps away from him. "You're mad."

"We haven't tried—not really. And what if it's just trying to be heard, to be understood? It's a newborn basically, but it's huge and it's trapped. I'd be slamming at the door too."

"This is a bad idea," Sasha says quietly.

"But shooting up the place is brilliant? And then running when the cops get here? Do you have any idea how—"

"It's the only way," I say, but Josh is undeterred.

He shakes his head, turns toward the door. "I'll do it,"

he growls. "Since no one else will. I've always felt like…I was born for something. Something more than wrangling boards of trustees and raising a few kids out of poverty. More than bodega runs and bad loft parties. I don't know what this thing is or what we can do but…maybe…maybe." He opens the door and slides in before anyone can stop him.

There's a pause, then a muffled word, "Hello," I think, and then another terrible crash, Josh's muted scream, then a wet thwacking sound. The door flies open and a huge gray form bursts out. Janey ducks out of the way and I let off a barrage of shots but the thing is fast as hell—a few pock marks erupt on its gigantic form without slowing it at all. Sasha and I dive to either side as it barrels through. Everything seems to slow; the monster moves at lightspeed but we are all wading through invisible mud. I fly through the air; my only thought is Charlotte.

A smashing noise, plaster crumbling, then an even louder crash and shattered glass.

Charlotte Charlotte Charlotte Charlotte.

I land hard, scramble to position the gun, see what happened.

Dr. Charlotte Ann-Marie Robateau Tennessee.

She stands perfectly still against the wall, a gaping hole beside her where the door we came in through used to be. Glass shards everywhere. She is alive, in one piece, eyes wide, chest heaving, hands fisted at her sides. I let out a sigh that turns into a tiny hiccup, maybe a sob. And then I know it without a question or doubt: this woman is my future. At least she will be if I can keep her alive tonight.

"Check the room," I say, rising. The world returns to normal speed; my heart returns to normal speed. Inside me, the snapshot of Charlotte, still alive, terrified but perfectly alive, recedes to the background as the urgency of now takes back over. The cops will be coming. The monster's loose. Josh is…

"Just…pieces…" Janey reports. Then she turns, bends over and hurls whatever was in her stomach onto the floor. It lands with a wet slap. Sasha's by her side in seconds. "We gotta move out," I say. My eyes meet Charlotte's, ask if she's okay. She gulps back whatever shriek or wail was about to come out, saves it for later, nods. "Five-oh could come knocking any minute. We lock this place down and leave." I start packing up my duffle-bag. "They probably won't have a specific location for the shots fired and hopefully they'll mark it unfounded and keep moving. Either way, we won't be here. We can come back later and clean up…Josh."

"Wait," Charlotte says. Behind me, Janey and Sasha get themselves together. "I'll stay. This needs to be handled now."

I clench my jaw, hating that between the two options, her being at risk of getting arrested at a grisly murder scene is the more palatable one. For a flickering moment, all the choices I've made to arrive at this moment flash past. I shake the threads of doubt away. Nod. Take out my work phone. "A huge Guyanese guy named Rohan will show up with a clean-up team to help you. And make sure you're safe."

"Sounds like a dream come true." She manages a smile. "Go catch that monster."

\* \* \*

It's late and a Tuesday, so the streets of Williamsburg are mostly empty. I screech around a corner onto Broadway, missing the huge metal leg of the train overpass by centimeters, then blast towards Bushwick. "Take this," I pull up a police scanner app on one of my phones and hand it to Sasha. "Put 11206 in when it asks for a zip code and then listen for them to freak out or any calls that sound like it could be our guy." She nods, perfectly calm, almost eerily calm.

Janey, on the other hand… "Fuck fuck fuck," she chants in a sputtering, rhythmic sequence from the back seat. "Fuck shit fuck."

Sasha puts an earbud in with one hand, reaches the other over the seat to rest on Janey's knee. "We gonna sort this out," she says.

"We already didn't," Janey says. "Josh is *dead.*"

Going on gut instinct alone, I hook a left onto a side-street, accelerate hard down two quiet residential blocks and then swing back around towards Broadway. "Tell me exactly what happened. Anything that might give us a hint about where it went."

"It's like I said," Janey says with a sniffle. "It was kind of a joke: we built this huge thing, and the kids were all into it and we were kidding around about bringing it to life and so I just…" She trembles, pulls it together. "I just did some of the prayers and things my grandma taught me and added some ingredients."

"What ingredients?" Sasha asks.

Janey scrunches up her face. "Cemetery dirt, for one."

A police car flies past, lights flashing. I glance at Sasha. "They're saying it's a pedestrian struck," she says. I swing the car around.

"Some pigeon feathers. Some honey. Rum. A few other things…some hair."

"Your own hair?" Sasha asks.

"Ugh! I feel so stupid," Janey moans. "I didn't think…I never thought…How could I…"

Up ahead, the blue police lights have stopped at an inter-section along with a few other squad cars. "You couldn't," I say. "You had no way of knowing." More pulsing lights converge; from the far end of Broadway, an ambulance approaches, its siren a muted wail in the night.

\* \* \*

Moose Ed lounges beside the police tape looking some-how both mystified and unimpressed. "Pedestrian struck? Ha. I guess you could say that." He spits. Nods at a passing sergeant.

I scowl at a crumpled Suburban in the middle of the intersection; its airbags hang like melting wax over the dashboard and steering wheel. Beside it, a big guy in a Yan-kees cap tries to wave off paramedics, insisting that he's fine, he's fine and then unleashing a thick stream of Dominican curses into a cellphone. "That's the driver." I say. "Where's the pedestrian?"

Moose Ed chuckles. "That's the thing: It was a hit and run but the one that got hit is also the one that ran."

"Which way?"

"Can't make this shit up, I swear."

With some wrath now: "Moose, which way did the pedestrian run?"

He eyes me. "Up Union and then disappeared down a sidestreet, the driver said. But he also said the dude was eight feet tall and gray and butt naked so you know...we gonna breathalyze him. We told the medics but they said it wasn't their job to chase huge naked gray dudes around Brooklyn and hey, I can't argue with them on that point, you know?"

"Thanks, Moose." I'm already halfway back to the car.

\* \* \*

"The worst part," Janey says as we swerve around the idling ambulance and up Union, "is that I...for the first time since I met him, I know what Josh was talking about... with the thing, I mean."

Sasha and I stay quiet, but I'm sure we're both restrain-ing ourselves from blurting out some form of *Get the fuck out of here*. Still, Janey doesn't strike me as the sentimental type. "I know that sounds ridiculous," she amends, once our silence has registered. "I don't...I can't explain it. And I know it's even weirder since the thing did that...to Josh but...it's like when those wild animal attacks happen, you know some fool wanders into a bear cave and gets ate and then they put down the bear and it's like, the bear was just bearing, you know? Homeboy needn'ta shown up in the bear's house. Not that Josh...never mind. You know what I mean?"

"Except you made the bear out of clay," Sasha says.

"And we're in Brooklyn," I add. "Not the Sierra National Park."

Janey nods, watching the dark streets whizz by. "I know... it's the I-made-it-thing, you guys." With those two simple words Janey has somehow invited me into a secret girls' club I've never been in before. *You guys* is the official direct address of the sleepover party. And here we are zooming around backstreets looking for a giant monster. Against my will, I am charmed.

"Nesto Jr. doesn't want kids," Sasha explains to me. Janey reaches over from the backseat and punches her shoulder. "What? You don't think that has anything to do with this?"

"That's not the...ugh!" She feigns indignation but a giggle slips through. "Whatever."

"If you're waxing mommytastic about a giant lump of clay," I point out, "you may need to put Nesto Jr. on ice."

"You mean kill him?" Janey gasps.

Sasha and I bust out laughing at the same time. I don't laugh much, but this night has already been unusual in so many ways. "Damn, Janey!" Sasha guffaws. "She meant curb him." She shoots me a look. "Right?"

I shrug. "Whatever works."

They both cackle and for a minute, the entire mess of this tragic night evaporates amidst our sudden fellowship. Then something huge and gray hurdles across the street and

I slam on the breaks, sending a cascade of cold coffee across the windshield.

"Jesus Christ!" Janey yells and then I screech the wrong way down a one way after it, my mind reaching back to the guns in the trunk, ticking off a quick inventory of what might take this thing down.

"There," Sasha says, ever calm and steady. The gray blur streaks up the block then launches into the air, lands on a car, nearly crushing it, and without missing a beat, vaults up to a fire escape and disappears into the darkness above. I double park, throw the hazards on and then I'm out the car, popping the trunk, grabbing my dufflebag. Sasha's beside me, then Janey, and we're sprinting down the block then squinting up past the orange glare of the streetlights. I use a grappling hook to pull down the fire escape and we clang-clang our way to the top without a word, the weight of what's about to happen heavying up the air between us.

It stands at the far end of the rooftop, the magnificent Manhattan skyline spreading out to either side like fiery wings against the night sky. We just pant for a few seconds, and then I put down the duffle bag, unzip it. The shotgun feels like an old friend in my grip, comfort. The thing turns when I *chuk-chuk* the barrel into place; it takes a step toward us. Beside me, Sasha stirs and then I hear the *shiiingg* of her blade coming out. The towering shadow breaks into a run. I lift the barrel, steady it, find the fast-approaching giant.

"Stop!" Janey yells, running out into the darkness.

I hear Sasha mutter, "fuck," as I try to find a shot over Janey's head. The monster's not moving though, the thing froze in its tracks…exactly when Janey told it to.

"Janey…" I say. She holds up a hand, gazing up at the clay giant she created.

"Kneel," she says. There's a pause, a terrible silence. Then the monster lowers itself to one knee before her. Janey shoots a wide-eyed gape back at us, then puts one hand on its head. "No more killing," she says. "Okay?"

"Not for now anyway," Sasha mutters. I just shake my head.

The monster nods. Around us, the city sparkles.

\* \* \*

"It's been a busy month," I say, glancing at Sasha. "All my regular spots are off limits right now." Charlotte and the guys did a helluva job cleaning up the place. Every surface shines, the reek of bleach the only remaining hint of what a horror show this place was a few hours ago. That and the trash bag full of what used to be Josh in the middle of the floor.

"It's alright," Janey says. "I got a place."

Sasha glares at her. "Really, bitch?"

She shrugs. "A girl can't have some secrets? Shit. Seriously though, it's better this way. Disposal sounds so cold. I know we weren't close in life—hell, I cursed him out more times than I care to remember—but the least I can do is honor him in death. He was hard to get along with, but he meant well, deep down inside." She takes a swig of Jack and pours some out. "To Josh." We all nod solemnly.

"Where's the…it?" I say after a few moments of silence.

Janey gestures toward the stairwell. "Basement. Emptied out a big ol' crate we had laying around. He's…sleeping."

Oh he's a he now. I refrain from commenting.

"Ahem." Charlotte stands in the doorway, looking exhausted and still utterly gorgeous.

"Dr. Charlotte Ann-Marie Robateau Tennessee," I say, crossing the room.

"Right, your,"—Sasha makes little quotation marks with her fingers—"*associate.*"

"I'll be that," Charlotte says with a wily grin. "And so much more."

I take her in my arms; she fits just right. "Even after all this?"

"Mmm." She kisses me. "Apparently so."

I nod my goodbyes to Sasha and Janey, smile at Dr. Charlotte Ann-Marie Robateau and then arm in arm, we walk out into the night.

# SKIN LIKE PORCELAIN DEATH

When Victor has something uncomfortable to say, he usually ends up eating and smoking a lot. Since his health-conscious girlfriend Jenny's bustling around in the bedroom, all he can do is stuff his wide face with those papery, tasteless organic chips that she fills the cabinets with. He flinches slightly after each bite, like the snacks have been charged with tiny electrical currents.

"Spit it out, man."

"You're dead, right, Carlos?"

I roll my eyes. We've half-stepped this conversation so many times and I'm tired of tiptoeing.

"I'm partly dead."

"Right, whatever, you're deadish."

The difference means nothing to him and I have to remind myself it's only 'cause he doesn't know any fully dead people. I deal with their chilly, translucent asses all the time. I nod at him to get on with it.

"And your job—you investigate, uh..."

You know what I hate? When someone stops mid-sentence and stuffs a bunch of food in his face. Then you're just stuck there listening to all that crunching and smacking, waiting for the conversation to start back up. "Victor," I say,

"I'm hung-over. Breakfast was delicious but maybe I should come back when you've rehearsed a little better whatever it is you need to talk about."

Victor swallows a little too quickly, sputters, and gets back in it. "My little cousin Jimmy...had a weird...experience."

"Tell him it's very normal and one day he'll be able to do it with a real live woman, but not to hurt himself in the meantime."

"No, Carlos, this is serious. He says he saw something. He's all freaked out, wouldn't even tell me what it was. He went over some girl's house and something real off musta happened. Came back pale as shit and stuttering."

"Also normal. Surely there's some pills he can take."

"Carlos!"

"Alright, Victor. He didn't say anything else?"

"He mentioned something about dolls. That's all I could get. I know it's a cliché, but he looked like he saw a ghost."

"That's why you asked me over here for breakfast?"

"Look, Carlos—I never ask you for nothing, and it's not like you don't owe us a favor or two."

Damn, he played that card. Most of the time when I show up at Victor and Jenny's door it's because some heavy supernatural shit went down and I need a little upkeep. Victor works overnights on an FDNY ambulance and Jenny has as many herbs and nerdy things to say about herbs as Baba Eddie's Botánica. It's a strange, fiery combo—new age and 911—but my half-dead ass can't just stroll into an ER and demand treatment, they might try to resuscitate me while I'm napping. "You know," he continues unnecessarily, "we had to get a new couch cover after you bled out on our last one."

"Thank you, I remember." It was a nasty little run in with a million-year-old ghost mammoth. And yes, I stained the couch, but this guilt trip, I don't need. Maybe I would be better off at an ER after all. "Alright, I'll talk to him. But look, he doesn't need to know about me and what I am."

"Carlos, you already know I keep your shit under wraps. HIPPA, patient confidentiality, I got you, bro."

"I have no idea what you're talking about. Bring him to Marcus Garvey Park in three hours. I'll see what I can do."

Jenny pokes her head in. She's wearing a flowy pajama thing and her blond hair's pulled into a tight and shiny pony tail. "I'm gonna do some yoga, boys."

"Try not to hurt yourself again, baby," Victor says. "I'm off duty."

"Fuck you."

* * *

I like Garvey Park because the spirits here are very old and very chill. They don't wile out and send kids hovering over swing sets or switch joggers' right and left feet just to pass time. They watch, nod their ancient, glowing heads, appraise the spinning world around them, and confer quietly amongst themselves. They're older even, than The New York Council of the Dead, that sprawling bureaucracy of the afterlife that keeps me busy with heinous errands in return for a modest income and a vague sense of purpose.

It's one of those languid Harlem afternoons in late summer that the whole world has come out to enjoy. The park is thronged with barbecue families, bums, and flirting teenagers. Each group orbits in little clusters around the picnic tables and basketball courts. The occasional sweaty, spandexed jogger huffs and puffs past. The sun sends a golden, gentle glow through the trees as it gets ready to turn in for the night. And here's when the nothingness sets in. These damn peaceful moments, when no bodies are dropping, no fanged fuckups are charging through subway tunnels at me. This is when I seem to be a sum of only negative parts:

Not dead, not alive. No memory, no past. A hundred miles away—at least inside my own heart—from the one woman I managed to fall for and the two adorable fully alive babies we created. Aloof even with my closest friends, unless we're laughing about some grim shit that just popped off. I think it's all the happy families around that do it to me. All that cheery wholesomeness clogs my flow and gets me nostalgic for a time that never was, for a potential that simply won't manifest. It's why I usually don't bother with the park 'til late, late at night.

In the woodsy slope above the playground, the ancient, blissed-out park spirits are watching the tiny theatrics play out and nodding silently. One floats just at the edge of the trees, staring back at me. Apparently onto my neither-here-nor-there status, his bearded face shines with serene uncertainty.

"That high-ass geriatric bothering you, C?" My partner Riley has materialized a few feet away. "Want me to fuck him up?"

I grin. "Nah, I'm used to it."

"He's either/or, abuelo, walk the eff along." If nothing else, it's good to have crude friends who stand up for you even when you don't really need them to. The gently bobbing ghost keeps staring, his ancient mouth forming a little concerned O from within a long translucent beard.

"He's not scared of you, Riley."

"He's bluffing, but we can let him have his moment. C'mon." Riley flips the old ghost off and floats towards one of the winding paths.

"What's all this about anyway?" he asks as we stroll along the outer rim of the rusty amphitheater.

"Victor's little cousin got into some shit with a lady."

Riley chuckles. "Okay, Anne Fucking Landers, but why am I here?"

"And he thinks there's something about it that might pertain to us."

"How's she look?"

"Who?"

"The lady, Carlos. Jesus."

"I don't know, man, she's probably a kid like the cousin. What's wrong with you?"

Every once in a while, being dead catches up with Riley. The few shards that he remembers from his life swirl in repeat through his head and he gets all agitated and perverse like a damn teenager. I don't think he can even really be horny, but something about that frisky interplay and all those gooey juices mashing up together just means life to him. It drives him even more crazy that it's a game I could play but don't.

"What's wrong with *me*?" he says. "What's wrong with you?"

Instead of responding, I light two miniature cigars and pass one to my partner. I do have a recurring fantasy, or perhaps it's a memory, who can tell? She's Puerto Rican, dark skinned, hair a black ocean of curls, eyes mahogany and penetrating, ferocious. She just looks at me, usually in that perfect dream-time between sleeping and waking, when everything is foggy enough to make thoughts and dreams indistinguishable. She floats towards me, always getting closer and closer but never touching. Her eyes bore into mine like delicious drills, evacuate everything that troubles me from the inside and leave me empty, wide open, charmed and with a huge-ass erection. Other than that and ignoring the thoughts of Sasha that constantly barrage me like barbarians at the gates, I'm all set. I don't pay much mind to ass on the street.

Riley and I make our round, smoking in silence. Victor's waiting for us by the half-shell stage. Beside him stands the tallest sixteen-year-old I've ever seen. His face is long, moose-like even, and he wears Malcolm glasses over a serious frown.

"Damn, Victor," I say as we stroll up. "You miss out on some genes?" Victor's not particularly short or wide but he looks like a fat midget next to his cousin. "You play ball?" I ask up at Jimmy.

"Chess actually."

"Oh well."

Victor rolls his eyes. "You done?"

I nod. "Let's walk."

We start a wide loop around the ball field. Riley floats along beside me, invisible to Victor and the giant. It's further into evening now; the little ones have been dragged off to bed and the park belongs to a few squirming teens and some quietly conversing homeless guys. The occasional rising firefly glistens against the darkening field.

"So me and this chick, right," Jimmy says, "we been talking, you know, for like, two, three weeks now."

"Talking means fucking in teenager," Riley points out in my ear.

"When you say talking," I say to Jimmy, "do you mean having a conversation or having sex?"

The boy flashes an awkward smile and waves his hand as if swatting the thought away. "Nah, we was just talking." He giggles a little. "Yeah, you know, speaking, with words, to each other. Or whatever."

"Gotchya."

Victor, I realize, has turned bright red and put his hands in his pockets, which means things will only go downhill for him from here.

"So then on, like, Saturday, was it? Yeah, Saturday. Mina—that's the chick, Mina Satorius—asks me to come over to her house and watch a movie."

"That also means fucking, by the way," Riley says. "Ask him what this Mina looks like."

"White chick?" I say.

"Yeah," Jimmy nods but not, I notice, with any particular

pride or boastfulness. "But she's, like, white-white, not just Caucasian-white. Not an albino either, but her skin's like fucking porcelain. Shiny and everything."

"That's kinda creepy," Riley says. I nod, which to Riley means I agree with him and to Jimmy means 'go on.'

"Like, she's definitely fine," Jimmy shrugs. "I mean, dudes always sweatin' her, so I was surprised when she started talking to me, 'cause I just kinda have, like, my boys I chill with and whatever, but we definitely not the cool kids, if you know what I mean."

I say I do but I really have no idea what he's going on about. High School, if I even went, is at the bottom of a pile of deleted memories for me.

"So whatever, you know, I go over there. She lives in Staten Island, so it's like a serious journey; had to take a train to Manhattan, then the ferry and *then* a bus."

Riley belly laughs. "And I know he was thinking, 'This better not be for no damn movie.'"

"She meets me at the bus stop. She's looking really fine, wearing one of them, what-you-call-it, spaghetti strap shirts?" Riley and I both shrug. Victor's still turning colors and chain smoking menthols with one of his FDNY rubber gloves on to hide the hand stink from Jenny. "We walk a few blocks through the suburbs. But it's, like, serious suburbs, like, manicured bushes on the lawns and tonsa space between each house, and mad pastels and shit. And I'm already feeling kinda on shaky ground, you know, 'cause clearly this place ain't seen a Negro since there was cavemen in it."

"True, true," I say.

"Not to mention a tall-ass Spanish-speaking one like me." We're all laughing now. I notice that the old park spirits have ventured out of their forest hideaway with the onset of dusk. They form a growing crowd of curious onlookers in our wake, marveling at this strange fellowship of night strollers.

"Her house was ornate, yo. I mean, like some kinda Disney movie shit: All fucking swirls and coordinated furniture and pearly crap in vases. She leads me inside, and yeah, I'm definitely thinking about getting ass, but I'm still shook from being this deep in unfriendly territory, *and* the house is just giving me weird vibes."

"Ah-ha!" Riley says. "Get into that!" Which I was going to do anyway, but I let it slide.

"What kind of vibe, Jimmy?"

"I mean, the shit just felt spooky, like I was being watched by a hundred tiny eyes. Like, you ever go into one of those emptied out apartments in the projects and you can't see 'em, but you *know* the wall's fucking alive with waterbugs and centipedes and shit, and even if they don't actually touch you, you can feel them all around? That's what this was like, but it was crazy, 'cause like I said, the shit was ornate."

"Now we're talking," Riley says. He is getting excited. So are the park ghosts; I hear them muttering and humming behind us in ancient languages.

"She leads me through the main room into a smaller one, and this one's real dark and draped with all kindsa heavy fabrics, blood red and burgundy colored curtains. But that's not even the thing with this room. This room is full, from top to bottom, of dolls. You know, like, the girly kind they're always hocking on late-night TV and you're, like, 'Who buys that shit?' Well, this lady does—all of 'em. Grandma Tess I guess, that's what Mina said. The old lady's, like, a serious doll fanatic. Mina just rolled her eyes like it was some annoying grandma thing, but I was, like, truly chilled to the bone, yo. It was deep, because like I said, I had felt all those eyes on me, and then we walked into the room and there they were, hundreds of creepy little girls, all dressed in creepy little outfits and posed in mid-gesture. And no matter where you move in the room, they all looking right at you, I swear to God."

"That's fucked up," I say. Riley nods in agreement.

"So babygirl starts getting all hot and heavy right then and there."

"In the creepy doll room?"

"*In the creepy doll room!*"

"Oh hell no!" Riley yells. Even the elder ghosts swish back in disgust.

"And I was, like, 'Oh hell no!'" Jimmy says.

"Good man," says Riley.

"But she's, like, fiddling with my fly, making like she wants to give me some brain."

I look at Riley. "Bobo," he says. I blink at him. He circles his fingers near his mouth and pokes his ghostly tongue out the opposite cheek.

I say, "Damn, son," to Jimmy, who's starting to wonder what I'm looking at. Victor shoves a fresh menthol into the dying embers of the one in his mouth and puffs 'til it's lit.

"And I'm, like, 'Don't you have a bedroom?' And she's, like, 'Yeah but ain't you want some right here?' And I'm, like, 'Ain't you feel like a million fucking porcelain freaks about to go Chucky on your ass?'"

"You said that?"

"Nah, but I was thinking it."

Riley's doubled over, slapping his knees.

"What'd you say?"

"I said, 'Let's go in your room, baby,' and you know, eventually she let up. But for a minute I thought I was gonna haveta choose between head in the dolls-of-death-room and no head at all. And I really don't know what I woulda done."

Riley clicks his tongue. "That's teenagers for you. I'm horny, but not that horny."

"So we went to her bedroom..."

"What was it like?"

"It was normal, you know, like your average teenage girl

shit: Band posters and half naked dudes on the wall. A few leftover stuffed animals from elementary school. Mirrors and makeup and shit."

"Nothing creepy in there? No dolls?"

"Nah, it was cool. And when we get in she lays out on that big poofy pink bed and does the one finger c'mere thing and we just... You know."

"You do it?"

"Well, you know, not all the way..."

"What base?" Riley says. I give him a what-the-fuck face. "Just ask!"

"What, ah, base?"

Victor scowls at me.

"First she went down on me. It was alright, but there was definitely teeth." Riley coos sympathetically. "Then it was third base, like, right away."

"That's French kissing?" I ask.

"No, asshole," Riley says. "Third base is finger in the pussy."

"Nah." Jimmy raises two fingers and two hopeful eyebrows.

"Right," I say.

"Alright," Victor finally pipes up. "Jimmy walk ahead a sec, I gotta talk to Carlos here." Jimmy looks confused but strolls a few feet along the dimly lit path. Night has dropped her cool darkness around us. The air is fresh with the swirling of plant life and the churning urban forest. The elder dead watch us anxiously, unclear on what the holdup is.

Victor smokes and waves his hands like he's trying to pick the words out of the air around him. "It's just..." he takes another drag. "Jimmy was born when I was ten. I babysat him 'til he was twelve. I changed his fucking diapers. I'm not really ready for him to be getting to third base yet. That's all."

"For a paramedic," Riley says, "Victor sure don't have a

very nuanced appreciation for the gooier aspects of human life."

"Riley says you need to get your shit together, ambulance boy," I tell Victor. "And I concur. Dirty diapers or not, the kid's growing up. So you may not be ready, but he is. Deal with it."

The funny part is, Vic can talk up as mean a sex story as any of us, and don't get him started on the nasty traumas he catches on the graveyard shift. But that's family for you. He'll get over it. We catch up with Jimmy, who was clearly overhearing everything we said. "Can I continue to live my life now?" he says to Victor. Vic nods wearily. The ancient park spirits gather closer around us.

"After third base, it was sloppy seconds."

Riley turns to the floating audience. "That means he licked her titties." They nod solemnly.

"They were a little on the small side," Jimmy reports, "but perky. Looked right at you. It was awesome. And I know this sounds corny, but the whole thing was just really sweet. Like, it was comfortable, you know? She didn't try to act all pornstar like some of 'em do. We just kinda held each other for a while."

"That's sweet," Victor admits.

"Then she blew me again 'til I nutted on her face."

The whole park lets out a collective hum of muted fascination. Teenagers really are another species entirely.

"We passed out—well she cleaned up and then we passed out—and I dreamt some heavy shit. I can't remember what was going on though, but this creepy carnival type song was playing the whole time."

"You remember how it went?"

"I actually can't get the fucking song outta my head. It's haunting me. And I can't figure out if it started before I fell asleep or not, like, you know, when you're almost passed out, but not quite? *That's* when the music started."

"How'd it sound?"

Jimmy whistles an eerie minor key waltz, slightly off time and dissonant. It gives me the chills. The park ghosts have widened their circle around us by the time he finishes. Riley and I trade concerned looks.

"That's evil," Riley declares.

"Word," I say. Jimmy looks confused. "That melody's got some power in it," I tell him. "But go 'head. What happened next?"

"When I woke up, Mina's gone and the dolls are all around me in the bed."

"Now that," Riley says, "is some horror movie shit."

"And I feel sick, like, physically ill. Not to mention terrified. I throw 'em off me and they're so cold—it's not natural. It was still dark out, just before dawn actually, and I just got up and fucking booked it outta there. I barely put on my clothes all the way, just was out. Out, son. My black ass was running down all them crazy Arthur Kill Road type-a streets and I wasn't even afraida no crazy white people anymore. I woulda been relieved to see some sheet-wearing mothafuckas, just to get away from those dolls, I swear, Carlos. I was shook."

"Then what?"

"I caught the first ferry home. Passed the eff out and tried to forget the whole thing happened."

"Alright," Riley says. "So some phantomified American Girl dolls jumped him after he banged their owner's granddaughter. He got away. It's spooky but not much else. Open-shut."

"Anything else go on since?" I ask Jimmy.

"That's the thing," he tells me, and I feel a little lump building in my throat. "I haven't really been the same since."

"What, you can't sleep? Nightmares? That'll pass."

"No, man, I'm telling you, I'm off. Look." He reaches his hand out to Victor and his fingers shudder dimly and fade into his cousin's shirt. "I'm disappearing!"

This is bad. This is bad in so many ways. I can almost feel Riley's gears turning at the same time as mine. The dolls. The girl. The grandma. And now our boy's slowly checking out.

No easy way to do this: I reach a hand I hope will be comforting up to Jimmy's shoulder. It doesn't pass through him but I can tell the flesh isn't fully there. "You're dying," I say. "You don't have much time."

Victor spits out his cigarette. "What?"

Jimmy just nods slowly. He's fighting to get that man mask on, the one that doesn't cry or feel anything, but he can't do it fast enough. His eyes get shiny. I'm sure he'd suspected as much, but it can't be easy to hear.

"The dolls kept your soul. Without it, your body won't last long. When you go," I feel horrible dumping this all on him, but it has to be said, "your soul'll be trapped in that house, probably in one of those dolls."

This is more than Jimmy can take. He starts trembling and tears flow freely now. "For how long?"

"It doesn't matter," I say. "Because we're gonna bust up in there and stop it before it happens."

\* \* \*

Staten Island really is a pain in the ass to get to, especially late at night. I'm fast on land, even with my crookleg, but that damn ferry goes from occasional to barely-ever after midnight and time is slipping quick for Jimmy. It's damn near 3 a.m. when Riley and I show up to stake out the premises. The quiet little suburb is all dark patches and occasional foreboding mansions with high walls and security systems. We perch on a hill just outside the gates of the Satorius house and take in what we can.

"It's bad," Riley says. "I don't like any of it."

"You think the girl's in on it?"

"Only by proxy. I'm guessing the old dame got the youngin involved in her shit, but baby Barbie prolly don't know it."

"Sounds about right," I say, "but here's what I really don't like: Let's say granny's stealing dudes' souls and keeping 'em in the dolls." Riley nods. "Now you and I bust in there, swords a-flashing, and me—I'm a body and maybe I got half a soul, give or take."

"Sad but true."

"But you, Riley, you're all soul."

"That's what they tell me."

"You know what I mean. It won't be a slow decline for you; you don't have a body. If things don't go our way in there, and there's a good chance they won't from what I can tell, it's gonna be a wrap for you quick."

"Now hold on a minute..."

"Second of all," I say, "I need you on the outside. I'm guessing a whole lotta souls gonna get released when things start getting hot, and I need you to be out here with Jimmy to figure out which is his and get it back to him. Feel me?"

"I feel you," he says. "But I don't like it. You wanna go in there all by yourself and you're not even sure if both of us could handle it. That don't make no damn sense either."

I'm opening my mouth to get into it when a voice behind me says, "Who's that?"

I look up, and then further up, at Jimmy's face. He'd walked up through the underbrush while we were arguing.

Riley says, "Uh-oh."

"What do you mean, 'Uh-oh?'" Jimmy demands.

"You can see Riley?" I ask.

"If that glowing floating dude you're talking to is Riley, yeah. What's that mean?"

"It's bad," Riley says. "The living can't see me."

Jimmy says, "Oh," so sadly I almost have to sit down.

"It just means we don't have much time," I say. "Even

less than we thought." I look at my partner. "Stay with him, man. That ain't no place for you to be with your dead ass."

"That's true for so many reasons," Riley says. "But I still don't like it."

Halfway down the hill I pause and look up at them. "You wanna call the COD for backup?" Riley and I toss the idea back and forth silently for a second. You never know what you're gonna get when you call in the Council of the Dead. They might come in all heavy, spirit blades a-rattling or they might not come at all. Usually it's whatever would be least helpful in the given situation.

"What's COD stand for?" Jimmy asks.

"Corpulent Old Dickheads," I say.

"Corporation of Ongoing Douchebags," Riley says.

"Nice one," I say. "Let's not. They'll find out soon enough." Jimmy just shakes his head at me as I turn and head off towards the mansion.

\* \* \*

Normally, we have all kinds of slick moves we do to get in a spot we're not supposed to be. I have my grumpy cop routine down pat and a range of fake badges and IDs in my coat pockets. But that's for when we have some time to find out what's going on. I hop the fence, limp-sprint across the lawn and kick the door in. One thing about houses that are heavily spirited up, they rarely have much in the way of earthly protection, A) 'cause they don't need it, and B) 'cause they don't want a bunch of cops up in there anyway.

Ornate is the right word. The kid was also on point about the icky, too-many-eyes feeling. I can almost hear them whirl around in shock and focus that sick stare on me from their perches. I pull a no-nonsense blade out of my cane and advance slowly forward, imagining ghouls lurking in every shadow. The next room is the doll house, but when

I walk in, the shelves are empty. I don't like that at all. I move through quick; don't need to linger to know about all the bad things that've happened here. The room still echoes with lost soul screams.

Next comes a dark corridor with two doors at the end. One goes to Mina's room, I'm guessing, and the other probably gets me to grandma's. The energy seeping out of the room to my right is hot and old—a crude mix of fevered sepsis and sterile medical equipment that can't have much to do with Mina. I click open the door and walk in, blade first.

It's all dark but for a muted TV in the corner by the door. The screen projects shuddering, colored lights that dimly illuminate Grandma Tess. She's sitting up in a steel outpatient bed on the far side of the room, staring at me. Long, loose-flesh arms wrap around the guard-rails. Her tightly wound bun and heavy makeup give her face that old-lady/demented clown look. The room is boiling hot.

"Ah, a visitor!" she croaks when I walk in. "How lovely! Come, sit by my bed. I do get so lonely these days."

"You know why I'm here," I say. Sweat has begun running unrepentantly down my face and back.

"I'm sure you're here to keep me company, my dear. You can put that sword away."

"You have quite a little operation going, lady." My eyes are jumping around the room, from her forest of see-through orange medication bottles to the stacks of sterile sheets and catheters, but nothing seems about to pounce. "Where's the dolls?"

"My children? I have quite a collection, you know. You'll meet them soon enough."

"This is what I figure," I say, winding a slow orbit around the room. "You're a lonely old lady..."

"Tut-tut," she chirps. "Where are your manners, young man?"

I pick up an old black and white photo of a beautiful smiling woman. "You used to be all the rage, when you weren't busted and bed-bound."

"I had my heyday, yes."

"Probably quite the man-killer. And then..." My eyes scan the family photos decorating her bedroom wall and land on a fading image of a teenage girl with her hair in a horrific topknot. "You had a pretty young daughter."

"Celeste."

"And you inducted her into your ways. Taught her the art of luring a man in. And once she had him here, you went about your creepy soul-trapping business."

"Nothing creepy about it, my dear. They all came willingly enough. Celeste was quite the little nymphette I'm afraid."

The air in the room is getting heavier. Things shift nervously in the dark corners above my head. "You trapped their souls in those damn dolls, and when their empty bodies decayed they belonged to you."

"Like I said," grandma's breathing comes in fast labored wheezes now, "it gets lonely up here. No one comes to visit. The young don't give elders the respect we deserve. Such a shame, really." Her edema-heavy hands reach over to the bedside table and retrieve a gold-lined, velvet jewelry box with dancing clowns on it and a crank sticking out of one side. "Such a shame." She absent-mindedly starts twisting the handle, staring at me with that bright red smile all the while.

The music seeps out in lurching, timid jolts at first. Jimmy'd had the melody down perfectly, with all its eerie, off time elegance. It comes from all around me, envelops me in a hazy cloud of uncertainty.

"Pretty song, no?"

I shake my head no, trying to steady myself. If I speak I might puke, and that wouldn't be a good look. "What happened," I gasp, "to Celeste?"

"Bitch got a conscience," Grandma Tess laughs. "Or more precisely: She fell in love. Broke the Golden Rule. I told her: 'Celeste baby, never, never fall in love. You can have all the men you want, my dear, just don't fall in love.' It worked for so many years. I thought when she had Mina, something would change, but when I placed Mina's father on my shelf with the rest of them, Celeste took it all in stride. I was so proud of her."

I let myself sink into a chair at the foot of her bed, because otherwise I would sprawl out across the floor. The melody trudges on around me like a dying ballerina.

"But then, a few years later, this Maurice character starts coming around. A mailman, of course. I knew from the start he would be trouble, with all his good natured smiles and gentle ways. She should've known better. Soon enough, it's 'Mommy, not this one, don't take this one from me, please.' And what did I always tell her? There's only one Golden Rule. A mother must be firm with her teachings in this day and age."

I have to stop the room from spinning or I'm toast. The walls swim with movement, and I can't tell if it's the dolls lurking towards me or my own weary head.

"Mina was eight at the time. I told her it was cancer that took her mommy and she was too young to question it, poor dear. Now I've spent nine long years with the same old irritating companions, waiting for my granddaughter to come of age and my daughter's ghost to stop moaning underneath my house. She's given me at least two strokes and probably caused the renal failure, the bitch."

It's definitely the dolls. I stumble to my feet and slash out haphazardly with my blade. They're moving faster than I thought they would, swaying and scurrying towards me like porcelain roaches.

"Now, now, young man," the old lady's voice rings out sing-songy and fierce. "No need for violence. We just want to help you sleep. I know you must not sleep very well, all that hard work you do. Sleep, my friend." The music won't stop. The dolls are everywhere.

Something deep inside me is calling out to get my attention but I'm too busy trying to swat away those tiny hands to notice. Finally, it gets me: Jimmy and Riley, waiting outside. In this moment of utter desolation, my soul has coughed up a stern reminder that folks are depending on me not to get myself taken down. People I care about. If I fail, not only will Jimmy be sucked forever into this Hell house, Riley will surely come in after me and get his ass evaporated too.

I force myself to stand up straight, block out the swirling melody with all my mental might and focus my eyes. Those shiny little porcelain faces glint up at me in the flickering TV light. I pick one and smash its head off with my blade. A bright ball of light issues forth, one of Celeste's poor lovers, and scatters frantically towards the ceiling. I slice again, crack another, and swing my body backwards, almost toppling, as the light bursts out and swooshes past me. In the new illumination, I see there are many more American Girls than I had thought, and my mind is still swimming, in spite of my best efforts. I begin whacking viciously at the crowd with both my blade and the cane sheath. Porcelain explodes around me as lights burst upwards.

I'm ignoring both the creeping melody and the old woman's screams but my energy is waning quickly. The dolls keep coming. Their little hands are grabbing at my ankles and their skin is cool and soft like dead flesh. It chills me, drains my drive. I have the notion that I'm hemorrhaging somewhere, which would be a quick wrap up to the situation 'cause I'm damn near anemic. But there's no blood. I tumble towards a window and smash it with my cane. The swirling balls of light flush towards it and burst out into the night like an explosion of stars. Hopefully, Jimmy's is in there somewhere. If so Riley will sort it out.

Meanwhile, the room has fallen back into darkness now that the shimmering souls have flooded out and the old hag switched off her soap operas. I swing my blade blindly for a second before an icy mound lands on my back and then another on my shoulder. I've lost all sense of direction. Tiny, frigid hands are working their way up my ankles. How many can I smash before I succumb? My knees are giving way, so I try to gauge where the majority of the little fuckers are gathering and aim my collapse that way. A terrific shattering greets my fall and for a second all I see is a giant flash of light, rising into the air. It illuminates the room just enough to afford me a glimpse of more legions of dolls scattering forward. As the world gives way to that horrific crawling feeling scrambling over my whole body, I hear Grandma Tess cackle and then the sound of a young girl screaming.

\* \* \*

My lady friend is sad tonight. We linger together like extras waiting for our cue, somewhere between asleep and awake. I have the vague notion that something horrible is going on all around us, but right now, I am safe. As long as she's here, it's inconceivable that anything bad could happen to me. Her light is just that bright. But she's been crying, or is about to—who can tell? She reaches out a hand towards me and for the first time in all the years that this beautiful morena has been blessing my dreams, she touches my face. It feels like I'm walking out into the afternoon sun after being in a basement for weeks. The warmth spreads over my whole body and I want to laugh and yell with joy but my friend looks so worried I clam up. I raise my hand to touch her face but there's blood laced between my fingers. It's my blood. That warmth all over my body...

I roll my head back to scream and then wake up pinned

to a wall in the flickering lights of the damn soap operas. The dolls are standing perfectly still around me. There are noticeably fewer than there had been, but I'm still outnumbered, surrounded and bleeding. Grandma Tess is talking urgently into an old antique telephone, and the thought that she's in communication with people outside of this house fills me with dread.

I'm trying to gather my strength and figure out where I'm bleeding from when Mina appears in the open doorway. She's absurdly skinny, has big gawking kitty-eyes and is still rocking that spaghetti-whatever tube top. Jimmy has some work to do on his descriptive powers. From the way Grandma Satorious says, "I'll call you back," into the phone, I gather Mina had been here earlier—scream-ing I vaguely recall—and wasn't welcome back.

"Can I help you, Mina?" the old woman says icily.

"I don't know what it is you do in here, Grammy," Mina says, "but it has to stop." Not bad for a mousy chick.

Grandma's not having it, though. "Go to your room!" she hollers with all the fury of a runaway elephant. "Get out of my sight! I'll deal with you later!" Mina has a lot to learn from this one. If I wasn't chained to the wall I'd be cowering to my room, but the girl stands her ground. Then I see why: All six and a half feet of Jimmy step firmly into the doorway behind Mina. For some reason, the first thought that comes to my head is: How did these two ever possibly get it on? Then the flood of relief kicks in. He looks good and solid so Riley must've gotten him his soul back.

Grandma Tess reaches frantically for her music box and begins cranking it as fast as her worn out old limbs will let her. That horrible song tiptoes eerily out. I'm about to yell to Jimmy when he pushes Mina to the side and launches across the room. The dolls clutter towards him. A few drop from the ceiling and find their mark on his shoulders and Jimmy misses a step and crashes forward. I'm pulling at my binds with everything I got but that's not saying much. Blood is still leaking steadily from somewhere.

Jimmy's up before too many dolls latch on to him, and he rips a few off and tosses them roughly at the walls. They shatter, sending light balls scattering out the window. Mina screams and runs towards him but he's already lurched the rest of the way across the room and is wrenching the music box from Granny's hands. "No!" she screams hoarsely. "No! Give it back, boy! That's mine! Mine!"

"Break it!" I yell. "Millions of pieces!" Little colorful bubbles are clouding my vision, which I take to be a bad sign, but I'm desperate to stay awake and see what happens. Jimmy aims at an attacking doll and brings the music box down hard on its head. Gears, springs and shards of wood explode across the room as the song finally grinds to a halt. I laugh drunkenly and am about to let myself slip into nothingness when a tall, glowing form steps into the doorway. I squint at it until the old bearded soul from Garvey Park comes into focus. Was he spying on us the whole time? If he's in on it with the fat witch, the deal is done; Jimmy wouldn't stand a chance. I'm about to say as much when the happy colorful dots mount a full takeover of my eyesight and I pass the fuck out.

\* \* \*

She's smiling now, my friend, but the sadness waits just behind her eyes like a persistent lover. Her hands are on my face, all that good warmth spilling sloppily over my cheeks, down my throat. I look at her longingly. I'm so tired now, I want to let the world slip away but only if she's coming along too. And her face tells me sternly that she's not. That we have to stay. If I was in bed I would roll over and pull the sheets over my head and then wait for her to come find me. Maybe I'm a child again. I just want to let go, let the darkness keep

closing in, but then she smiles and I can't. I can't be anywhere if that smile's not with me. I fight the bleariness away
and reach out, put my hands on her waist and pull her close
to me. Turns out she's naked and that sacred warmth wraps
around me like a steamy bath as I enter her. We move in
slow motion, find our rhythm and then fall into a breathless, joyful, steady fuck that seems to go on forever. I wonder what base this is and then I wake up drooling, grinning
wildly and staring into an ancient bearded face.

I scream and the face curves its little O shaped mouth
into what must pass for a smile in old spirit expressions.
Riley peers curiously down at me. He looks truly concerned,
but he's not worried about old beardy being there, which
means I don't have to be either. I become vaguely aware of
the forest breathing in and out around us. Riley speaks but
it just sounds garbley to me. He's looking at the park spirit.
Then the spirit says something garbley to Riley. Why can't
they bring back my new girlfriend and garble at each other
somewhere else?

"How you feeling, bruh?" Riley asks me.

"I feel like God stepped on me."

"You lost a lot of blood."

"I didn't have a lot of blood."

"Yeah, well now you have less."

"The boy?"

"Saved your ass. Soon as his soul burst out that window,
we separated it from the fray, I worked it back into him and
he bee-lined for the house. Brave kid, Jimmy. I barely had
time to tell him to aim for the music box."

"Ah, glad you picked up on that."

We're definitely in some remote corner of the park, deep
in the underbrush. I test out turning my head. It works, but
I don't like what I see.

"We're...not on the ground." Not by about twenty feet
from the look of it.

"Yeah, this fellow brought you up here. The COD was so pissed off about the sudden flood of dead souls at Intake they didn't even want to deal with your hemorrhaging ass."

"Charmingly Official Devastation."

"Exactly. So we brought you here. Well, this old guy brought you here. He'd been watching us the whole time. He took care of the kid too."

"Jimmy's okay?"

"He's fine. But he can still see me, which is odd." I'm strangely relieved to hear that. It makes everything a little less lonely knowing someone else will now have to put up with this in-between shit. Even if he's not half-dead like me, we'll be able to compare notes. And he saved my life.

"You got the heffa?"

"Heffa got away," Riley reports with a twinge of shame. "Seems she had someone swing by and pick her up. Made herself scarce while we were hauling you out of there."

There's that vague sense of dread again. "She was on the phone with someone," I say, "right before Jimmy and Mina came in."

"Yeah, the boys at the Council are on it, but you know how that goes. The daughter's ghost popped up from under the house as we were leaving. Celine?"

"Celeste."

"Whatever, she took off after the old hag in a hurry. She was going on about unrequited love and a mailman named Morris or something. Looked to be a nasty cat fight in the works, but not the kind you pay money to see. The wee, skinny chick stuck around, though. She's spooked, kept saying she shoulda seen it coming, though I have no earthly idea how. She'll be alright."

The old bearded spirit stirs slightly and warbles at Riley. It's a low moaning sound, like air blowing past a flap that keeps saying *fworp fworp fworp* over and over again.

"What is that?" I ask irritably.

"It's old ghost talk," Riley says. "Very old. Mostly forgotten. Few phantoms even speak it anymore. Lucky for you I had a crush on my ancient languages teacher in the academy."

*Fworp-fworp-fworp*, goes the spirit. Maybe it's changing intonations slightly.

"Turns out he's some kind of family of yours. An ancestor."

"What?" It never occurred to me that I have ancestors. Of course, I do—everyone does. But why bother trying to find them when I don't even know the first thing about who I am? It's all too much. I look up at his peaceful old face and smile. "He knows about my life?"

"Not much, I'm afraid," Riley says. "But he's been dying to meet you. Says he's sorry it had to be under these circumstances." Speechless, I study him for signs of me but come up short. "He's been keeping you alive for a few days now."

I reach out a trembling hand to touch this brand new, very old piece of myself. All of the sudden, I am not the errant, half-dead weed in God's garden I'd thought I was; I'm a link on a spiraling, ancient web. I have a towering young friend who saved my life twice. I have a partner that can make me laugh when we're both about to die and a chain-smoking healer man that lends me his couch when I'm hurt. A woman loves me, even if she's imaginary or long dead, she stays with me when everything else goes dark. I have roots. The old ghost puts his glowing hand to mine. It's icy cold and barely there, but it's real.

# GRAVEYARD WALTZ

Janey finds me at my spot on the graveyard hill late one Sunday afternoon. It's true, I owe my future daughter-in-law for getting me that nice job at the care center for troubled kids, and I owe her even more since I got my ass fired for holding midnight salsa classes, but that's another story.

As she gets closer, I retrieve a Malagueña from my pocket and turn down the music. When I got the graveyard gig, my boy Ernesto'd bought me an i-thing, a slick little music player, and loaded it up with all my favorite old salsa guys, but it never sounded right—those tiny headphones and even though it's supposed to be higher caliber, you can imagine what becoming so many zeros and ones does to a song. Instead I just bring my record player to work. Yes, it's a pain, but the quality is incomparable. The i-thing sits in my jacket pocket; I keep meaning to accidentally leave it outside the middle school across the street for one of the kids to find.

"Gordo," Janey says, puffing her way up the last steps to where I stand chuckling. They call me Gordo because I am gigantic in the old world of rumba and salsa, a legend. Also, because I am fat.

I can see by Janey's face she's come to collect up on that favor so I head her off at the pass. "I thought we were straight after I got you that jar full of cemetery dirt," I say, winking.

"Yeah," she says, "turns out that was just you being nice."

"Really?" I say.

"Turns out I need a bigger favor, and then we'll be straight."

\* \* \*

Janey works at this swanky save-the-children spot on Lorimer, teaching kids how to be well-behaved, properly speaking little robotrons. But of course, when the grinning overlords aren't looking she always slips in some Malcolm X shit or a little hint about how to get one over on the cops. Anyway, the kids she was working with, they decided to build this monster—that's what the cemetery dirt was about apparently—they needed all kindsa ingredients to make it work. It was supposed to be like a team building exercise or something, you know from one of those corny books. But then Janey ended up throwing in a little of that Panamanian juju she inherited from her bruja granny and the damn thing came to life, Frankenstein style. But she says they just caked it together from mud and clay, not a body.

\* \* \*

Whenever I start a new job, I like to find The Perfect Spot. You'll see me circling the place like a dog looking for somewhere to sleep. I'll try one, smoke a Malagueña, take a nap, let it settle into my body. Then I'll try another. At the cemetery, the Perfect Spot is on top this tombstone speckled hill—a little sheltered outpost that affords me a terrific view of the passing midnight traffic on the BQE and beyond that the sparkling city. From here, it's obvious that those skyscrapers are just lit up graves, different books in the same library.

The sky grows dark over the city as Janey tells me her

story. The beast was supposed to help their community. Something that would look good in a brochure, I suppose. But instead it cut loose, took out into the Williamsburg night. Janey and her friends went after it, and what does it do? The thing ate a hipster. Hipster is what they call these new-fangled white people that've been moving onto the block—the ones with the tight pants and big glasses. Now Janey has a serious clean up job on her hands.

"You know," I say, "the river's really good for that kind of thing."

She says it'd bother her not to give the kid a proper burial, being that she was partially responsible for his death. And knowing Janey, he'd probably start troubling her dreams.

\* \* \*

So here I am, at 3 a.m. on a soggy late April morning, lugging two ominously heavy trash bags up a remote hill towards a grove of trees. I have a shovel and a flashlight and I'm trying to ignore the way one of the bags is knocking against my back as I walk, like it's trying to get my attention. Still, the thrill of adventure is tickling me like it hasn't done since Nesto's mom made me give up breaking and entering. Perhaps it's tinnitus, but the dead seem to be humming excitedly, a quiet droning accompaniment to my journey. Most people sneak around graveyards to steal bodies; here I am bringing one in. And I work here. If I'm caught, at least they will be confused. But then they may think I'm the one chewed up the boy. I walk a little faster.

Untold stores of ferocious grace remain in these old bones, however hidden beneath lard and cholesterol. The hole gets dug pretty fast but I'm a sweaty disaster when it's done. Just as I heave-ho the two bags in, the crunching of tires on gravel announces the imminent arrival of grave-yard security. I probably know the guys; I play dominoes with a few of them at shift change, but still, this would be difficult to explain.

I'd like to say that I grappled my way down; even a controlled tumble would've been something. There wasn't time for any of that though: I plummeted. I felt sure my girth traveling at that speed would've given the planet a jolt, but the splintering bones and squishy body parts I land on break my fall, saving my ass in more ways than one. I try to breathe as quietly as possible as the patrol jeep rumbles close and then wanders away.

It's a few hours from dawn and I'm lying in a fresh grave with two trash bags full of severed hipster parts, so I sit up and light a Malagueña. I'm pretty sure I haven't had a stroke or heart attack. Everything hurts slightly more than usual; perhaps I'm bleeding internally. That, at least, would be poetic. I close my eyes and pull a stream of smoke down my trachea to survey the damage. Things seem to be in working order.

I exhale and follow the cloud up into the dark sky, above the tombstones, above the trees, above the sparkling city. Souls are rising into the night. It's just graveyard souls at first, but then I start seeing people I know. There's Old Corrales and Ruben, my bass player. Sylvia Andaluz, who used to give me head in the back room at El Mar. By the time Nesto Jr. and Janey float by, tears are rolling down my face, which hasn't happened in a few eons. All I hear is the swarming hymn of the dead and the clackity-clacking body parts beneath me. White pus is oozing from the torn up hipster's limbs and slow-mo flooding through the streets of Brooklyn; a rising tide. The last few scattered souls float up into the sky and all that's left are kids, thirteen and under. It's a whole orchestra of the little guys, each armed with instruments and they're putting up a fight, coming at the pus with everything they got. I hear them laughing and chattering as they blast homemade fire bombs from trombone cannons and beat back the waves with flame-throwing tubas and sharpened guitar spears.

The chattering and laughter of children blends with scattered birdsong as morning breaks around me. Everything is back to normal, but nothing will ever be the same. I sit up, take in the crisp new day air. It's a beautiful morning, but something terrible is coming. Perhaps Janey saw the same vision, and that's why she does what she does. Either way, my own path is clear: I'll drop off this i-thing in front of the middle school. While I'm there, I'll see if they need anyone to teach music or sweep the floors or both. Maybe at the school there will be a nice spot for me to smoke and ponder in between classes. I'll see what this new day brings. But first I have to get out of this hole.

# PROTECTED ENTITY

Short, sullen-faced child ghosts are hovering around my legs. They don't speak, just stare through wide, horrified eyes at the misty warehouse around us. I don't like kids that much, especially not dead ones, but I still have to force back the urge to just wrap my living arms around them and tell 'em it's gonna be alright. It's not. They're dead; prematurely, horrifically dead, murdered probably. What do you say to a murdered child? I just stay quiet; try to ignore those questioning eyes.

"Carlos," Bartholomew Arsten floats towards me from one of the offices. Bart's one of the Council's more reconciliatory ghosts upstairs, always trying to make like he's doing his best to work things out for us soulcatchers in the field. I don't trust him. "Thanks so much for coming down, we really appreciate it." He looks nervous, skirting carefully through the crowd of youngins like he might catch something if he touches one.

"Whassup?" I say as if the answer weren't hovering all around me. It's more fun to make him explain.

"Well," says Bart, "it seems there's been some kind of incident, er, spiritual incident, you know, of some kind, in the African-American community."

"What makes you think so?"

You'd think we were playing tennis, the way those wide eyes bounce back and forth between me and Bart.

"Well, all these..." he gestures helplessly at the air, "children. These bla–African American...children."

"Looks like someone having a damn celebrity adoption open house down here."

Bart laughs, but only for show. He's too busy being uncomfortable to really pay mind to what I'm saying. "Of course, yes. Yes. Anyway, Agent Delacruz, that's why we brought you in, as you can see. And Agent Washington, of course, is on this too, he's just otherwise occupied right now, but he'll meet you at the scene."

"Buncha black kids get offed so you bring in the only two minorities you got, huh?"

"Yes! No! Well, of course I mean, because...no. No."

"Whenever you're ready, Bart."

"We don't know what to do, Carlos, they won't even speak! And they keep showing up! There's what, seven, eight now? It's crazy. We just want to help them, but you can see how the situation's getting, er, untenable... It's horrible really, whatever's going on. And we don't know their names, where they're from... Nothing."

I wrap my hands around one of those little cloudy waists and lift up the child to my eye level. He squirms, tiny arms waving in the air, and lets out a few pathetic chirps. The others get quiet and watch to see what I'll do. "What's your name, kid?"

The boy lets out a heartbreaking sob, his little icy body trembling in my hands. I close my eyes, blocking everything but the gentle vibrations radiating back from my hands. It's mostly emotion coming through, all that brand new fear, but there's relief there too. Seems like all the boys know each other somehow, besides having died together.

"God, I just want to do something for them, you know, like, start a program or something, you know?"

I put the kid down and grab another, ignoring Bart so as not to encourage him. This one's a little more together. Perfectly twisted ghost locks dangle from his round head. He doesn't cry, just glares back at me like I had something to do with this mess. But when I close my eyes, it's like looking through a slightly smudged window into him. It's a block, a pretty damn fancy one; gorgeous brownstones stand proudly on either side. BMWs, SUVs and Mercedes are parked along the grassy, tree-lined curbs.

"I mean, like, a program for the underprivileged, you know? Like, for ghosts who were poverty stricken in life? A way to, like, help them to help themselves." Bart's words flutter around me like a stupid flock of moths—one I can ignore for now. Might be in Harlem, this block, maybe up by 125th, on the west side. I squinch up my closed eyes, trying to clear up the image enough to make out a street sign but it's still pretty murky.

"They're not poor, Bart."

"Huh?"

"Here." I extend little man to Bart. He looks pleadingly at me for a second and then grudgingly reaches for the child. "I gotta go. Tell Riley to meet me uptown."

"Come back soon," Bart says, trying to keep the desperation from his voice.

\* \* \*

This part of Harlem's mostly white now. Homeless black guys wander aimlessly, pretending they didn't get the memo to clear the fuck out. Cops wear vindicated grins as they stroll triumphantly up and down the quiet, sunshiny blocks. Comfortable young white people flutter around in sandals and shorts, doing little chores, heading to outdoor cafes, staying casually but carefully within the designated borders of their territory.

"Malcolm X Towers?" Riley scoffs. "Luxury apartments?

Are you serious?" We're standing at the foot of a monstrous glass fortress on Fifth Ave.

"You know ghost Malcolm's ready to fuck a tower up," I say.

"If only..."

"Well, at least they had the decency to put in an exercise room, Riley. And a spa."

"Let's go, man. I'm 'bout to have a Nat Turner moment."

We wind westward through the sidestreets. I'm blending with the bums, a limping weirdo in a long leather jacket, talking and joking like there's some dude next to me. No one pays me much mind; strolling madmen are an endangered species in this part of town.

* * *"Black people live here?" Riley says as we approach the first spiraling mansion. It's a holdout: Several of the richest black families got together and bought up all the property on this one block as a last ditch effort to hold on to the old spirit of West Harlem. "Shit, if I'd known that when I was alive I would've found a reason to come over and marry their daughter. This place is made outta money."

"Maybe you did," I say. "Hell, maybe you lived here."

"Carlos, I don't have to remember my past to know that this brother was broke, OK? Don't press me on it."

"I don't really see how..." I start, but then the door swings open and a tuxedoed white man appears.

"No...fucking...way!" Riley yells at the top of his lungs.

The butler can only see and hear me though, and he doesn't look amused. "How may I help you, sir?"

"These cats went ahead and got a white man to serve them hand and foot!" Riley gasps, doubled over with laughter. "Son!"

"I'm Agent Delacruz with the NYPD's Special Crimes Division." I flash a fake badge that the Council of the Dead secured through one of their nefarious, un-talked-about connections with the cops. "Just want to ask Mister and Missus Ballantine a few questions about the disappearance of their son." It's utter nonsense of course but usually gets us in the door.

"The Ballantines have already spoken to the police," the butler says in a severe monotone. "They don't wish to be further disturbed."

Riley stops laughing. "Oh really, motherfucker?"

"I understand, sir," I say. "However, I'm afraid I have to insist. Given the recent media coverage about the number of kids gone missing on this block, it's crucial that we rule them out once and for all as suspects in the investigation."

The butler raises an eyebrow. I really haven't said anything, just laced the words "media" and "suspects" into a sentence together so Jeeves'll know I mean business. He chortles unintelligibly, opens the door and stands to the side. I walk in, exaggerating my hobble. I don't feel any imminent danger, but I've fallen into the habit of giving anyone I meet plenty of reasons to underestimate me.

\* \* \*

A few minutes later, Riley and I are waiting in an eerily immaculate sitting room. Nothing around us looks like it's supposed to be touched. The air is acrid with cleaning solution and perfume, so I light a cigar and blow some smoke towards Riley.

"This place is icky," my partner says, flowing over a pristine forest of crystal tchotchkes. "Let's do what we gotta do and blow on to the next one." I nod slightly instead of answering, because I know someone somewhere is monitoring our every sniff and tremble on little black and white screens.

Mr. John R. Ballantine looks rather ghostlike himself

when he shows up. His thin face creases into a perma-frown that radiates over his entire body. "I've already said all I need to say to the police," he says without leaving the doorway. "All I've gotten in return is stupidity and bureaucracy, none of which will bring back my boy. You can show yourself out."

"Sir," I say, but he simply walks away. Riley and I exchange a look and then I walk out and he floats to the corridor that Mr. Ballantine disappears into.

\* \* \*

Outside, the block is completely still. Even the breeze is keeping its distance out of respect to the grieving. It's the end of summer, and the late afternoon sun plays a dazzling light show across the Hudson River. If I'd been able to touch Ballantine, I would've had a chance to penetrate his wall of grief and find something out, but the man was unapproachable. I close my eyes and take a long pull of smoke. The sorrow must be seeping from house to house like a biohazard, making families keep their children locked up in crisp air-conditioned bedrooms, throwing silence over dinner tables, wreaking havoc on fragile, middle-aged sex lives. Or was that how things were even without a spate of child-killings?

"It's the third house on the left," Riley says, breaking my reverie. "Some dude named Calhoun. New on the block."

"What about him?"

"I dunno, but sounds like everyone thinks he's to blame for all this. Let's take a look."

\* \* \*

The Calhoun estate is every bit as magnificent as the rest of the block. Spiraling towers poke out above a terrace garden. This time we're ready when a white man comes to the door. "Could you tell Mr. Calhoun that the NYPD would like a word with him?" I say in my formal let's-get-this-done voice.

"You're talking to him," the white guy says with a grin. Yes, the Hawaiian shirt and khaki shorts should've tipped me off that he wasn't the butler, but the whole day has thrown me for a loop. John Calhoun's in his mid-forties and sports a quickly retreating flop of light brown hair.

"Right, Mr. Calhoun."

"John," the guy says.

"John," I say. "You're..."

"Can I help you?" A touch of menace flickers around Mr. Calhoun. Riley catches it too. I get my game together and give him my cop spiel. He sizes me up for a moment and then flashes a cheesy smile and beckons me inside.

"Really horrible stuff, all this business with the young black kids dying and all," our host says as he leads us through an expansive foyer towards some glass-paneled sliding doors. I believe him—there's no anxiousness or guilt radiating out, and his voice is slightly detached but not forced.

My eyes dart across the room and Riley does a flash fly around. It's hard to describe what we look for in situations like this. Something that's not right, is the best way I can put it; something that may be harboring a malicious spirit or used to commit mass murder. But that could be anything. I've extracted some vengeful afterlifers from an old boot and executed a whole nest of errant house ghosts that were infesting a microwave. You have to learn to pick up on the little clues that things are not as they should be; tiny cries for help. Then there's the obvious ones, like the dried up animal parts that some bored traveler dragged home thinking they'd look cute on the mantle, or the blatantly haunted grandfather clock that shows whoever's near how they're going to die. Those are the ones that make you roll your eyes and try not to think about how the fool deserves whatever supernatural ass-whupping he ends up getting.

John Calhoun has none of that stuff though, at least not on the first two floors. He leads me up a winding stairwell, all the while chatting about the different families and how welcoming they were when he moved into the neighborhood and what a terrible shame it is about those black kids. We pause on a landing and I say: "Mr. Calhoun."

"Please," throwing his hands up, "just John."

"John, you are white, correct?"

Calhoun lets out a laugh like I'd just told a dirty joke. I half-chuckle, more out of discomfort than anything else. From somewhere above us, I hear Riley squirming and clattering around. "I mean," Calhoun says, acting like he's still reeling from the preposterousness of the question. He makes a show of checking the skin on his arm. "I am!" he says, still yukking away. "By golly!"

"Is this guy for real?" Riley says, floating down next to me.

I shake my head, at a loss for words."How is it you came to live on the last remaining all black block in West Harlem, Mr. Calhoun?" I really am curious.

"What is this, the 1960's?" Calhoun laughs. "Did I break a zoning law? Are you going to charge me with desegregation? Guilty as charged." I just stare at him. "Okay, look, in all seriousness," he says, wiping the big grin off his face and waxing professorial, "I have a great respect for African and African-American culture. I teach Pan-African history at Columbia. I've written several books on Nigerian culture and the Caribbean Diaspora. I've spent three of the past seven years doing field-work on one end of the continent or the other. I wasn't about to move into some hood, but I feel comfortable around black people. So here I am. I asked permission from the block council before buying the place, and frankly they were quite impressed with my extensive knowledge of pre-Colombian civilizations."

"Let's kill him," Riley says in my ear.

"Now, Detective," Calhoun finishes triumphantly, "if you will kindly step into my office, we can further discuss the tragedy at hand."

\* \* \*

Riley and I both stop and let our jaws hang open. An entire army of sacred African masks and statues clutter around us from every corner and crevice. I recognize a few from the Afrofantastic table stores on 125th, but most of it's clearly some collector shit. A small cadre of cowry shell-eyed stone heads gape up at me from the floor around Calhoun's writing desk. Wooden Masai warriors guard either side of his file cabinets. Elaborate masks glare from the walls. Any number of these items could be covertly housing some irritable, child-killing demon. The air's thick with old wood musk, Calhoun's self-satisfaction and a chaotic mix of colliding spiritual energies. None of them jump out at me as being particularly malevolent, but there's still plenty to sort through.

"What's the matter?" Calhoun jibes. "Never been in a room with so many sacred objects at once? It is a little overwhelming at first, but you get used to it." Somewhere in the clutter of masks, digital fish float lazily across a screensaver.

"Did any of the kids from the neighborhood ever come up here?" I ask.

"Do you have any idea how valuable just one of these items is, Detective?"

"That's not an answer."

John Calhoun smiles. "No, Detective, none of the children ever came up to this room. I have had a couple of the families over for dinner in the past few months since I moved in, the Robinsons, the Eltons and the Ballantines, and I suppose I showed the adults my collection—I'm a bit of a show off—but none of the kids came up that I recall."

Riley's milling in and out of the statues, trying to untangle all the spiritual data colliding around us. Judging from his cursing, he's not having much luck. "The last officers I spoke to told me I wasn't a suspect," Calhoun says as he walks past me and holds the door open. Then I feel it: A wash of brittle frustration and rage. The suddenness of it almost knocks me into a battalion of statues. "Whoa there, guy!" Calhoun says, reaching out good naturedly as I right myself. "Told you it was a little overwhelming at first. Why don't you have a seat in my thinking chair?"

I don't like the sound of that at all, but the nausea's so intense I don't have much choice. I slump into an antique wooden chair with ornate pink cushions. Of course Calhoun would be one of these doofy intellectuals that needs his special chair to get anything done. If anything though, sitting makes the spiritual cringing even more fierce, like two giant sets of teeth grating somewhere at the core of my being. I leap up out of the chair and walk unsteadily to the door.

"Detective!" Calhoun calls after me, but I'm already making my way back out into the fresh early evening air.

\* \* \*

"What you think?" I ask Riley as we stroll the Hudson River walkway.

"I think we have a problem." Shadows grow long around us. The water turns a murky purple beneath the graying sky. "There's definitely something up there but there's too many statues and masks to sort through."

"You felt it, right?"

"Yeah," Riley says. "Powerful shit. Like a caged animal or something. I know one thing: I never seen your ass move out of a room that fast." We both have a good laugh. "What'd you get from Calhoun?"

"The guy's all kindsa trapped in his head. He's got this lingering discomfort though—"

"Another shocking discovery by Carlos."

"No, I mean there's something else. When that festering rage passed through the room, it didn't come from him, but it knew him. Or he knew it. Something. There was a familiarity between them."

"Maybe," Riley says, "he paid some charlatan to spiritually bind him to one of those masks and the shit worked."

"There's definitely something he's not being straight about."

Riley's nebular glowing body straightens suddenly. He's getting a message from the Council of the Dead.

"Those telepathic motherfuckers want an update and an answer ASAP," he reports.

"Imma do a little archive work," I say. "But we need some time in that room without Dr. Africa's prying ass around."

Riley nods. "Tonight."

\* \* \*

The basement research section at the Harlem Public Library is incongruously tidy. It lacks the towering stacks of coffee stained parchment one would hope for in a historical archive, and the antiseptic smell and glaring lights would better suit a hospital. But that's only if you stay in the main reading room. If you down with Doctor Tennessee though, you don't stay in the reading room, you go into the backstacks. "The reading room for suckas," Doctor Tennessee told me when I first came through for a visit. "The backstacks where all the good shit hiding. If you workin' anything deeper than a middle school book report..." she peered over her bifocals at me to confirm. I was trying to track down an angry architect ghost at the time, so I nodded. "...Well then you gonna need to go into the backstacks. You smoke?"

"Cigars."

"Gimme one." The little Doctor ambled quickly down a corridor and around a corner. A second later she poked her head out and waved at me. "Well, c'mon then, mister. Ain't you gonna join me?" I looked around the crisp, sterile reading room and then ducked under the counter and followed the old woman out the door. That was the first of many, many afternoons spent sharing smokes and jokes in the little hidden atrium between the main library and the backstacks. Mostly I just let Tennessee talk, rambling stories about her childhood outside of Memphis mixed in with animal fables, historical anecdotes and musings on the history of jazz. Then I make my request.

"Calhoun," I say. The good Doctor has wound down and is now sitting peacefully, sending little smoke cities up along the gray bricolage of air ducts and fire escapes.

"John Calhoun?" She spits back at me. For all the spiraling stacks in the labyrinth surrounding us—there is an even larger library inside the doctor's head.

"The very same."

"The cat that wrote all the books 'bout Africa or his plantation owning great grand-pappy?"

"Come again?"

"John Richard Calhoun III is a preeminent scholar of West African culture and religion. You can't draw a smiley face on a paper plate in Benin without the guy writing a book about it. Lives around these parts I hear. His great grand-pappy ran one of the most heinous and successful slave plantations in the North. Name was known far and wide. Made a fortune off it. You know the deal, Carlos. God may work in mysterious ways, but when He feeling ironic, the shit just become straight predictable."

Lost in thought, I make a neither-here-nor-there

hrmphing noise.

"I can see you into something there, C. You run along, do your thing. I'll take a look at the collection." Doctor Tennessee knows better than to ask too many questions about what I do.

* * *

Riley and I hole up in one of those 24 hour spots under the tracks. We eat eggs and sausages and drink bottomless cups of coffee as the night drifts past. I've gotten used to being the weirdo who orders two of everything and sits there talking to himself. Riley's gotten used to taking little tiny bites and sipping his coffee with the cup on the table. "I think we been barking up the wrong proverbial tree."

"Oh? What'd the good doctor have for you this time?"

We tumble the situation back and forth a bit before straying into an extended imaginary musing about what our lives must've been like.

We shoot the shit 'til quarter to three. That's when an older lady comes in surrounded by a squabbling entourage of toddlers and pre-teens. A tall, sour-faced twelve year old girl walks beside her. They both look exhausted but not altogether put out as they shuffle into the table across from us and try to simmer down the slew of bouncing youngins.

I'm about to get up and be out when a little guy with a bigass fro and corduroy overalls clamors up onto the seat beside Riley and stares at him. Riley looks back at the kid, first with his angry squint and then gradually softening to a sort of Rileysmile. "Wooga wooga," he says. The boy chuckles, holding eye contact. "Boogady boogady boogady." More chuckles. The girl and her grandma are busy with the other wee ones. Time seems to have slowed for my best friend. Ever so carefully, he reaches out a shining, see-through hand to the kid. The child reaches back, still gurgling and giggling away, and wraps his own little hand around one of the glowing fingers. His expression doesn't change, but I can tell something just shattered inside Riley.

"Let's go," he says, when the spell is finally broken and the child wanders off to some new distraction. "I wanna get this over with."

* * *

At three, we trudge through the humid Manhattan night into West Harlem. Once again, even the trees refuse to rustle on the mourning block. All the houses are dark, but inside restless limbs strain beneath too hot bed sheets and anxious heads play out horrific fantasies in never-ending cycles.

I can be as quiet as any ghost when I have to. Patience is really all it takes. Move like you're made of molasses. Sound just falls away from you. You catch your rhythm and eventually, you're wherever you need to be and no one's the wiser. Riley pops the door and we slow-mo it up the winding stairs to Calhoun's office. I turn the knob ever so gently and soft foot in, Riley at my side. It's completely dark save the little blinking-light city of the computer terminal and modem.

Riley's mingling with the statues again and I'm about to start in on the masks when I feel it. Riley stiffens and readies for combat. A wave of revulsion sweeps over me. I close my eyes, investigating the churning ripple of rage that has suddenly become a presence in the room. We both turn around and there, in the easy chair, sits a very old, dimly glowing man.

* * *

As I'm sure you've noticed, death isn't the great equalizer it's made out to be. Layers of hierarchy remain, interlaced by the tangled webs of power and privilege. The dead, after all, are human, and what could be more human than an unnecessarily oppressive bureaucracy at the end all be all of existence? Anyway, through whatever combination of sinister string-pulling and luck, this particular departed old-timer is obviously immensely powerful. If nothing else, you can tell because he's completely unfazed by the presence of two no-nonsense COD soulcatchers in his living quarters. The guy's from way-back-when, judging by his threads. He has on an elegant 18th century type jacket, complete with poufy nonsense at the collar and doily cuffs.

The wretched feeling only grows stronger as he sits there, smiling and looking off into nothing. I like to do things cleanly, gather what information I can before slicing an afterlifer into oblivion, but wave after wave of nauseating bitterness is fouling up my flow. I notice Riley's glow flicker wearily. This'll have to be quick.

"What's up with the dead kids?" I say, pulling a shiny spirit-killing blade out of my cane. He doesn't speak, but I got his attention. Without moving his eyes, the old ghost focuses all his energy and concentration on my weapon.

"Listen," Riley says, producing his own glowing saber and directing it at the easy chair, "we being nice by talking to you right now instead of just getting this over with, but we could certainly—"

*You dare address Captain Jonathon Arthur Calhoun III, boy?*

The voice is a sharp slither inside our heads. The old man just sits there smiling.

"Excuse me?" Riley demands.

"What do you want?" I say.

*The Calhouns were once a well-respected family.* It feels like a knife is cutting away parts of my brain with each word. *Kept New York harbor a central point in the transatlantic slave trade. Ran a de-facto empire from our estates in the Hudson Valley. A name known all over the civilized world. Three generations later, my fop of a great-great grandson has further disgraced his noble lineage.*

"Is he talking to us?" Riley whispers.

"I don't know," I say.

My knees are starting to give out. I'm not sure if I'm holding off ending him from fascination or fear, but the no-turning back point's fast approaching.

*And now: Here I am in this faggotine city of corpulence, cross-breeding and cowardice, shackled to a worthless, slave-loving progeny. Still: I manage to have my fun, wreak my vengeance in a manner fit for pharaohs.*

"The first born sons," I say. "The tenth plague. You're a dipshit just like your great grandson."

The old man turns his shaggy sneering face towards me for the first time and I almost double over with nausea. *The extinction of the black race has to begin somewhere. Why not in the uppermost echelons?*

I'm done finding shit out. Time to endgame the situation. As I step forward to engage the ghost, the office door swings open and John Calhoun bursts in. He's wearing tighty-whiteys and a stained, white t-shirt. He looks pissed. Gone is the forced smile he had flashed again and again that afternoon. "What the hell do you think you're doing in my office, Detective?"

He stands directly between my blade and his slave-trading, child-killing ancestor. A cruel laughter erupts in my brain like a bomb going off. "Get out of the way," I say. I'm trying to put on a calm front but a shiver has found its way into my voice. Both Calhouns hear it. The laughter in my head gets louder. "I have to destroy that chair."

"That chair is an heirloom!" John Calhoun screams.

"I bet," Riley mutters.

"I'm calling the police," Calhoun announces, as if that settles the matter. He produces a cell phone and I swat it out of his hands with my cane. He glares at me in total disbelief. I swat him again, higher this time and he falls out of the way and cowers in a corner.

"Let's get this over with, man," Riley says. He's beside me now, weak but ready to move. "Hold off Captain Underpants and I'll deal with Grampa." I feel his icy hand on my shoulder, steadying me.

The transmission comes in blaring and staticky: *Councilman Arsten to agents Washington and Delacruz.* We both straighten to attention at the sound of Bart's nasally voice. *Be advised, the entity known as Captain Jonathon Arthur Calhoun III, deceased 1846 of New York State, is a confirmed protected entity. He is not to be touched, harmed, or insulted.* I try to concentrate on holding my blade steady, keeping both Calhouns at bay. Riley starts breathing heavily. *Under no circumstances is he to be dispatched into non-existence. This concludes Emergency Executive Order 203-14 of the New York Council of the Dead. Failure to comply will result in banishment and termination.*

When the transmission ends, all I hear is the ghost Calhoun's piercing laughter. I lower my blade slightly and then bring it back up. I feel Riley bristling and burning like a fireball beside me. There's a pause. Then Riley lurches forward. I see the blade flash and the old man's face suddenly looks frail and desperate. You ever notice how old people do that? Act all powerful until things don't go their way. The ancient phantom moans, gurgles and then shrivels out of existence. On the floor lies the crumpled pile of wood and fabric that had once been a Calhoun family heirloom. I feel suddenly light on my feet. The whole room takes a breath, like the steam had been let out of the pressure cooker.

John Calhoun, still cowering in the corner, stammers nonsensically. Riley and I look at each other. I can't decide if that's disappointment in his frown or just the sullen satisfaction of a grim job well done. I had hesitated. When he moved, the whole world had moved with him to deliver that divine justice; I could feel the sacred pantheon reveling in his victory around us. But the repercussions of defying the Council are devastating. We don't have much time. Death's angry bull's-eye is already swirling towards Riley.

Calhoun screams and I realize that Riley has made himself visible. I guess once you've tossed the rulebook out, you might as well go all the way.

"You've caused a lot of problems," Riley says.

"Jesus, what are you?"

"It's not about me. Maybe if you'd spent more time studying your own people before you came studying mine, we wouldn't be in this mess."

"I-I don't understand!"

"I think you do, but I'll let it slide. I'ma need you to do me a favor, though, Mr. Calhoun."

"Anything."

"Put some of the degree'd-up intellect of yours into dealing with your shit," Riley says, "and move out."

\* \* \*

"What are you going to do?" I ask. We're strolling slowly back down towards the darkened river.

"I don't know yet," Riley says. "Get the hell outta here, for starters." We both laugh weakly. I light a cigar.

"About what happened back there..."

"I did what I had to do," Riley cuts in.

I know those words are gonna haunt me. We walk a little further in silence. I try to ignore the image of that great warehouse with all its misty apparitions flickering into a frenzy as word of Riley's disobedience spreads. Icy fingers will twitch anxiously. A flurry of messages will broadcast out. The gears of supernatural war are about to begin thundering towards the ghost beside me.

"They're gonna send me after you," I say.

"I imagine so."

"Things will get messy between us."

"They don't have to."

I nod. We shake hands and walk in separate directions, drifting off into the New York night.

# MAGDALENA

In a couple of hours, Magdalena will walk out of a forest and into a field. I've imagined the moment so many times now. One of her spaghetti straps'll be hanging down her shoulder and she'll still be carrying the machete. She won't be smiling. Face so serious you'd wonder if she'll ever smile again. But she will walk out into that field and far, far away, and leave the terrible past behind her.

"So you're saying you still think about her?" Big Cane breaks into my imaginings. Probably because he's bored. We've been floating amidst the manicured bushes in front of this library for two days now, waiting, watching, watching, waiting. Not glamorous at all, this ghost hunting work.

"Every mothafuckin' day, B. Well, okay, not every single one. But many. And especially as today started coming up."

"This was when you were still alive that you knew her?" His enormity demands he always be looking down at whoever he's speaking to, but otherwise, Big Cane is the least condescending white person I've ever met, dead or alive. When he looks at me, I believe he really does see me, not some cavewoman cartoon he caught on TV in whatever century he lived in, not some pitiful, overweight, punk rock black chick that needs saving.

It's something in his eyes.

"Yeah. This boarding school I went to." I always pause there. Don't ask me why. "For troubled teens."

I hope I'm right about Cane, because I've told him more about my life than I've ever told anyone else ever. He has a way of just prying stuff out of me, probably because he really doesn't try, just makes his little noises and occasionally sews together sentences and then I get to babbling. Which I swear is really unlike me, except when it's not. That particular grunt means, *I see* with an added connotation of *What are you gonna do about it, then?*

We spend a lot of time together, me and Cane.

I shrug and move my neck in circles to ease the soreness of so much of the same. "I don't know if I'ma do anything, yet. There's something to be said for letting go."

"Hm." *Amen.*

At the coffee shop across the street, life bumbles along its insanely dull daily routine. We're in Riverdale, a gushy suburban corner of the Bronx and not a damn interesting thing has happened here since 1947. Probably not true: A few night clubs and assorted shenanigan holes are scattered around on Broadway, not far away, but this block right here? Duller than death. You'd never guess that at the daycare center behind the coffee shop, three parasite phantoms are poised to feed on an entire room full of toddlers.

"Oh, look, that same mom with the two kids from yesterday," Big Cane points out.

"Mm." I'm getting to be more like him with each passing day of this insane stake out. Good thing we're cool.

"'Cept she's a little later today."

"Indeed." Kill me now.

Cane adjusts his position, stretches those gigantic arms forward and then up above his head. "So...I think you should do something." A rare declaration of opinion from the ancient giant. "About Magdalena, that is."

I frown. "Suggestions?"

"Nope."
"Great."

* * *

Magdalena strolled into fifth period English class late and chewing gum one chilly Friday afternoon, and slid into the seat next to mine. She wore a purple dress and you could tell she had those kind of breasts that just lay there against her chest and that she didn't give a fuck what people thought about that. Halfway through the class she slid a folded up sheet of lined paper onto my desk with a drawing of a penis riding a mule, its grotesquely hairy nutsack straddling the saddle like fat little legs. I tried to suppress a cackle, caught some saliva in my windpipe and erupted into a coughing fit.

When I recovered and Mr. Davis stopped glaring at me, I drew devil horns on the donkey and a backpack on the penis with a little baby penis poking its head out, papoose style.

That was the first time I saw Magdalena smile. It exploded like the tearing of two tectonic plates across her face; transformed her in seconds from a snarling teenager to a bright little girl. Her two front teeth were huge and one laid slightly on top of the other like it was trying to hold it back from picking a fight with the world. Then she disappeared the smile, perhaps never to be seen again, and concentrated on drawing the mama penis and her mule.

* * *

"I think it's time," I say, more because I'm bored than any real reason.

Big Cane shakes his big head. "Not yet."

"Soon?"

A nod and the slightest of smiles.

"How will we know?" I'm not usually this impatient but Magdalena's big moment is rapidly approaching, and it's drenching my thought process with a swirl of gruesome images. Not the walking out the forest ones. Other, uglier scenes, that I'd rather not think about. "The Council gonna send us a message or something?"

Cane lets out a gentle chortle and rubs his big fingers into his eyes. "Council ain't tellin' us shit except come to XYZ location, wait and move when it's time to move. The parasites been holed up in there for two days, gathering strength while the kids come and go. And you and I are the eyes and ears of the Council right now, Krys. That's it."

"So we just wait 'til some magical moment? How do we decide what to do?"

Instead of answering, Cane says, "Look, you wanna talk about what you're really talking about?" I hate that he can see right through me. I also love it, but right now I just bristle and shrug. I am, after all, still a teenager.

Cane shrugs too and it looks like a mountain range going for a stroll. "Suit yourself."

I let a moment or two pass, because I don't want to seem too anxious, and then say, "It's an anniversary thing. The day and hour she turns eighteen and... The day something horrible happened to her, years ago." Cane nods and I say, "On her eleventh birthday, actually." I'm not sure why I added that detail; maybe I needed to see Cane flinch like that, to know there is still some living, feeling thing under all those translucent layers of muscle and fat. But then I feel bad, because now the sadness in his eyes won't go away and it's too late to go back. "Her father."

Cane looks like he's been slapped and for what it's worth, a part of me is relieved. You never know how someone, especially a man, is gonna react to information like that, and I was afraid he'd just go on being the big stoic impenetrable badass he always is and that I would hate him for it.

* * *

I wasn't crying as Magdalena finished telling her story but I was definitely making stupid little sobby noises and frowning a whole lot. It was 3 a.m. on the morning of her sixteenth birthday. We'd snuck out of our dorm and holed up in a little makeshift nest made of stolen blankets and flickering candles in the cramped props room behind the auditorium. I hiccupped and sniffled but Magdalena just sat there calm as could be. Then she told me about the promise she'd made to herself. A covenant, she called it, fiddling idly with one of the silver spikes sticking out of her lower lip. A covenant. Then she frowned.

She still had babyfat on her face and her hair was tied back beneath a red bandana. I felt so big and solid next to her wispy little frame, but for the first time in maybe ever that bigness didn't feel like a bad thing, an awkward thing, it just felt like what I was. I wished in that moment that I could bottle the certainty in her eyes that made it so simple and obvious to just be me. Wished I could make a lifetime supply for every moment a stranger's gaze told me the opposite.

* * *

"It's time."

I look up from my memories. Cane is poised like a giant tiger that's about to obliterate some unknowing gazelle. The bastard's actually smiling about the magnificent ass-wh-upping he's about to deliver and that's why me and Big C are peoples. Because I'm smiling, too. Life, death, struggle, whatever: It's comp-licated, laden with strife and dis-agreements, regret, poisoned hearts and betrayals. We're all survivors of something. And nothing helps all that muck disappear into the ether, at least momentarily, like truly wailing on some deserving fool of a soul-sucking phantom.

I don't know what silent cue Cane took from the universe to tell him our moment had come. He never gives me a straight answer when I try to ask; instinct, I guess. A thing I'm only beginning to understand. Either way, like he says, he just knows.

At a nodded signal, I pull my bow and arrow from my back and aim at the sky above the coffee shop. Feels so good, so right to stretch my arms after so long sitting and waiting. Just right. I take an extra second to double check my aim, imagining the havoc I'm about to unleash. I don't really need to, but this is no time for arrogance. Children's lives are at stake.

I release, feel the projectile erupt from my bow, stretch upwards in a glorious arc, cut through the late afternoon sky above the heads of a dozen oblivious passersby. It hangs there for a solid second, as if unsure whether or not to give in to gravity, and then plummets. The warhead at the end is a sharpened canister: The spiritual equivalent of a shock grenade. It won't do any real damage but should stun everybody enough to give us the upper hand.

Inside the building, fourteen kindergarteners stand in a tangled shadow web. They can't see it of course, can't see anything in their semi-comatose state, but those misty lines stretch between the three hunched over phantoms. The parasites are fully in some kind of hellacious meditation, all bent on their soul-sucking ways. They're draining these kids of their life force. The kids'll live but they'll just be shells, no vitality. Failure to thrive, it's called in medical textbooks. The rest of their sad lives will be a failure to thrive. At least that's what would've happened. Instead, my warhead comes dancing out of the sky, swoops through all those layers of concrete and wire mesh and finds its mark smack in the middle of the feeding.

Cane and I burst out of our hiding place. People walk down the street like it's just another day in Riverdale, strolling, shopping, going about their business. We cut through them, a sudden breeze against the flesh of the living, and push into the building. The arrow has done its job well; the parasites stumble every which way, their long interconnecting tentacles flapping in the air uselessly. The kids blink awake; a few start crying and running around in circles.

I bring my bow down hard on the first parasite I pass, smashing it into the ground in a pathetic ghostly heap. The next one is recovering some; it lurches up at me and I meet it with a fist in the face. The thing crumples again and I move on, stepping gingerly over the collapsing ghost web.

\* \* \*

After Magdalena told me about her plan we sat quietly for a few minutes. This band she likes, Culebra, screamed and wailed on a gritty little speaker box and the only other sound was us pulling on the joint, coughing occasionally. If it had been totally quiet, no music, no smoking, nada? I think she would've been able to hear my heart sobbing. No tears came out, although Magdalena's story has pulled the floor out from under me. I just let the sadness become a sleeping snake, curled up inside me. I let it rise in my chest; let it squeeze a little tighter with each puff of smoke.

After a few minutes, Magdalena opened up that big smile once again. "The other part of my plan is this..."

"Tell me."

"Every year until then," she said like she was coming to the end of a really corny ghost story, "on my birthday, I will make love to a beautiful woman."

I burst out laughing, but Magdalena had folded her smile back away. I stopped laughing and we just looked at each other across the dark room.

\* \* \*

"Go," Cane says. He has his own covenant, the protocols of manhood. He follows them religiously and they don't allow him to put words to what's on his mind. But he doesn't have to. A certain tremble erupts in those ghostly pupils and it tells me everything I need to know. "Go," he says again, but he's really saying *Go, because it happened to me too. Because I survived and lived a long healthy life and so should she. Go.*

When I hesitate he nods towards the last writhing phantom and says "I got this" in a voice so hoarse and serious I almost hug him. But that's not the move right now and I know it. The move is get out of here and find Magdalena. Fast. So that's what I do.

* * *

"Actually," I said when Magdalena put her pretty, uneven lips against my neck, "I like boys." I still cringe when I think about it.

"Me too," Magdalena said between slurps.

I was lying on my back. Lying perfectly still, because if I moved, the whole moment might shatter. "I mean I'm not gay."

Magdalena didn't say anything, just worked her mouth down my shoulders and along my arms.

I didn't know whether I was relieved or disappointed when she stopped kissing my toes and nuzzled up on top of me like a kitten sleeping on a baby bear in one of those feel-good postcard photos. I mean, I was praying the whole time, to an entity I knew no name for, and cringing too, and I suppose all my prayers and my shame and pleasure got mixed into one sultry, complicated sludge that got sent up to Whomever and that was that.

I said, "I thought you were going to make love to me," trying to make my voice neutral.

"I did," she said and I felt her smile against my chest.

First, I felt sad because maybe, in her strange, broken world, that's what making love was. No vaginas, no ins and outs, no gooey juices; just a whole mess of the gentlest kisses in the world placed with the utmost care on each available body part and then a good cuddle. I watched the top of her head rise and fall with each of my breaths. I had never felt so peaceful in all my life. Maybe that was what making love was in my strange, broken world too, and it was everyone else who had it wrong. I smiled and was grateful it was too dark for her to see the tears sliding out of my eyes, down my face and onto the stolen blankets.

\* \* \*

This is where she said it would happen. I move quickly through a clearing; just a translucent flash in the darkening sky and then I'm gone, disappeared into the shadows of the forest.

Perfect spot for a killing, really. There's no one around for miles; we're well away from the main road in a vast park in the murky nether region where Brooklyn becomes Queens. I glide forward on intuition mainly, because once I enter the woods it's anyone's guess where she might be. Maybe it's the beginning of Big Cane's magic being born in me too; I feel myself getting closer. Then I see her.

I'm too late. Sort of. Magdalena's standing by a concrete opening in the forest floor, maybe the foundation of some building that never got built. It's full of murky rainwater that looks like it's been there for eons, all sludge and dead leaves and trash. Doesn't matter. What matters is the lifeless collection of limbs piled in the mulch at the edge of the pool. The ground is dark with blood and blood is splattered in a frantic design across Magdalena's white t-shirt. She's crying. Wipes a hand over her sweaty brow, slathering blood all across her face. She's still got the machete in one hand, and as I move towards her, she places the tip of the blade against her belly and closes her eyes.

This isn't how it's supposed to go. I admit I had no plan. But I thought maybe I'd make it here before the deed was done. I'd figure out some way to prevent it but still cause the stupid guy enough holy terror to keep him from ever doing anything so foul ever again—maybe castration as a last resort—and then Madgalena would walk away, out to the field and on into the rest of her life.

I wrap around Madgalena, feel her shudder as my translucence covers her. She can't see me; I'm only a memory, a whisper, but I'll be a whisper at the forefront of her consciousness, I'll be memory enough to blot out all the seeping terror. She trembles, her body still stiffened, ready to strike.

I'm just new to the afterlife but I have some swagger to my magic. I squeeze tighter, throw all my spiritual strength into making my ethereal almost-nothingness break through into that flesh and blood dimension. And Magdalena still stands there on the line, wavering slightly in the early evening breeze like some baby oak tree.

It's a few minutes before I realize that whatever I'm doing isn't working. She'd thought there would be some sense of relief, some triumph and closure after all that waiting and plotting. Instead there's just an emptiness so deep it infects me too: A total devastating void. Magdalena lets out a sob and tightens her grip on the machete.

I was a pretty devout atheist in life. That night in the prop dock was probably the one prayer I could put my name to. Since I died I'm not so sure. Hard to deny that there's something else out there when you are that something else. Cane, on the other hand, was a true believer all through life and still hangs out in the back of some church in Inglewood on Sunday mornings, smoking his hand rolled cigarettes and trying not to get mistaken for the Holy Spirit. He says every soul is like a tiny shard of glass that reflects God. He says when you're dead, you're just a soul, and the reflection is even stronger, not muddled by all that flesh and blood and living people shit.

Right now, at this moment, I'm gonna go with Cane's view of the world, because it's the biggest source of strength I can find. I'll be that super-magnified shard of divine light if that'll make some glimmer of hope filter through me into Magdalena's sad soul. I'll be that. That emptiness keeps trying to overtake me, the sudden absence of life lying in a crumpled pile in front of us, the sudden absence of mission and fire in the girl I'm surrounding. My mind keeps trying to get distracted by the horror that just happened, but I force it back into focus.

At first I think I'll imagine-up a beautiful future for Magdalena, one where she's peaceful, not haunted by today or that day eight years ago or anything else that's happened in between. But I need something more solid than a dreamy sunlit apartment and a warm cup of tea. Instead, I dig up a memory: The last week of my life, when every cell in my body wanted so badly to live. Cancer won, but the imprint of that desire, that thirst for life bubbles up inside me now and I let it overflow into Magdalena.

I slide my arms down hers, ease along like a second skin across her. My whole being is vibrating with that memory, the lion's roar to live, and I let it vibrate from my core all the way through Magdalena and out into the forest around us.

A minute passes, or maybe ten. I lose track. Lose track of my own trembling, transparent body and all my joys and sorrows. Lose track of which is me and which is her or whether it matters, which of us is teetering on the fine line between life and death. Both I suppose. And then Magdalena lets out a long, shaky breath and I know we've won. Death will have to wait its turn for her. She lowers the machete, squats down and pushes the pile of limbs that was her father into the green water. The last pale appendage disappears with a gurgle. Magdalena stands and then walks out of the woods and into the field.

# THE COLLECTOR

As another burst of gunfire rang out, Victor threw his defibrillator and medic bag into an unlocked door and ducked in. He did a quick glance-glance to make sure no one was around, brushed himself off and walked a few cautious steps into the room. It looked like some busted sultan's brothel. Elaborate, weathered curtains hung morosely from the ceilings. Cigarette burns and an archipelago of stains decorated a faded Oriental rug. The stench of corner-store incense, perfume and Pall Mall cigarettes colored the air.

Not only was no one coming to force him back into the streets, no one was around at all. Most decent, life-loving people would be curled up in their bathtubs for protection this far into a shootout, anyway. Victor took a few more steps, his eyes darting back and forth. A very comfortable looking recliner beckoned from the center of the room. It was even in layback position, footrest out. The scratchy voice of another medic came crackling out of his radio, trying to give a damage report and call for backup. Victor sighed, then turned his radio off and walked over to the recliner. He let his body collapse into it and lit a cigarette.

It had been a terrible week. The past two months of escalating turf wars and passion slays in the South Ward were culminating in these last days of summer. For the first time in his nine-year career, Victor had lost track of how many bloody calls he'd done. It was all beginning to feel so useless. Somewhere in there, he must've gotten some sleep too, but only in short, tormented bursts, always interrupted by the radio crackling out another assignment. Jenny was visiting her parents in Wisconsin, so Victor had picked up as many shifts as he could. The smoke curled thickly out of his mouth, obliterated the whole thought chain, left him giddy and relaxed at the same time. "Now if only I had a coffee," he said out loud.

"A little late for coffee, no?" a voice croaked from behind some dangling tapestries. Victor let the smoke continue to swirl out. His eyes scanned the shrouds around him. A moment passed.

"Um..." He rasied his eyebrows. "Can I help you?"

"You're in my house," said the voice. "Don't you think I should be the one asking that question?"

"Fair enough."

Victor smoked and waited. A slight rustling waved through the drapes, but nothing else moved. Outside, the street battle had dwindled down to a few scattered shots. That'd be the winners finishing off the wounded, Victor thought. Almost over now. "You have an ashtray?"

"Beside the mahogany bookshelf to your left."

Victor eyed a frozen cluster of dusty furniture and some exotic metal statues. "Don't...see...one."

"It's the Buddha."

"You mean this kitchy fake gold thing?" asked Victor, rising from the chair and approaching a four-foot tall meditating Asian.

"Yes, and it happens to be real gold."

"Well, that may or may not be true. But either way, are you sure you want my ashes in it?"

"That's what it's there for."

He tapped out the cigarette and walked back over to the

chair. The nonchalant routine was starting to feel strained but he kept his mouth shut.

"Ready," said the voice, and the draperies swung open to reveal an elegant four-post bed with a flowing canopy. A pale shriveled woman hovered in the air just above the bed. She emanated a sickly, fluorescent glow. A flimsy white cloth swayed gently from her shoulders and she wore a yellow and red dashiki around her waist. Her breasts dripped down her emaciated chest like melted wax.

Victor took the whole scene in solemnly. This would definitely have to top of the list of strange shit he'd seen ("ridiculous floating white lady," right above "man running around without head" and "dude stuck in his cat"). Her unwavering stare scanned him like a searchlight for signs of fear or surprise.

He furrowed his brow. "Why you floating, ma?"

"I'm dying."

"Alright, but why you floating?"

"I'm called the Collector." She emerged from the flowing bed canopy towards Victor.

"Alright, lady, just ease up now," Victor said, taking a few steps back. "How 'bout you put a shirt on and come down from up there, huh?"

"What are you called, young man?" Her eyes continued to burrow into him.

"Bob," said Victor.

"Ah, Bobby," said the Collector as if she'd just tasted one of those shrimp in bacon whatchamacallits. "That's lovely."

"No, it's Bob."

"Tell me, Bobby, have you traveled much, in your life?"

"Been to PA a few times."

"I have traveled all over the world, Bobby, from Bolivia to Bangladesh, walked the Highway of the Gods, cavorted through the Tierra Del Fuego with a glass of wine in one hand and a bamboo walking stick in the other." She carefully pronounced each name in some approximation of what Victor imagined to be a native accent, and it irritated him. Matterafact, everything about this lady was starting to tick him off. He took another step back and she continued to hover towards him. Her face was fully made up, layers of powder and cream caked on top of each other. She threw her head back and let out a laugh that sounded like it was supposed to be carefree.

"Listen," Victor said, "you didn't notice there's a small ground war going on outside your door? Why don't you crawl under something like a normal person and die of natural causes as planned?"

The Collector didn't seem to hear him. She closed her eyes and spread her thin arms out to either side. Translucent dollops of loose skin dangled from her bones. Something on the other side of the room caught Victor's eye. It was one of the antiques, an intricate metal statuette, floating up into the air. Outside, steady popcorn bursts of gunfire rattled out. Victor made a small mental calculation and decided that he might be better off back in the gunfight. He took a few more steps towards the door.

The woman opened her eyes and smiled. "It's locked," she said.

Panic rose like a flock of startled birds inside Victor's chest. He fought the urge to make a break for it. More objects began floating up around him.

"You don't want to go out there anyway," the Collector said, leveling her gaze at him. "As you say, they are deep in the throes of combat." There was something to the way she said that—throes of combat—that chirped out at Victor. Perhaps it was that know-it-all smile creasing the corners of her mouth.

Victor reached two fingers into the front pocket of his uniform shirt, retrieved a cigarette and lit it. "Smoke?" he said, raising his eyebrows up at the floating lady.

"Thank you," said the Collector, "I have my own." She alighted into an elaborately carved medieval wooden chair. One emaciated hand upset a collection of knickknacks piled on a nearby nightstand until it found her opened pack of Pall Malls and pulled one out. She lit it and then directed a sharp look at Victor.

"You are from Puerto Rico, Bobby?" Her pronunciation was gratingly precise.

"The DR actually," Victor lied.

"I have been to Puerto Rico many times—it is there that I began learning about the secret magic of the world."

"Oh, I see," Victor said.

She studied him carefully. "What do you see?"

"I see that you're one of those lemme-ask-you-a-question-but-really-it's-so-I-can-tell-you-a-story-about-myself type of people."

"Once I began to learn, I could not stop. It was like a drug, Bobby. The path led me from Puerto Rico to Africa, the cradle of civilization, like a reverse Middle Passage."

"In so many ways," Victor muttered.

"In Africa I was ordained a priestess and consecrated in sacred river waters."

"I mean, no offense, the Collector, but from what I hear you can get consecrated anything you want in Africa if the price is right. It's like the internet."

"I made my way along the Silk Route across the Indian subcontinent throughout Asia."

"That's where you got all these knick-knacks?"

"These knick-knacks, Bobby, are the spiritual DNA of all humanity. Surrounding you is one of the most extensive collections of divine objecture on the planet."

"Then why don't you dust them off every once in a while? This place is a mess."

The Collector took a deep drag on her lipstick-stained cigarette. "I have become so frail, Bobby, so frail. My time is not far now." She sounded excited.

"Yeah, well, you're like what, eighty something?"

That all-knowing smile crossed her face again. "Thirty-one, actually." She let out a laugh, her most genuine one yet, but it quickly deteriorated into bronchial hacking.

Victor dropped his ass back into the easy chair and let his mouth hang open. "Jesus, lady, what the fuck?" The floating shapes hummed and spun in long gyrations around the room. Outside, the gunfight was heating up again.

"The secrets of our planet grant one great powers, unimaginable powers, but it is not without a price." Victor watched a small porcelain globe hover past his head. "The sacred materials don't like to be tamed." The Collector started rising like a rag carried by a slow updraft. A rustling came from the doorway and then a succession of very loud shots burst out. "We have been engaged in a kind of cosmic—how would you say it?—warfare, for a few months now."

"Looks like they're winning," Victor said, lighting another cigarette off the embers of his last one. A shiny wooden mask drifted by. Carved lines formed spiraling labyrinths on its forehead and cheeks. The shooter taking cover in the doorway kept firing until a large blast, probably a shotgun, rang out. The whole room shuddered and a few glasses exploded from a bookshelf.

"There is great chaos in the spiritual realm, Bobby." The Collector's voice became alarmingly calm. "Static, spiritual static like nuclear fallout, penetrates every element, every realm in its path." Victor realized that the objects had created a little solar system around the floating white lady. Each spun in faster and faster orbits, circling their dying sun. It wouldn't be long now. The cruel fluorescent glow around her grew dimmer and dimmer every second. "The sacred materials," she said again, "do not like to be tamed." Another shotgun blast shook the house, followed by the rat-tat-tat of a semi-automatic a little further away.

"You mean to tell me," Victor yelled above the humming of the tiny spinning universe, "that you hoarded all these doodads and got 'em to work for you and now they rebelling?"

"That is more or less correct."

"That's why they spinning 'round you? They trying to kill you?"

The Collector chortled. "Oh, quite the contrary, my friend. They are trying to keep me alive because that's the only way they can defeat me. I have appropriated their power and am using it to spin gloriously towards divinity. They know my death will be the final step towards infinite awareness. My powers will increase tenfold and manifest like burgeoning hurricanes across our city."

"Great."

"No longer confined by this physical prison—"

Something clicked in Victor's head. "Wait. Go back to the part about burgundy hurricanes."

"My powers will increase tenfold and manifest like—"

"No, sorry, earlier—you said you're causing spiritual static on every realm. This static, it affects the whole neighborhood?"

"About a ten block radius, yes."

"You're the one been causing all these shootouts? How many bodies have we had to pick up in the last two months—twenty? Thirty?"

"There are always unforeseen consequences to spiritual growth."

"Lady, you're a plague! It's no wonder the universe is teaming up to make you miserable. And if you die it'll only get worse?"

"I'll disperse myself like so many seedlings scattered in the wind. I will be a martyred inspiration to the others like me."

"Jesus, there's more of you?"

"More than you can imagine."

The humming grew louder, blurring out even the constant burst of gunfire, and soon the whole building trembled along with it. Victor looked up expecting to see the Collector explode in some scattered star orgasm. He shielded his face with his forearm in case any errant chunks of her projected in his direction, but the explosion never came. The fluorescent light flickered on and off a few times and then sputtered out. The objects spun furiously fast. The Collector's lifeless body collapsed in a heap on the Oriental rug. Then all hell broke loose outside.

* * *

Victor had never done CPR out of spite before. He'd worked up cardiac arrests in dark hallways, stalled elevators, even once at a nightclub, pumping the chest to the throbbing techno while dancers grinded on each other around him. But trying to get someone back so that they wouldn't become some magnanimous hood-destroying demigoddess? Another new one for the list.

He worked quickly, throwing the defibrillator pads on her crooked little chest as soon as he'd finished two rounds of compressions. Her veins were bright blue and squiggly against her pale skin but he managed to find a juicy one to put an IV in. As he worked, the sacred objects spun and hummed above his head. Outside, bullets ricocheted up and down the street. Young men screamed and cars screeched.

As he squeezed a few breaths of oxygen into her lungs from a small tank, it occurred to Victor that he had not stumbled into this strange little room by accident. He was a pawn in a great divine plan to keep some kind of spiritual order in the South Ward, and if that meant thwarting this irritating white lady from world domination that was alright with him.

He pumped a few more times on her chest and then took a look at the monitor. Perfect: Ventricular fibrillation. Those ridiculous squiggly lines that could be shocked back into a normal rhythm. Victor charged the defibrillator to its highest setting, made sure he was well out of the way and pressed SHOCK. The Collector's body jolted. The lines on the monitor recomposed into a healthy blip-blip-blip.

One by one, the floating objects began dropping to the ground. The Collector had already begun to change when Victor looked back down. Her skin had smoothed out and she had gained about 100 pounds. She let out a low moan.

"No!" she sobbed. "No, no, no, no!" She raised her face, now with the proper careening-towards-middle-age look to it. Her eyes were blood shot and tear stained. She pounded the floor with her fists.

Victor stood up and gave her some room. "Things didn't work out like you planned?"

"Get out!" moaned the woman, newly not-old, half-naked and awkward on her bedroom floor.

"Whatsamatter?" Victor said, "You not the Collector anymore?"

"No, I'm not the damn Collector. I'm Emma. Emma Fastbinder. I'm from Vermont." Emma Fastbinder needed a bath. She didn't make the flowy shoulder cloth look majestic like the Collector had, and her makeup was splotched messily across her face. She looked like she'd just woken up after the wackest bachelorette party ever.

Victor noticed suddenly that the shooting had stopped. He felt like he hadn't known this kind of peace and quiet in years, like if he were to walk outside he'd hear the rustle of soil nurturing a young tree, the slow progress of a worm along the pavement, the beginning of a new morning.

"So much...work to be done," Emma groaned. "Must start

all over...from the very beginning. Must contact the others." She looked up groggily. "Bobby, do you have a phone I could use?"

A flush of childlike joy came over Victor. He felt fresh, ready to go and see the world, even if it meant having to step over a few bodies on the way. He smiled down at Emma, clicked his radio back on, lit a cigarette and then turned around and walked out the door.

# RED FEATHER AND BONE

There it is: A flash of crimson against the gray, gray sky. I jot down some notes and squint back into my eyepiece. Its ragged siren song reaches toward me through the cold skyscrapers. The cawing replaces my irritation with sorrow—a gentle blues that reminds me that I'm every bit as singular and lonesome as that bright red flicker of feather and bone.

I'm not used to this bird watching shit. I'm the guy the New York Council of the Dead brings in for the really nasty jobs. The headless bastards trying to make it back to tell their ex-wives some bullshit, the homicidal midget house ghost—all these wayward souls with grudges that won't stay where they belong—that's my turf. Unlike the rest of the NYCOD, though, I'm only half dead. Yes, my skin is more gray than brown—a weird neither-here-nor-there hue, just like me, and I'm eerily cold to the touch. But I've perfected the forced easy grin of the living, the authoritative cop snarl, the just-walking-by shrug. In short, I pass. It allows me access to places that fully dead COD agents could never get their translucent asses into, so the ghouls upstairs dispatch me only on those good juicy messes.

At least, that's how it was right up until three weeks and four days ago, when my partner Riley Washington disobeyed orders and did away with the child-killing ghost of a long dead plantation master. Riley went rogue and the Council went batshit—sent the full raging force of their soulcatchers on him. Everyone's been out there looking, except for me. They knew I'da sooner hugged the dude than taken him out, so I'm stuck staring at the Manhattan skyline, watching this stupid long-necked bird trouble the skeevy business men with its beautiful, pathetic song. Below me, the tall shadows of the elite COD soulcatchers roam back and forth, looking for my friend.

To top it all off, it's the middle of day—that horrible, bright lull when there're no shadows and no mercy. I put down the binoculars and walk back to the rooftop shed. A small, translucent child is waiting for me inside. He's about five or six, sipping absentmindedly from my two-day old coffee and staring much too closely at the scribbled over maps and bird drawings plastered across my walls.

"What you doing there, youngin?"

"Minding mine," the child says.

"Actually, you're minding mine. Why don't you go help some dead geriatric cross the street?"

The boy gives me such a haunted, intense stare that I'm not sure what to do with myself. He looks familiar—one of these lost soul child phantoms that haunt the outer boroughs running odd errands for folks like me in exchange for toys and candy. This one, as I recall, is only interested in rusted-out car parts and electrical wiring.

"You want a light bulb?" I try. He scoffs and hovers his little body to another corner. His bulgy eyes scan the floor plans to a building my bird was sighted in.

"What do you want?"

"You think the ghost bird came from the burial ground?"

"Seems likely," I say. The thing started its midday cooing in a high-rise beside the weird shaped, corporate rock that comemorates some forgotten African slaves. "I don't know where else it would come from down here. The thing is old, from what I can tell, and not any species I can find in the bird nerd books. All the buildings it shows up in are within a five block radius of the site. It's starting to add up." The boy grunts thoughtfully and floats over to an old map I found of the financial district in 1863.

"Where'd you get this map?"

"Ganked it from the research room at the historical society. But this is a nonsense assignment, kid. What you care?"

He hovers for another minute and then turns, looks up at me and says: "Just curious. Thank you for the nice visit." He moves out the door and then pokes his little head back in. "Oh, and I have a message for you. Almost forgot."

It can't be from the Council—when they want to get in touch they just blare another staticky transmission directly into my head with that creepy dead people telepathy they got. My slow, slow heart quickens by a fraction. Could it be—

"It's from Riley?"

"Gimme a battery charger."

"I don't have one, man, just tell me who it's from."

"Give to get, get to give. You got a blender?"

I briefly consider going for my blade. It's that kind of day. "You want my extension cord?"

He considers for a few seconds. "Yes, it's from Riley."

I unplug the cord from the wall and my lamp and start wrapping it around itself. "I'm really not in the mood to bargain any more—what's your name, shorty?"

"Damian."

"Damian, I'm done playing." I toss him the cord. "What's the message?"

He sizes me up carefully. "Where ass meets Anderson at eight." A pause. "Bring that map along." And he's gone.

*  *  *

In the Chambers Street train station, commuters are cluttering around a street musician. The music is wack, but the crowd is huge, which means it's either a midget in a costume or a hot chick. Turns out to be neither. When I shoulder my way deep enough in to get a good look, I find a half visible, shiny fellow doing an old fashioned jig to some scratchy canned music. He's tall and frail, dressed in baggy, rotting trousers and seems to have some kind of circus makeup on. Folks are just gaping at him obtusely and he's yukking it up.

If there's one thing the COD is really, really uptight about, it's dead folks appearing to the living. Course, the high-up afterlifers do it whenever they see fit, work their way deftly through and around whatever bureaucratic loopholes they can find, but those of us on the streets know there's no leeway when it comes to human interactions. So I'm not surprised when a burly, translucent team of patrol ghouls comes swooshing down through the turnstiles towards the giddy dancer. The crowd feels the chill circulate and begins to disperse. The performer chuckles, grabs his radio and shoots off like a rocket into one of the train tunnels. The patrol team disappears into the darkness after him, cursing and snarling as they go. I shake my head and get on a Brooklyn-bound train. Something is definitely fucked up in ghost world.

* * *

When Riley and I first started working together—back when I was still coming to terms with having died in some horrific, unknown way that wiped out all my memory and then been partially resurrected—we used to have a constant caller named Anderson. He was a suicide—I think he'd been a banker or something in life—and he was crazy about Puerto Rican ass. He couldn't even really do anything with it, being a ghost and all, but for some damn reason the dude wouldn't stop showing up at this one spot in Bushwick and harassing the girls. It was dumb shit—tying two ponytails together or giving invisible wedgies—but it was noticeable enough to show up on the COD's disturbing-the-living radar and land me and Riley out there again and again.

Now it's a quarter to eight, a dim September night and Bushwick is alive with bustling, laughing, gossiping Puerto Ricans, Dominicans and Ecuadorians. They mingle in and out of the cuchifritos spots and fruit stands, sending ruckus spanglish prayers and flirtations up into the rumbling train tracks above. I'm quiet and a stranger hue than the rest of them, but still: I am home. I never get the stares here that I do downtown. The occasional brand new whitey wanders past, sometimes in cautious bands of two or three.

I'm not surprised to see my old friend Riley sitting in the little triangular park just off Broadway where Anderson used to pester women. I am, however, a little disturbed to see his ghostly ass sitting directly across the chessboard from an overweight and very much alive fellow in a bulging guayabera. They're both laughing, probably each thinking he's got the other one's king three moves from checkmate. I reconcile competing urges to hug and slap Riley by pulling up a folding chair and lighting my smoke like it's no big deal.

"Whaddup," Riley says without looking up from the game.

"It is what it is."

He gestures towards the big guy sitting across the table. "Gordo, Carlos, Carlos, Gordo." Gordo extends a hand to me. I don't usually touch the living. I'm corpse cold and can find out way more information than I'd ever need to know about someone from a casual tap. But this man's face regards me with such genuine kindness I'm caught off guard. I shake his hand and he doesn't flinch when he feels my chilly skin. He looks me dead in the eye, smiles, and then helps himself to one of my cigars.

"I'm done with the invisible bullshit," Riley replies to my unasked question.

"So I see."

"It's not like they don't know we here. Especially chubby old Cubanos like this motherfucker."

Gordo chuckles. "It's true!"

"And COD coming for me anyway. What I got to lose?"

I just shake my head. He has a point. "You wanted to talk 'bout something?"

"Yeah, what you have on the bird situation?"

"It's BS. They just throwing grunt work at me. Why's everybody so interested in it?"

"What you got?" Riley's still staring at the game but I can tell his mind is elsewhere.

"What I told the Damian kid. He didn't let you know 'bout his spy mission?"

Gordo's lost in thought. I can see the strategic little lines twirling around his head and by his self-satisfied grin I'm guessing it's paying off on the chessboard.

"Alright, I'll level with you." Riley finally looks at me. "I didn't want to get you too deep in this, for your own sake, but we need your help."

"Check," Gordo says.

"Fuck." Riley lurches a pawn one square further into a suicidal last-ditch get the queen back mission.

"Mate."

"Fuck-fuck. Alright, we have to go anyway. C'mon, Gordo, let's show Carlos what we building."

* * *

"The kid's been working on this thing for a while actually," Riley says as he sends a metal gate clamoring loudly out of our way. "I guess Gordo here started helping him out a few months back, just putting pieces together that the little guy couldn't manage with his little ghost hands." He makes pathetic flapping motions with his arms.

"I can hear you, dickface," a voice says from the darkness inside. We're somewhere along the ambiguous line between Williamsburg and Bushwick, down a deserted backstreet. The empty warehouses will soon be swank million dollar lofts, but for now they're just canvas for young graffiti writers.

Gordo leads us into a vast, open room that was probably once full of either endlessly-sewing Chinese ladies or churning machinery. Tiki torches throw flickering illumination onto a pile of junk sitting in the back of a rusty old pickup truck. Damian is floating circles around it, appraising each piece and occasionally tinkering with a little silver tool.

"You guys are opening a mobile second hand store?" I say. "That's exciting."

Riley and Damian look miffed, but Gordo lets out a grandfatherly belly laugh. "No, no, Papi. It's a machine!"

"What's it do?" I think I see my extension cord in there, along with a few car parts I'd traded to Damian the last time I needed a message run.

"It opens things," Riley says, looking at me as if I should know what the hell he's talking about. I make go-on-with-it hand motions at him. "It makes new doors. To things."

"No." The meaning is slowly trickling down to me now. "Doors to...places?" I say. Riley nods. "Places where dead people live?" I need to sit down. "You're building an entrada-making machine?"

An entrada is an entrance to the Underworld. There's only about a dozen in the city; they're all old as shit and very well hidden. I've never met anyone that can remember when or how they came about—had always just figured it was a natural phenomenon actually. "Are you sure?" I say, cocking an eyebrow.

Damian floats over to me. "Allow me to explain the situation, Carlos, because Riley would prefer being cryptic and Gordo's just gonna sit there and chuckle."

"It's true," Gordo confirms. He eases his wide ass into an easy-chair and lights up a Malagueña.

"About three weeks ago, the ghost bird starts showing up downtown."

"Right."

"NYCOD puts their best man on it. He is perhaps of questionable allegiance when it comes to certain recent defections, but when it comes to getting the job done, second to none."

"Now, that I'm gone, of course," Riley puts in.

"Go on."

The boy's more animated than I've ever seen him. He floats in little figure-eights around his junky invention as he speaks. "Strange, right? Such a star agent on something as trivial as an irritating bird?"

"That's what I'm saying."

"And all those patrols downtown..."

"Right!"

"Well, you and I both got wise to the bird having something to do with that Burial Ground Memorial, as we spoke about earlier. Turns out the thing ain't supposed to be around at all. It's like the one that got away, three hundred years later."

"Eh?"

"Let's drive and chat," Riley says. "We don't have much time."

* * *

The Williamsburg Bridge is backed up with party kids

trying to make it on time but still be fashionably late. The city sparkles on either side of us, those emptied-out sky-scrapers looming like old gods in the later-summer night. We're squashed four across the front seat of Gordo's old pickup, the two ghosts sandwiched in between the one and a half living bodies. Damian partially unrolls a yellowed piece of parchment and hands it to me.

"What's this?"

"The missing piece, I believe." It's a chart of some kind. Little squares with writing scribbled over them sprawl across the page in a crooked hectagon shape. "The place-ment map for the African Burial Ground." I squint at one of the boxes. LITTLE THADDEUS, B. 1730 - D.1746, ORIG: DAHOMEY is written in tiny, elegant script. The one below it says: MISS LUCY TRINIDAD, B. ? - D. 1750 APPROX 82 YEARS OF AGE. HEALER. ORIG: KONGO.

I look at Damian.

He nods. "Everyone."

I unroll further. The little boxes go on and on. "There's thousands of them!" Damian nods again. "Where did this come from? Who made it?" Damian puts his tiny finger to the bottom left corner of the map. CYRUS LANGLEY, it says in the same delicate handwriting. MADE WITH LOVE & LIGHT THAT THE CHILDREN OF OUR CHIL-DREN'S CHILDREN MAY KNOW FROM WHENCE THEY COME & UPLIFT THEIR SPIRITS & OUR OWN.

"Who's Cyrus?" I ask, but Damian's already directing my attention to a box near the center of the map. CYRUS LANGELY, B. 1725 - D.1755. CONJURER IN THE OLD TRADITION. ORIGIN: UNK. EDUCATED IN THE MAGICAL ARTS OF BOTH WHITE FOLKS & THE NEGRO. BORN SLAVE DIED FREE & FREE WILL 1 DAY AGAIN BE.

Gordo leans on his horn, breaking my reverie.

"Get the fuck out of the way you scrawny hipsters!" Riley

screams out the window. "Tell 'em, Gordo, I don't think they heard me."

"¡Comiendo mierda y gastando zapatos!" Gordo yells.

Riley eyes him suspiciously. "Did you say what I said?"

"Basically," Gordo chuckles. The mini-coop in front of us jolts into motion and catches up with traffic further down the bridge.

I could drown myself in this map. The names and histories seem to go on endlessly. "It's bigger than I realized."

"Bigger than anyone realized," Damian says. The line of cars is picking up pace again.

"So the monument itself..."

"Just the tip of the iceberg," Riley says.

"And this Cyrus fellow?"

"Made the map after he was dead and buried down there obviously," Damian says. "They discovered it with the first few bodies that came up at the construction site, tracked down some surviving descendants of Langley and returned it to them. This is what I think happened: When the last African was interred at the burial ground and the property started looking juicy for real estate, the COD from way-back-when did their little lockdown spell maneuver, entrapping the dead within. Far as anyone in the afterlife is concerned, the place never happened."

"Which is basically what they did up here too," I said. "Best I can gather."

"Right, but then some pesky bones turned up in the nineties and they had to make amends."

"So they picked a choice few," Riley says, "you know, fill the color quota, and let the rest rot. The Council of the Dead basically did the same thing. The burial site is still sealed shut, no souls get out, no souls get in. Without interaction, without change, movement, they'll all go into a coma-like state and eventually waste away."

Some folks die and never show up in the afterlife. They

just float out into nothingness. The ones that do make it through as ghosts could turn up any damn place, and usually end up somewhere within the district limits of whatever city or county they end up in. But to have your soul locked perpetually in your own subterranean grave? I shudder just thinking about it. Thousands of imprisoned spirits, cramped into a tiny space after a lifetime of slavery—they must've gone insane with rage.

Gordo's smoking again. "It's a very sad estory," he says.

"But?"

"But," Damian says quietly. "They didn't count on Cyrus the Conjurer."

"That's Cyrus The Mothafucking Conquerer, crackers!" Riley yells out the window. The car full of hoochies next to us exchange concerned glances. "I think they heard me that time."

"It must've killed him not knowing where he was from," I say. "Seeing as how he put down an origin for most of the others buried down there."

"We think he's gotten out," Damian says.

"Gotten out?" I stammer. "The only way he could get out is..." Oh, the pieces. Turn them. Rearrange them. Fit them together. "...by making an entrada."

"With whatever combination of traditions he ended up mastering," says Damian. "But still—it must be tiny. Even with all that magic."

"Too tiny for a human spirit to fit through?"

"Exactly."

"Hence, my brightly-colored little friend," I say.

"Indeed," mutters Damian. His spooky little eyes are elsewhere though. "He must've been down there for years, watching all his contemporaries waste away, gathering strength, preparing. Drawing from their wisdom."

The river below is as inky black as the sky around us. Little flickering reflections of the city dance and disappear in the current. "Council must be pissed." I say, smiling.

"They throwing everything they got at him," Damian says. "That's why we have to move fast. I believe they're quite close to catching their prey."

Of course! All those swarming patrols weren't looking for Riley—they were on the same assignment I was. "That's why we're driving downtown with that machine?" I say. "We're going to finish the job Cyrus started and break open a new entrada to release thousands of entrapped souls of the first African New Yorkers?"

"Exactly," Riley and Damian both say.

Gordo just laughs.

\* \* \*

It's still the wrong century for two brown men to be driving a pickup truck with mysteriously tarped cargo towards lower Manhattan. Angry, suspicious eyes whirl around to glare at us as soon as we cross the bridge. Gordo cuts a hard left on Allen and barrels towards Canal. I'm relieved no one can hear the obscenities Riley's yelling out the window at them.

"You got the map I told you to bring?" Damian asks as we jolt to a halt outside one of the federal buildings. I retrieve the photocopied, taped-together sheets from my pocket and unfold them across the dashboard. Gordo switches on the inside light. "No one knew how large the gravesite really was," our tiny companion explains. "At least they never demarcated its true borders on any of the white people cartographies."

He places Cyrus's ancient, yellowed chart on top of my crisp printer paper. "The entrada should be over Langley's grave. We have to line these two up. Look for landmarks."

A silence falls over the cramped front seat as four pairs of eyes scan the two pictures. Riley's transparent finger traces a diagonal line marking the edge of the African Burial Ground on the conjurer's map. "This looks like it moves along the coast here, the South Street Seaport."

"Yes," I say. "That would make the memorial site about here." I stretch my hand from the border of the map halfway across towards the middle."

"And Cyrus's grave..." Riley tiptoes his fingers along five paces, checking back and forth between the two documents as he goes. "...here."

Damian looks past Riley at Gordo, who's fallen into a pleasant nap. "Ernesto," he says.

"Eh?"

"You brought the map I asked you for?"

"Glove compartment."

I pop it open and find an MTA train map. We spread it across the other two and dart our eyes back and forth.

"Chambers Street train station!" Riley and I yell.

Gordo's eyes pop open. He cranks the gear shift into drive and speeds off down Broadway. We all throw our hands to the ceiling as the truck two-wheel tips, screeching around a corner to Chambers. We blow through a light and pull up beside the subway entrance on Church, heaving collective sighs of relief.

We hop out of the truck and that's when it hits me. "Of course!" I yell, slapping a palm to my gray forehead. "Could Cyrus return to his man form once he was out?"

Little Damian considers for a moment. "I imagine so," he says. "But his powers would be diminished. Probably he couldn't leave the immediate area."

"I believe I saw our man earlier today." Everyone spins around to stare at me. "He was dancing to bad 80's music for change on the A train platform."

"Damn," Riley says, "times really are tough."

"He's reaching out any way he can," Damian says. "The birdsong. The train dance. He's trying to let us know he's ready."

Gordo lumbers over to us from the driver's side. "How we going to get this damn thing down there?"

It takes me, Riley and Damian hauling it step by step down the stairs and through the handicap entrance while Gordo runs interference on the station agent, pretending not to speak English, but we eventually make it with the entrada-maker intact. We stand at the edge of the platform, gazing into the utter blackness of the tracks.

"I'll cover the entrance with Gordo here," Riley says. "Carlos, you and the youngin head in. Something comes that we can't handle, I'll give a shout."

"What if a train comes?" I say.

"Ju kidding?" Gordo laughs. "It's after midnight. We have plenty of time."

We all nod gravely at each other and I hoist up the machine and follow the kid down some metal stairs into the tunnel. It's completely dark except for his little glowing form ahead of me. He's got both maps stretched out and he's muttering quietly to himself. We round a bend and my eyes start to adjust. It's all drip-drops and scurry-scurries in the shadows around us, plus the distant rumbling of late night trains.

"How'd you get this map away from the family anyway?" I ask Damian.

"I didn't," he says simply and quietly. "It's an heirloom." I'm left to ponder the significance. Connect-the-dot constellations form around my head. I stagger along behind my little floating glow-in-the-dark guide. *That the children of our children's children may know from whence they came and uplift their spirits and our own.* Langley hadn't been kidding. Maybe it's because it wasn't so long ago that I stumbled upon a long lost ancestor of my own, but the realization that Damian is in it for his bloodline strikes a chord deep inside me.

"How this mechanical doohicky gonna do anything in the spirit world?" I ask.

"A little sorcery will help."

"Another heirloom, I presume."

Damian doesn't answer. A few minutes later, he stops and hovers perfectly still, scanning the dark walls. "Should be... right about...here!"

I place the machine carefully on the damp ground and step back. Damian is on it instantly, fuddling around, muttering to himself, pouring little vials of liquid into some plastic piping. Soon, a mechanical churning grinds out, accompanied by a low, angelic hum. A dim glow emanates from the wall in front of us.

"It's working," I whisper. Damian just creases his little brow with determination.

I'm trying to fathom how many years this moment has been in the making when Riley's voice comes echoing down the tunnel.

"Company!" he hollers.

"What kind?" I yell back. My hand wraps around the blade handle that's stored securely in my walking stick.

"Soulcatchers. I got this." He does, too. Riley's been waiting for an opportunity to get into it with some COD loyals ever since he went on the run. The clanging and groaning sounds of spirit warfare drift out from around the corner. "Yeah, what?" Riley's yelling. "What? Thought so."

The light is burning bright from the tunnel wall, now. Damian's still fiddling with levers and liquids, looking up occasionally to see how the work is progressing.

"More company!" Riley yells. There's an uncomfortable pause. "Lots more!" Reinforcements. Those dickheads always roll deep. If they see me it's a wrap. I had just begun having visions of all the good work I could do from the inside, especially being linked up on the DL with Riley's band of rogue ghosts. So much to consider and so little time. "I'm coming to you, man; there's too many of 'em." Another pause. "And they got cops with 'em too!"

That's bad. "Real cops?"

"No rent-a-cops. Of course real cops. Transit, I'd say. Two of 'em."

"Ew. What's Gordo doing?"

"Pretending to be homeless and mumbling to himself."

"Works. Come to us, we're better off closer together." I look over to Damian. "How we looking?"

"Close. But not there." It's downright bright in here now. The light's throwing giant shadow versions of me against the far wall. When Riley comes flashing around the corner I throw myself into one of those sarcophagus-shaped inlets and wait. He pants up and we both draw our blades.

"How's it look?"

"Looks bad," he says. I resist the cheesy 'just-like-old-times' remark that I know we're both thinking. "A lot of 'em out there. Probably got tipped off when Homeboy the Magnificent decided to put on the A train minstrel show."

"Almost...there," Damian reports. I peek around the corner and see the anxious flickering of flashlights. Boots are echoing towards us, along with the ominous swoosh of many, many angry spirits.

"What's going on down there?" an authoritative and terrified voice demands. "Come out and let us see your hands!" The two cops burst around the corner, guns drawn, faces contorted into tense frowns. They immediately throw their arms in front of their faces to block the sharp glare of the brand new entrada.

"Done!" Damian yells. The glow becomes unbearably bright for a moment and it sounds like two tectonic plates are getting it on somewhere beneath us. The light dims slightly and I see the skinny dancing ghost from earlier burst out of the wall and hover directly in front of the stunned policemen. Further behind them, a crowd of fuming soulcatchers hovers in wait.

"What the fuck is that?" one of the cops yells.

"I'm the magic Negro from all your worst nightmares," Cyrus laughs. "Now scatter!" He swirls his arms like he's gonna shoot a fireball at them and they take off, tearing through the ranks of NYCOD agents and disappearing around the corner.

"I like this dude," Riley whispers.

Cyrus directs his attention at the angry ghost mob that's glaring him down. "You want some too, fools? I got some for you, don't worry." The mob advances towards us and I flatten myself deeper against the wall. Cyrus floats away from the glowing entrada entrance; there's a swooshing sound like an invisible rocket just blew past and then a flood of old African souls comes surging forth. They pour out into the tunnel, thousands and thousands of them, and barrel through the COD goons without stopping. They're wearing head scarves and raggedy clothes, carved jewelry and beaded necklaces; a few even have chain links around their arms and legs. I feel the wind of hundreds of years of pent up rage and frustration release across my face. Riley's screaming as loud as he can beside me and we're both laughing hysterically and crying at the same time.

Everything is bright light and holy terror and then the souls scatter through the tracks and out into the fresh New York night. When the air finally clears, a peaceful silence descends on us. Riley and I let go of each other's hands and smile awkwardly. In front of the entrada, Damian has his arms wrapped around Cyrus. His little body is heaving with occasional sobs. Cyrus just smiles that big grin of his and pats the boy on the back. "Hush boy," he says. "It's all over now. We're free."

"¡Coño, mi gente! The fuck happened?" It's Gordo, stumbling blindly towards us around the corner.

"Go help him," I tell Riley.

Damian has collected himself by the time Gordo and Riley get to where we stand near the entrada. The entryway is just a swimmy black void now that the souls have all escaped. Cyrus looks the four of us over carefully. He's replaced his rags with an elegant zoot suit. A bright red feather sticks out of his crisp Stetson hat. Tightly wound braids stretch around the back of his head. "You've done well," he says. "Each of you played your part." He died young, but Cyrus's deeply-lined face beams like a proud old grandfather. "A very capable team."

"What're you gonna do now?" Riley asks.

"Oh, there's so much mischief to make; this is only the beginning." Cyrus looks like he can't control the grin breaking across his face. "I believe I'll stick around in this city for a little while. I think I could be a very unpleasant presence for certain deserving individuals and institutions."

Riley beams at him. "I was hoping you'd say that."

"Besides," Cyrus says, "this isn't the only entrada I been working on." We all perk up and gape at the ancient conjurer. "There's one go straight into the New York Harbor. Been slipping through as a little guppie fish, pestering the cruise boats and them. It's a whole other kinda gravesite out there, boys. You can only imagine."

We make our way slowly towards the platform. Each of us is in our own little daze, dreaming up futures pregnant with Cyrus's swashbuckling adventures and the roles we each could play. For the first time, I can imagine using this ridiculous both/neither status for something I believe in. The idea gives me an unfamiliar feeling, like a hundred baby birds are jumping up and down in my stomach—giddiness, you could call it. "There's much to be done, lads," Cyrus is saying, his voice fluttering with laughter in the dark tunnel around us. As we walk together towards the station lights, the old spirit starts humming—it's a gentle, melancholy blues, a ragged siren song that reminds me that I'm every bit as free as that bright red flicker of feather and bone.

# THE PASSING

Something is very wrong. When I wake up, the knowledge is waiting for me, lurking. All my bones scream it. My gut is clenched with it. It's all over me.

Outside, the sky is still gray. A little light comes in through the window, hits the bare tiled floor. I sit up in bed, feel these old muscles groan with the sudden effort. At first I think maybe this wrongness is in me, with my own collection. I try to steady my mind. Lay back down, close my eyes and go inward to check. All the stories are there, hovering around peacefully, and I breathe a happy sigh. There's hundreds of them, but I know the ins and outs well enough to know at a glance when something's off, and it's not. Not with me anyway. But there it is, that nagging something-or-other. A very terrible thing is happening.

I ease myself up again, slower this time. Drop my legs over the side of the bed. The cold floor sends little gasps of surprise up through the bottoms of my feet. The day is breaking behind the skyscrapers across the river. The city wakes up all around me. I am alive.

But this badness pursues me out of my bedroom, hangs over me while I brush my teeth and sit on the toilet for my morning tinkle. In the shower it recedes some but then it's back when I'm putting the coffee on. Slithering around my ankles. Crawling up my spine. Diablo. I fight off restlessness while I eat my mushy stuff, because that's not good for digestion. My kitchen is pale and bathed in sunlight. I can smile for a moment, appreciating the bright geometry my windows create with those rays, but only for a moment. Then the feeling's back.

From somewhere inside, a story rises. It was an old guajiro back in Cuba. 'Simpático' is the best word for him. It means 'nice' in English, but nice is such a pathetic word. Nice. It just lives and dies in one breath. Simpático is a whole story unto itself. It has panache. This old man was simpático until the day he died. You know, I think he had a thing for me? I was already very old at the time, and this was way back when, understand, but Tomás had his eyes all over me and that hunger radiated off him in hot waves.

His story—it was about his first love. He was old now, and alone, but he carried it with him everywhere he went, and not in a bad way. It walked along beside him like a faithful friend, that story. Never held him back or distracted him from the present tense, but just remained, a gentle reminder that his heart was alive and well, in spite of whatever hardship may come. Sometimes, before going to sleep, he would think of it and smile his old wrinkled smile. I came to him late at night. Inhaled all that fresh earthy perfume of the countryside breathing through the big open windows in his little house. Put my hand on his forehead and out it came: A whole wily early-twenties romance, complete with messiness and passion, but all in all quite tidy and to the point. I thanked him, and he smiled at me with sleepy eyes.

They always smile when I'm done. They must know that their stories will live on long after they do, that they're sharing a little part of themselves with the great patchwork quilt of humanity, and it must be very pleasant indeed.

Old Tomás's story winds through the chaotic finale and then slides back into the ether and I'm done with my mushy stuff and almost done with my café and the icky feeling is back. Fine. It is here to stay, apparently, so I will investigate. That's all that negativity wants anyway: a little attention. I don't usually pay it much mind because when you do, it feels good and keeps coming back for more. But this is... different. It's someone else's shit, first of all, so I don't know why it's come to trouble my morning.

If it's not my shit, it must be one of my sisters'. I admit I've been a little out of touch recently. It's just that I like it up here in my twenty-first floor apartment, with its cold linoleum floors and the burner that you have to ignite four times before it finally lights, and the occasionally leaking faucet. Most mornings I wake up and am simply content. I have my stories; stacks and stacks of them. Plus I have many memories of my own to wander through. I've been married six times and I still get letters from the offspring I've left scattered around the world. Sometimes different friends or family members stop by for obligatory visits that I can will to be suddenly fascinating tête-à-têtes. Yes, I can still be surprising after all these years. I'm still profoundly in love with life even for all the death I've seen. It still gives me a thrill to feel the cold floor against my bare feet every morning and know that I am alive.

So I don't trouble much with the others. They're fine, I'm sure. They have their occasional meetings, every few decades or whatever, and sometimes I pass through, but mostly, eh, I could go without. There'll be a day when we're all together again, I'm sure. Whatever it is we're holding these stories for will come to pass and we'll convalesce and compare notes. Until then, though, I'll just make my café, eat my mushy stuff, and mind mine, thank you very much.

At least, that's what I would do, if I could shake this feeling. Okay. I rise, supporting myself with one hand on the table, and pad across the apartment. I say pad because I'm wearing these slightly frayed pink slippers, and when you walk around in slippers, you're padding. I hear the dust shuffle beneath them and think I'd better sweep up soon. When I reach the window, the one next to the couch, my mind starts moving fast.

I scan the rising and falling buildings beneath me and realize that whatever's gone wrong, it's gone wrong with Hyacinth. It's a fact I'd been actively trying to ignore, but when I let my mind relax over the cityscape the knowledge just swims right to the surface. Hyacinth is my elder by decades. She's prim and proper to a fault, down and dapper with all the protocols. She's unshakable. I'd say it's even come between us some over the years; I simply tired of her being so thoroughly *her* all the time, and I'm sure she feels the same about me. Truth is: We're probably too much alike to be around each other for very long, but there was a time I damn near worshipped that woman. Anyway, she's the last of my sisters I'd think would fall prey to some simmering stupidity. Or whatever this is... What I need is a way to see things that are going on in Hyacinth's real physical world, because all this psychic-ether shit is great but only takes you so far.

Beside me is a desk with a computer on it that my niece brought me and I never bothered to set up. Really, what am I going to do with it? I don't type. I have no need for company that's not flesh and blood. I thanked Janie profusely— it was very touching how she said, "Now we can keep in touch!" all excited like—but then I never set it up. My bad, as they say.

Now though, I eye the sleeping contraption with new interest. They have ways of doing things these days, I know. This internet is full of surprises. Perhaps I could send an email of some kind and find out what's going on. Or whatever it is people do on those universal airwaves. Twit? Twat? It doesn't matter; it might work, and right now I don't have much else to go on.

Juan-José is standing there when I open the door of my apartment. He's wearing that beat-up old Yankees cap and the same humongous headphones and wrap-around sunglasses as always. He's got a little plastic yellow flower and he holds it out to me, trying to smile with that toothless caved-in gap where his mouth should be.

I really don't have time for this. I crane my neck and yell "Mirta!" towards the next floor up. "Miiirtaaa!"

"¿Qué pasó?

"Juan-Jo se escapó."

"¡Ay carajo me cago en la madre de Dios!" Mirta yells back. Then she punctuates with a curt: "¡Coño!"

I step past Juan-José as Mirta's flip-flopped feet storm down the stairwell.

\* \* \*

Benjamin is on the phone when he opens the door, probably with one of his boyfriends back in Wisconsin or wherever. When he sees me he wipes the irritated look off his face very quickly and says, "Hold on a sec, babe." Then he furrows his eyebrows. "Fine! Look... I said hold on. Can you...can you wait? For two seconds, please, my neighbor just... Look!" He looks down at me apologetically. "Look, just hold on. Can I call you back? No? Fine, then hold on."

"It's okay," I say, and turn to shuffle back to my apartment. Maybe I sag my shoulders a little more than necessary. Perhaps I frown some and shake my head.

"No, wait. Babe, I'm going to call you back and we'll finish this later, okay? Fine. Yes. Goodbye." He lets that irritation slide out in a long sigh while staring at the cellphone and then composes himself. "How are you, Ms. Cortázar?"

"I'm fine, Benjamin. I'm sorry to trouble you but I remember you said once that if I ever needed help setting up that computer I should come knocking?"

Benjamin is wearing a puffy vest over a superman t-shirt. He's got on sweat pants and a baseball cap sits on his wily brown hair. I was wary of him when he first moved in, mostly because he wears vests and sweatpants at the same time, but he's a genuine enough soul with his little greetings in the hallway and nervous politeness. He looks puzzled for a second. I can see his mind wavering back and forth between me and the cellphone and finally he scrunches up his face and says, "Sure, hang on one sec. Lemme just send a text." He taps away at the keypad, disappears the phone into one of his vest pockets and follows me across the hall to my apartment.

After the pleasantries and obligatory offering of coffee, Benjamin gets this very serious look on his face and sets to work. He's a computer something-or-other, it's what he does, and you can see that even a simple task like this grants him a certain determined vitality. While I watch, another story surfaces. It's a difficult one, and I wonder briefly if it's a foreboding sign before giving myself over to it. A young girl, Brazilian, who'd had a very terrible childhood. She's killing, systematically killing people who hurt her, one by one, but none of the peacefulness she'd hoped for comes when it's all over. She's just empty. There's something at the end, before it fades out, a little glimmer of hope there, some hint of her new life, but it's fleeting and when the story's over I feel empty too, and very sad.

"You okay, Ms. Cortázar?"

I snap out of it. "Of course, Benjamin. How's it looking?"

"Um, almost done actually."

It's impressive: A whole cascade of wires goes from the screen to the keyboard to the big bulky box on the ground and then a few more connect to a smaller black box with lots of blinking lights on it. "That was quick."

"Well, you know." He looks pleased with himself. "It's what I do." Then a little buzzing noise erupts from his vest and he scowls and pulls out his phone. He taps another message into it, frowning, and apologizes without looking up.

"It's fine. You sure you don't want any coffee?"

"No, thanks, Ms. Cortázar."

"Benjamin?"

"Hm?"

"Do you think, will I be able to be connected to the internet, when it's all setup?"

He laughs a little and puts away his phone. "Of course! It's already mostly done and what I can do..." He slides into the wicker chair I'd set up by the desk and reaches down to flip a switch somewhere. "...is set you up with your own wireless network. Let me see..." The computer lets out a heavenly chime and blinks to life. How sweet!

"This network setting-up thing, it would take a while? I hate to be impatient but there is actually something with some urgency I need to deal with."

Benjamin turns around in the chair to look at me. "Is everything okay?"

"Yes yes, just a friend of mine. She might be in trouble. It's complicated."

"I see." Of course he doesn't, but okay. "Well, then, I can connect you through my own wireless and that'll be quicker, since your router is already set up."

"Okay." Whatever that means.

\* \* \*

I used to be so proud when people would mistake Hyacinth and me for sisters. We didn't even look that much alike, but we're similarly complected and both slender and have a spry quickness. I didn't really understand who she was or why she seemed so interested in me at first, I was just awed by her easiness with the whole world, that supernatural calm she carried. Then came the Night of No Return.

I don't remember a lot about it except there was so much music playing and I was surrounded by women. More women than I'd ever seen. They were all shapes and sizes, so many glorious shades of brown and speaking so many different languages. I remember feeling smooth, ready for whatever may come, and realizing I had clicked at least momentarily into Hyacinth's perpetual state of elegant ease.

I'm sure I knew somehow that nothing would ever be the same after that night, and I'm sure I didn't care. I felt those tambores radiating through my body, whispering their secrets. The guitar let out an ocean of notes, dancing with me as I strode through the crowd behind Hyacinth. An enormous woman was playing a horn of some kind; it let out raw, guttural moans that sounded like the swoons of lovers in the act.

We came to a chalk circle where the crowd had cleared some space. A very, very old woman lay on cot propped up on some pillows in the middle of the circle. She was smiling, watching the beautiful tide of womanhood swirl around her, and when I approached she winked at me and said something in a language I didn't understand. No one had to tell me the old one was dying—it was written, in the most peaceful way possible, all across her wisp of a body. "Lay down," Hyacinth said, nodding at an empty cot beside the woman. "This is how it all begins."

* * *

Ben says, "Ha!" which apparently means I'm connected to the internet and now fully a part of the 21st century. A page appears on the screen with little animated characters and colorful letters.

"So this is the world wide web I hear so much about," I mutter.

"You should be all set, Ms. Cortázar." I let a moment pass

and Benjamin turns around. "Unless you need something else done?"

"I do. But I don't know how to explain it. I'm sorry to trouble you, I know you have other things going on."

"Oh, it's no trouble at all." He takes out his phone and makes a face at it. "Just drama, you know. What do you need to do?"

"Well, I have a friend..." Already this sounds like one of those horrible stories you tell a late night call-in show that's really about you. "...And she's in trouble. I think. Well, I know someone's in trouble, and I think it's this one friend of mine."

"Oh."

"Sorry to be so vague."

"How?"

"What?"

"How do you know someone's in trouble?"

Because the knowledge is a cancer creeping through my insides. Because I know things. Because it's true. "Ah. It's hard to explain. Maybe one day. But my friend: If I could somehow, I don't know... Check on her. Is there an email that could do that for me?"

Benjamin does some things with his face that I assume mean he's trying not to laugh. Nice kid. "Not an email, necessarily, but maybe an app." He turns back to the screen, his eyebrows arching in concentration. "I wonder..."

"Maybe the app could ask someone else's email if she's okay?" I suggest. He's too deep in thought to answer that one so I just let him do his thing.

"There's this one app," he says, a few hmms later. "It not only links up with satellite imagery of a particular location, that's pretty basic Google maps shit, uh...excuse me."

"Oh, it's fine, Benjamin, I curse all the time."

He visibly relaxes. "Oh. You can call me Ben, by the way, only my mom calls me Benjamin anymore."

"Ben, okay. Do you want a beer?"

He chuckles. "It's nine-o'clock in the morning."

"I know that."

"Well... Sure."

"Go on," I say as I pad across the room to the fridge.

"Oh, well this app, it's super secret actually but I know some of the guys developing it. Still pretty new and probably vastly illegal, but anyway, it hacks into all the security cameras in the vicinity and can actually give you a semi-complete 3-D map of what you're looking at. Pretty amazing shi-stuff, uh, shit." He finishes with an awkward giggle.

German really fucked up the English language. A beer? I mean, it's simple, so that's nice. But nothing compares to cerveza with its mischievous regality. Cerveza. It's dignified. I hand Ben a cerveza, a Presidente in fact, which perhaps is not the most dignified of them all, but not bad. He nods and takes a sip. When he finishes a crown of foam ejaculates from the spout and spills onto his sweatpants. "Oh, shit," he says, "I'm sorry."

"They're your pants not mine," I laugh, padding back to the kitchen for some paper towels.

"Alright let me see if I can bring this app up."

I give him the paper towels and the address of Hyacinth's Queens apartment and he clacks away for a few minutes.

I'm getting itchy. The terribleness trembles along my spine; it's a jagged clanging that won't go away. Deep breath. Stifle impatience. Breathe.

"Pow!" Ben yells. There on the screen is a whirling image of Hyacinth's building. I say whirling because it looks as if a helicopter is circling the place, panning every possible angle with startling accuracy.

"Amazing," I gasp. "Tell your friends they have made a very excellent app."

Ben laughs. "I will." He gets out of the chair and I sit, narrowing my eyes at the screen. Hyacinth lives on the third floor, I believe. Her living room window had a fire escape outside and view of the... There! I lean even closer to the screen and the image becomes blurry, full of fat, ungainly squares. But there's something there.

"Can you, Ben, can you make it clearer?" Not so frantic. The poor boy will get scared.

He leans forward and does a few things with the mouse. The image stops rotating and swooshes forward toward the spot I was glaring at. First it's still all messy and then, by some means of that weird digital magic, it resolves into a crisp, perfect picture.

"My God," I whisper. Probably, Ben doesn't see it. It's just a tiny sparkling sliver, like a thread of silver caught in the sunlight. It outlines the form of a man standing perfectly still on the fire escape outside Hyacinth's window. A taker. This one would be the look out. That means that at least one other is either on the way or already inside. This is much, much worse than I thought.

"What is it?" Ben asks.

"Nothing," I say. The lie is plain, though. Ben reads the horror on my face but doesn't say anything

I stare at the screen for another few seconds, making sure I saw what I saw. "What's the quickest possible way to get to Queens?"

"The G train, I guess, but you'd have to take a bus to the station. Um, you could take a cab but it'd be pretty expensive I think." Stupid New York City public transportation. Ben considers something and then says, "Or we could take my super-scooter."

I'm a little put out that an adult man has something called a "super-scooter," but listen, I'm in point A to point B mode, so I don't really give a crap what he calls it as long as it moves faster than the B48. And then we're downstairs in the basement storage area and Ben is pulling a tarp off something quite huge and there it is in all its glory. If a Harley Davison had its way with a prehistoric swan, nine months later you'd have a Super Scooter. "Technically, it's a personal hovercraft," Ben is saying as he once-overs it with an old rag. "But you know, they call it the Super Scooter I guess 'cause it sounds cool."

"I didn't know such a thing even existed." I'm trying not to sound like too much of an awed schoolgirl, but the thing is amazing.

Ben looks around and cranes his neck towards me. "Technically, it doesn't yet. But I know some people who know some people in the tech world, and...this is basically a prototype of something that'll be on the market a few years from now. I'm not really supposed to have it at all, just holding it as a favor for a guy. And I kinda swore I wouldn't ever go joyriding on it, but...you said this was an emergency, right?"

We just stare at each other for a couple of seconds and then I nod ever so slightly.

"Well, hop on." He sits on the cushiony seat and pushes forward to the edge so there's room for little me. I am frail, older than anyone imagines. Still, there's some room for thrill-seeking left in me. I'm both terrified and feverishly exhilarated by the thought of putting my life in this strange, skinny fellow's hands. I put my own wrinkly old hands against his torso to steady myself while I mount the thing. It hums and vibrates like a living animal beneath me— not an altogether unpleasant experience, I have to admit. Ben clicks a button, the metal gate crunches open and we swoosh out into the sunlit streets.

At first I can't breathe. Or maybe I don't want to breathe, or just plain forget. Everything is moving so fast around me, these streets I know so well just blur past and are gone. And then I realize I'm smiling. Hugely. I must look like a babbling moron, the wind flushing through my old face, my gray and white hair dancing miraculously behind me. I'm zooming through the streets of Williamsburg at mach

10 holding for dear life onto a 6'3 130 lb white boy from Wisconsin. The universe does indeed bring you to strange places.

"You must have wonderful joyrides on this thing with your boyfriend," I say once I catch my breath.

"Oh. I'm not gay."

For a few moments all we hear is the wind whipping alongside us, the occasional horns of midday traffic. "Oh."

"That was my girlfriend Diana I was um talking to on the phone earlier."

"Of course."

Maybe it's better if I don't speak. We zip along side streets and alleyways 'til we're in Polish Green Point, mostly quiet little houses and occasional butcher shops and bakeries. Then, very suddenly, we're flying, literally flying across the Pulaski Bridge. It's a tiny one, as far as New York bridges go. There's some industrial business going on down by the canal, along with the obligatory declaration of love and territorial dispute graffiti. The water is crisp in the midday sun and all the factories and parking lots sparkle dazzlingly along the surface. And then it's all over because we're in Queens, blasting past some warehouses and then cutting through traffic beneath the 59th Street Bridge.

Stories are rising up inside me. They're agitated; maybe they sense the danger. Whatever it is, they need to stop. I can't concentrate when I keep getting whiffs of chocolate, whispers of rain against a window, stomach-clenching jolts of passion and indignation. I close my eyes and will them to back up off me for a bit, smile as the scattered threads of life settle back into place.

"Ms. Cortázar?"

"Yes, Ben?"

"We're here."

* * *

The door to Hyancinth's apartment is ajar so I ease it open and poke my head in. It's much worse than I thought. The room is a mess, but not the kind you find after a struggle. There are piles of food-crusted dishes, discarded tissues, crimpled up papers. The blinds are pulled and the whole place seems dusty and grim, like you have to wade through the air. Hyacinth has been wallowing. I step in, bracing myself against the fetid smell of neglect, and gingerly cross toward the bedroom.

There're three of them. They're just barely visible, more glinty flashes of silver thread in the half-light. The lines describe three tall bodies crouching along the floor. Hyacinth lies on her back in the middle of them, her mouth open, her breath coming in irregular bursts like a dying fish. The takers have their hands on her, holding her old body down, although she's so far gone I don't even think they have to. Their heads are nestled against her ribs like suckling pups. They're sucking her stories out, emptying poor Hyacinth of all the hard work she's done over the centuries.

I don't bother being quiet. Anyway, the rage is in me; I don't think I could creep if I tried. The first one rises, all sluggish from so much feeding but still fierce like a cornered street-hound. I narrow my eyes, find where the glimmering contours insinuate something solid and drive my open hand into it. Catch the thing full across the throat and hear it gasp. Those invisible hands reach out towards me so I throw myself forward, feeling my old body crackle and grumble as I go. The taker is thrown off balance and we collapse across one of its still-feeding companions.

On the way down, my leg brushes against Hyacinth's. It's cold and I know if she's not gone yet, it won't be long. I can't be troubled with that now. The two takers are pinned beneath me; it feels like a horrible breeze, writhing up from the floor against my chest. They're pathetic, these wraiths, given over to their gluttony and barely able to stand, let alone fight off a nice old lady like me. So they don't put up much struggle when I place my hands over their faces and press down, releasing all my power to destroy through my palms and whispering fevered prayers.

They squirm, twitch, begin to give over to nothingness. I feel the last raging gasps reverberate through my slender body. An echo clatters along my bones, rattles me, and then they're gone. The third one has wrenched itself away from Hyacinth and is stumbling towards the door. There's so much crap on the floor, the taker has to keep throwing his weight from one side to the other to sashay around things. I walk slowly towards him, watch as he pitches forward and lands in a nebular heap.

It's so easy, I almost feel bad. Then Hyacinth gasps again. The rage wells up inside my chest, a red rising tide. It swooshes through my arm and explodes out my hand and into the back of the taker's head and annihilates him instantly. I rise, scan the piles of laundry and old newspapers. I'm about to take care of Hyacinth when a tingling voice in the back of my head whispers one word: *Window.*

The lookout. I turn towards the window as it cracks and then shatters. I hear the bedroom door swing open behind me and like an asshole, I turn around. Of course it's Ben. But when I realize that, it's too late: The lookout is on me. He's not fatigued and fatted out like his brothers. Those long arms hold me fast from behind and his cold lips are on my skin.

"Ms. Cortázar!" Ben is frozen in the doorway. I must look like a crazy person; I'm sure he can't see the taker. I open my mouth but a sudden shock of pain erupts through me. The taker has sent some sliver of itself inside, is burrowing through those precious stacks of stories. I wait for the panic but instead an unsettling complacency comes over me. The pain subsides and a pleasant haziness takes its place.

"Ms. Cortázar?" I'm sure my eyes have glazed over. I'm not really focusing on anything in particular, because why bother? Everything is taken care of. The boy in front of me suddenly looks at the floor and gasps, "Oh my god!" He runs past me. I think I might turn, at a leisurely pace. Maybe see what the excitement is about. I do, slowly because I'm a little dizzy and the room becomes a blur when I move too fast. Something heavy is weighing on my back but I'm very, very content.

A foot. A woman's bare foot, grey brown and calloused, with overgrown toe-nails. It's all I can make out because Ben's crouching over the rest of her. He turns, in slow motion, and shoots me a terrified glance. That's when I see the woman laying on the ground. The whole situation seems so familiar to me, like I saw it in a movie once. Or perhaps it was a story someone told me as I fell pleasantly asleep. Then I see her face.

*Hyacinth.*

Just a whisper. That voice. That's my voice. My whisper. *Hyacinth.* I know her. She is my friend. My sister. Just then, the sad old face trembles slightly and a hoarse breath escapes her open mouth. *Hyacinth.* And I see it: She's full of stories. Well, not full anymore, but there are still some, dancing in there like children left at school after all their classmates have been whisked away.

I have stories in me. Sweet Jesus!

That weight on my back. The taker. The situation flashes back to me and I'm suddenly consumed by panic. Ben is standing, staring with wide eyes. I drop to my knees, my arms are flailing. No. No flailing right now. I will my arms to reach behind me, find the thing, the...

Everything is so pleasant. My hand catches something in the air behind my head. A form. I'm sinking towards the floor. Ben reaches out to me. Behind him is Hyacinth, my sister.

This old hand finds its mark and my brain shoots a trembling blast of death through it. And something releases inside of me. Terror floods back up; the room is suddenly crisp. I wrench myself free of the taker's grasp and whirl around, still on my knees. He's shaking his head, trying to rally for another grab at me. I put my hand on him and when he looks up I let the death out, let it crease through him, watch him crumble and dissolve at my knees.

"Jesus!" Ben says. "What the fuck is going on?"

I try to stand but it's not working. This combat shit wore me out. Ben offers his arm and I clutch it, pull myself up. Hyacinth takes another breath. I kneel beside her, my whole body trembling, and have a look. She's mostly gone, my sister. As I gaze over that unkempt, tragic body, her withered hair and dry skin, I understand. They've been here for a while now, weeks maybe. That gnawing wrongness I woke up with was just Hyacinth's death knoll. Too late. She didn't even have any fight left in her. The takers found their way in, poisoned the air with that sweet-sensation morphine-type stuff they have, and feasted on poor Hyacinth's stories at their leisure.

Amazingly though, there's still quite a few stories in there. I can sense them twirling and tingling as I get close to her sad old face. She's been around a lot longer than I have. I can't even imagine how much traveling and collecting she's done. The sorrow of the moment suddenly rushes up on me. Hyacinth, for all her pain-in-the-ass perfectionism, taught me so much. There was a time that she was the one I went to when the pressure of all that living felt too burdensome to bear. Her face would crease into a smile and those eyes would glint a little and she'd spit out some silly old aphorism, more potent for its tone than meaning, and I'd feel somehow revived. I'd walk out fresh and the air would seem chilly and crisp around me and the world wouldn't be closing in anymore.

I let it pass. This isn't the time for century old recollections. Hyacinth really only has another couple moments left and I need to figure out what to do with her stories. I can't keep them all, I know that for sure. The suddenness of that overload, the two collections colliding, would be a shock to my system that I may never recover from. I could just let them go: As soon as her mortal body expired it would release them like spores out into the world. Most would evaporate. Some might carry off into the early Autumn wind and become dreams or fits of inspiration. But all that work, all that collecting... It seems a shame to let them go.

"Should we call 911?"

Ben is crouched across from me, staring intently at my face. I must have let my sadness slip out. "No, Ben. There's nothing they can do for her."

He nods like he understands. I suppose, in some way, he must've figured out by now that I'm not your average abuelita next door. I study his face for a second, blocking out all the chaos and carnage around us.

It's an intriguing third possibility, but I have my doubts.

Not because he's white, mind you.

Well, partially because he's white, yes. I've never seen a white storykeeper. I'm sure they're out there, they must be, but they're probably part of a whole other network than me and Hyacinth. Who knows? Also, he's a man. Never seen one of those keep stories, either. Again, I'm not saying... Well, let me stop apologizing for myself. Men don't necessarily have that same impulse towards nurturing the inner garden, so to speak. Particularly not the pale ones. At least, none of the ones I've met.

It's not just that though. He's very flimsy, Ben. I don't know if that little body could handle the sudden influx of stories. Even then, long term, there's no telling what would happen.

"What is it, Ms. Cortázar?"

He's genuine, I'll give him that much. Not trying to be anything but his own strange little self. Maybe, over time, he could develop some more spine and grow into the tremendous responsibility. Maybe. It's cruel, in a way, but crueler things have been done for much worse reasons.

"Ms. Cortázar? Why are you smiling?"

"Lie down, Ben." I say very gently. "Here, next to Hyacinth. This is how it all begins."

# TALL WALKIN' DEATH

## 1

In the back room of El Mar, the walls around us bumpy with fake coral reef and starfish, the drinks strong and ongoing into the night, we make light of every topic known to man. It's a machine gun strategy—any of these awkward taboos could be the one to a lay us low in a dark, too-much-thinking hour, so we rat-tat-tat through each with slick comments and useless insights. It's a thing we do. Sex, death, crying, true love, growing up, not growing up, sports, drugs, politics, race, sex,—we take it all on but tonight's discussion is about the secret pleasures of women.

"Look," Riley announces. "It's all about this." He wraps a translucent arm around his face, peers around to make sure everyone's watching and then enthusiastically slobbers all over his elbow pit.

"Snorkeling?" I suggest.

"No, Carlos. Head. Head!"

Gordo chimes in: "I agree, actually, with Riley. If a man does not give head, he is really not being considerate to the woman."

"Why'd it get called head anyway?" Jimmy asks.

"'Cause if you do it right the chick's head explodes," Riley explains.

"That's fucked up," Jimmy says.

"It's true," I confirm.

"Only in a manner of speaking, yes," Gordo puts in.

Cyrus Langley is characteristically quiet. Cyrus's one of these slow moving strategic ghosts, right up until it's time for war, and then he's all fire and fun. After more than a hundred years being bottled up in his own grave, watching his fellow forgotten and enslaved ghosts rot into ether, the man's gonna need his time to readjust. Tonight he looks content though, a serene smile pasted across his face, his fingers wrapped around a glass of pure absinthe. "Head," Cyrus says with a soft chuckle. "Don't know where you modern day Negroes come up with this shit."

I order another round of rum and cokes for me and Jimmy (Gordo's still nursing his) and a vodka shot for Riley. The table is littered with empty glasses and ashtrays full of stumped out cigar butts.

"You working tomorrow?" Riley asks.

I nod solemnly.

"Say fuck you to the Council for me."

"Done. Anything else?"

"Getting a new assignment?"

Nod.

"Anything we can cause trouble with?"

Shrug.

"Well what is it, you cryptic motherfucker?"

"I dunno, Riley. All I know is I'm working with Big Cane."

Riley splorches his drink across the table. "Big Cane! No way, that ol' ghost been around, like, two thousand years. He doesn't even work much anymore."

"Well, he's working tomorrow."

"Who's Big Cane?" Jimmy asks, wiping vodka and ghost saliva off his glasses.

"Seriously, Jimmy," Riley says, "you're underage and fully alive. If you wanna hang you're gonna haveta do better than just sitting there asking questions all the time. You need to contribute to the conversation too."

Jimmy puts his glasses back on and glares at Riley.

"You ever work with him?" I ask.

"Nah but he's a legend. Supposed to be quite the ol' badass."

"Why he called Big Cane?"

"'Cause he's tall and white. Why you think?"

I doubt that's really it but it gets everyone chuckling again. The waitress shows up with our drinks. She's short, round and delicious. I try to tell her how much I like her whenever she comes back with another round but it only comes out in stupid grins.

"If you don't let that young lady know how you feel," Cyrus muses after she hustles away with a wink, "I'm going to do it for you."

I roll my eyes.

"If they bringing in Big Cane," Riley says, "that means something has got The New York Council of the Dead truly unnerved. 'Specially if they pairing him with you."

Cyrus hovers up into a wavery standing position. "Gentlemen." The old conjurer's soft, squinty eyes are watery from the absinthe but his glow is fierce as ever. "Friends." He raises his glass to the center of the table. "A toast, to our unruly band of supernatural warriors, spies, magicians and griots." Our five glasses meet with a ruckus clank.

"Who's the warrior and who's the spy?" Riley asks.

Gordo says, "I am the griot."

"We're each all of them," Cyrus says gamely. "And a toast to a future where our destinies, in life and in death, are not governed by some foul sprawling bureaucracy but rather by our own collective passions and morals. This is the future we fight for."

Another clink and a chorus of here-heres and tell-ems.

Jimmy takes a swig and passes his drink to Riley.

"What's this?" Riley says.

"For my homies who passed away. I was gonna spill on the floor but you right there. Just take it."

"Har har," Riley says.

Cyrus just smiles.

\* \* \*

At dawn we stumble out into the stilldark streets in that sprawling mess of houses and shops where Bushwick meets East New York. Cyrus and Riley float off together, singing some ol' time conjurer song in careless, slurred howls. Gordo watches them disappear, chuckles his goodbyes and then waddles off towards his cramped apartment by the train tracks.

I look up at Jimmy. He's just seventeen but his face has grown so serious in the few months I've known him. I wonder, for the thirtieth time this week, if I'm making a mistake in bringing him under my wing. "You drunk?"

"Nah," he waves the idea off like it's an angry moth and then relents. "A little."

"Me too." We head towards his bus stop, him with that long loping stride and me with my half gimpy grace, cane clicking along. "You know you can back out any time you want."

"I know, and if I'da wanted to I woulda, Carlos. But I don't. I'm in it regardless. Gonna be seeing ghost ass moth-afuckers floating around the city, I might as well know how to deal with them." He's right. And he's getting really good with the short blade I gave him. And I really don't want him to stop, because somehow showing Jimmy the ropes makes this whole mess-with-the-Council-from-the-inside idea a lot more bearable.

"Alright," I say, lighting the night's final Malagueña. "It's the last time I'm gonna ask. What's this?" Jimmy has passed me what appears to be a miniature graphing calculator. "Thanks but I'm not taking the SATs any time soon."

"It's a phone, asshole."

"Ah."

"I swear, man, sometimes I really do wonder what century you were alive in."

"A mobile phone?"

"Look, I have one too." He reaches a long arm into his jacket and produces an identical phone. "This way, we can talk to each other. When we're not around each other. It's brilliant."

"Yes, I grasp the concept."

"It's to thank you," Jimmy looks somewhere else, 'cause that way it's easier for two men to be nice to each other. "For teaching me and everything. It really means a lot to me. I set you up with a plan, it was no big deal."

All I got is half sentences. "Jimmy, I... You didn't have to...really this is...wow." It's just that I haven't gotten many presents since I resurfaced. And the most important one is a cassette tape haunted with too many good memories of a woman long gone. And the rest of my life is a big erased blackboard, so that makes this the best present anyone's ever giving me. I can't quite put that into words though, so I just reach up and pat his shoulder in a way that I hope conveys how I feel.

We walk along in silence for a few blocks. The beginnings of gray creep along the eastward sky, a gentle glow over the houses. Little particles of rain flit in the morning air around us and the sleeping city stirs with the first chills of approaching winter.

\* \* \*

Death always wins. Life is just a blip. It's a shiny, hyperactive blip, but a blip nonetheless, and no matter how strong or wily or rich a life may be, the slippery slope always leads to the great nothing. That's why when the dead see some clothes they think they might look slick in, they simply gank 'em and sit with the shit nonstop for a while. And since death always wins, pretty soon the threads'll take on that eerie translucent quality and start feeling nice and comfy against shiny barely-there flesh.

The girl sitting next to me outside of Botus's office looks like she stripped a whole military platoon and then went t-shirt shopping at a Metallica show. Her desert storm fatigues are fashionably huge and tucked into steel tipped boots. An angry winged skull grins out from her chest, haloed by the words ANGELS of NO MERCY in neo-gothic sprawl. She's about Jimmy's age; heavyset with dainty little glasses. She's also cradling what may very well be a bazooka, or perhaps a rocket launcher, against her shoulder. Its butt rests on the ground. The business end features a red and white projectile of some kind—looks like it probably explodes on impact, whatever it is. I stand up and put a few seats between us.

The girl raises a mischievous eyebrow and grins at me. "Whatsamatter, halfie, Greta here bother you?"

"Greta looks temperamental."

"Nah, she got the safety on."

"Either way..."

"You meeting with Botus too?"

"I am."

"Hate that greasy fuck."

I cast a suspicious eye in her direction. She sounds genuine, but a) I'm already under scrutiny for being of questionable allegiance and b) only a reckless bastard would diss the all powerful Chairman in his own waiting room. She may be here to flush me out, but I am intrigued regardless.

"He's definitely one to watch out for."

The effect is startling. The girl leaps up and rushes over

to the seat beside me, Greta in tow. For all her urgency, she does wield the thing with the fluid ease that only a professional could muster. "You think so, too?" she whispers.

"I mean..."

"It's just that I signed up for this thinking, you know, I'd get to play with guns and kick some ass for sure, but also do some good for people. But seriously, man, it's been one bullshit after another from jump. From jump, son, you feel me? And quite frankly, there's just some shit they had me do that I ain't even comfortable thinking about. I just... I just ain't with it. I ain't. And yet I'm stuck, you know, 'cause once you in, you in. Game over. And I definitely don't trust the corny old ghost on the other side of that door but he the one got me taking out all kindsa errant phantoms and shit. It's troubling me, man."

She pauses to breathe. "I'm Krys by the way. Krys with a kay. Short for Krystal but since I'm neither prom queen nor pornstar, it's just Krys." Flashes that awkward teenager smile at me and offers her fist for a pound.

"Carlos," I say, putting my chilly flesh-and-bone knuckles against her icy see-through ones. "And you need to be careful who you unload to."

"I know." She rolls her eyes toward the misty warehouse ceiling. "But I knew who you were when you sat down. There's not that many half-dead dudes walking around HQ—none actually—besides you, and well, not that I'm not a stalker or nothing, but I've read all your case files."

"Oh?"

"Oh indeed. And I know something about you."

"Really?"

"Well, I can tell a thing or two. You can see it in the case work, the way you write your reports. The way you carry yourself."

A fury of self-consciousness creeps over me. Am I such an open book? Have I been incriminating myself this whole damn time? "What do you think you know about me?" I try to keep the words even but the menace lurks out anyway.

"Relax, man. No one else knows. I got you. You've done your homework. I'm just very perceptive." I shoot her a doubtful look. "Trust me," she says. "And I been talking you up to the other soulcatchers, starting rumors about you massacring motherfuckers and taking unholy vengeance on anyone that challenges the Council's authority and shit—you know, throw 'em off the path."

"Are you serious?"

"Dead ass, kid. You can't be too careful."

I grunt in agreement.

"Anyway, there's lots to talk about. Maybe we could meet up later or something?"

High School's awkward phraseology carries over in death, apparently. "Maybe," I say, mostly 'cause I'm still trying to work my head around the idea of a random teenage girl ghost talking me up to cover for my supposed rebellious activity.

Botus's office door swings open and his big stupid head pokes out, toothy grin first. "Carlos! What's up man thanks for coming c'mon in we ready for you!" The man just vomits phrases with total disregard for their meaning. I try to tune out as much as possible around him. Krys rolls her eyes.

"Maybe I'll see you later," I say, and follow Botus into his office.

\* \* \*

Big Cane really is fucking huge. You couldn't even call it sitting, what he's doing to that chair. He's dominating it. The thing looks like it's about to give up. His hulking mass would qualify as both fat and beefy—the only ghost I know you could actually describe as solid. And he's tall. His pale shiny skin wraps around that monster frame in thick loafs.

He stands when I walk in, dwarfing the shit out of me and Botus. A wide, genuine smile stretches all the way across his face, creasing thick canyons into his cheeks.

"Agent Delacruz," he says, extending a slab of a hand towards me. "I am so honored to meet you finally. They say you're the smaller, Spanish version of me."

"Hardly," I chuckle, although I have no idea what he means by that. I cringe as I reach out and take his hand but his touch is surprisingly gentle. I'm sure he's been taken to task for crushing more than a few ghost hands.

"Alright, blah blah blah, nice to meet you, let's get on with it," Botus blathers as we both take our seats. "Listen: This mess is deep. I was just updating Big Cane on it, Carlos, while you were running on Puerto Rican time or whatever you call it."

"I been waiting outside your office for fifteen minutes!"

"No matter, but don't make it a habit, 'kay? This one's a doozy. A true doozy. A steaming hot pile of horseshit, this one. Otherwise I wouldn'ta called Cane in." Cane belly laughs for no apparent reason. I settle into my fuck-you face and sit back. "We're looking at one Joseph Anderson Green." He slides a photo of a very much alive yuppie across his desk at us. "Rich kid. Momma's boy. Yale, Cum Laude whatever, Wall Street, corporate lawyer now. Serial killer."

"He's alive," I say.

"Well, thank you, Agent Delacruz, for that insightful piece of evidence you've uncovered. You know, you and that two-timing two-bit afterlifer Riley you used to run with— guys think you're all deep 'cause your death was so fucked up you can't remember your life. That doesn't make you any more special than the rest of us. It just makes you forgetful. I died slow and painful, pancreatic cancer's a bitch, and I remember every damn second of my life and here I am: Your boss. So put the attitude in a little box for later, 'kay?"

If I launch across the desk and puncture a thousand holes

into Botus like I want to, I will definitely blow my cover. Plus Big Cane would probably sit on me. But if I don't do anything, I'll appear uncharacteristically comely and become suspicious. "Fuck your mother," I settle on. A happy medium. I put the vicious stabbing in a little box for later.

Seems to settle it. Cane shifts uncomfortably in his chair, but Botus continues unhindered. "Anyway, yes, as Agent Delacruz helpfully pointed out, Mr. Green is still alive. Alive and well. It is not Green that is our target, exactly. The illustrious young maniac has managed to dispose of no fewer than seven females—a prostitute, a one night stand, three ex-girlfriends and two fiancés—in the past ten years."

"Jesus," Cane sighs.

"At least four of them ended up back in this city as ghosts and now, somehow or another, they've banded together." The shady Chairman leans both hands on his desk and rises to signify we're getting to the crux of the matter. "This quadrangle of murdered females is threatening to disrupt the very fabric of our afterlife in New York."

An uncomfortable silence follows. I'm hoping Cane's in the same muddle of astonishment that I am. The big old detective removes a filterless cigarette from his jacket pocket and puts it between those big meaty lips. He raises his eyebrows to see if I want one too but I wave him off. "How exactly are they doing that?" Cane says slowly as he lights up.

"They're trying to go public. Trying to make a fuss 'bout this guy. Say he's gonna kill again so they think it's their god-given duty to mess with him. They're still fairly weak as ghosts, so it's little things, you know, poltergeist shit, but it adds up. People are starting to notice. They have to be stopped."

"I'm sorry," I say. "Just to clarify, you want us to stop the dead women. Not the serial killer."

"Oh, don't get all Ghandi on me now, Carlos. If taking

out Green is what you have to do to make this shit stop, take him out."

"Kill him?"

"Whatever."

"I don't usually kill people." I took out a fellow halfie last year under these assholes' orders and ruined whatever shambles were left of my life. Left a bad taste in my mouth, to be honest.

"Really? Only us afterlifers, huh? How you like that, Cane? Carlos here is too high and mighty to take out a living soul but he'll send one of us to whatever great unknown awaits beyond death in a hot second. You're a piece of work, Carlos. Real classy."

"What happened to all those 'don't fuck with the living' rules you won't shut up about?"

"Make up your mind, kid," Botus shoots back at me. "You either want to deal with the serial killer or you don't. You can't have it both ways. The dead bitches are causing us trouble. The living kill each other every day; it's not our department to deal with. We are the Council of the fucking Dead. Period. Not the Council of the Happy Make Your Grandmother Soup Douchebags. Clear? Your job is to stop the shenanigans. One way or the other. Any means necessary, and all that."

"Seriously," I mutter, "never quote Malcolm again."

"Any questions? You start the stake out tonight."

I nod at Cane and exit, gripping my blade handle.

* * *

Krys is waiting for me when I walk out off the Council's ragged old warehouse HQ. I'm relieved to see she didn't bring Greta. She glides beside me as I amble along the backstreets of industrial Sunset Park, trying to calm my head. I don't know why I let Botus rile me up this much, but he manages to get at me every time. I wonder if somewhere deep down inside he knows I'm gonna fucking kill him one day, and he's just trying to get his digs in while he can.

"You all right?" Krys asks when I've stopped muttering and furrowing my brow. I'm not ready to get into it with her yet, much as my instincts tell me to trust her.

"Did you get your assignment?"

She scoffs. "Some nastiness by the river they want me to clean up."

"When they say clean up, they mean utterly annihilate. You wanna get a sense of what's going on first."

"Thank you, Yoda, I'm not actually the brand new fool I appear to be."

"Just a thought. Which river?"

"Hudson."

"Why you following me?"

Krys tucks her lower lip under her front teeth thoughtfully. "I was thinking about some shit. Been thinking 'bout it for a while actually. I mean, I know you're disgruntled..."

"No, you think I'm disgruntled."

"Whatever, you're obviously a subversive. I know a like-minded motherfucker when I meet one."

"You mean when you stalk one."

"Yeah, yeah. Look: I am relatively new but I'm through with this shit. I'm done. But I don't wanna just give up and walk away, you know? I wanna fuck some shit up first. Work it from the inside. I wanna leave the Council something to remember me by when I go. I mean, I'm one of their best hunters. A fucking natural—not to toot my own horn, but it's true. Who better to tear shit up? And you're a legend, even besides your freakish dead/alive thing, and that limp—and even that only adds to your mystique.

"I see through you, Carlos. I know you want to tear shit up too. Maybe you already have. It's hard out there alone." She looks a little pre-tantrum. "It's not easy having all these thoughts. But I know you understand. We don't have to be alone anymore though. We don't have to be alone."

I take a long hard look at Krys, toss around about twelve scenarios, from terrific to catastrophic. Then I light a Malagueña and say, "We're not. Follow me."

\* \* \*

By the time we reach El Mar, I've explained as much as I can about the ragged band of supernatural warriors that I've spent my last few months being a part of. She oohs and aahs throughout each twist in the road, from the time Riley sliced that sick old plantation master against direct COD orders to the momentous escape of Cyrus Langley. She appears to be in a state of awed silence as we stroll into the perpetually dim bar and make our way to the back room. Langley's there all by himself, sitting in a single ray of afternoon sun from the barred windows, reading an ancient tome of some kind. He rises when we walk in, his grandfatherly grin already spreading like a stain across his face.

"I'm honored," Krys says before I get a chance to introduce her, "to meet such a tremendous individual as yourself, Mr. Langley. Honored. Speechless."

Cyrus laughs—it's a thin, wispy wheeze, but warm in its own right. "Hush now, my dear, the pleasure is all mine."

"Cyrus, this is Krys. She's a soulcatcher prime with the NYCOD. A coworker. And she seems to have dreamed up the same dream as us, all by herself."

"Splendid," Cyrus says. "There is much to be done. Two insiders will be a tremendous asset."

"Don't you need to test my allegiance or something, make sure I'm legit?"

Cyrus swats his long hand in the air. "Now, now, child. We trust each other. If Carlos trusts you then so do I." Krys looks disappointed. She'd clearly had some wild plot ready to prove her worth to us. It's probably for the best that Cyrus's mellow 'bout the whole thing.

"Where's everyone else?" I ask.

"Young Damian doing some work in the sewer system. You know that child's always got some project he on. Won't say whatall it is he doing down there though. Riley napping, and Gordo in rehearsal with the band."

"Jimmy?"

"Jimmy with the chess club, son. It's only three in the afternoon. Can't spend all his time cavorting and drinking with us dead folk."

"It's three?" Krys backs towards the door. "Damn! I gotta head to the river." She looks eagerly into my eyes. "Carlos, thank you. Thank you so much. I can't tell you... And Mr. Langley, so nice to meet you, sir, truly. I'm out, y'all. Peace."

"Come back anytime," Cyrus calls after her. "I like her."

"Yeah, she's weird," I say, "but I like her too."

## 2

I can't stand midtown. It's a void. An endless black hole of utter nothingess. Soul death. The dead don't usually fuck with the place, not if we can help it. The half of me that's still alive fucking hates it too. But here I am, holed up in a weird little backroom on 32nd Street with this gargantuan gumshoe ghost. Passing fucking time. I meant to bring one of those dingy detective dimestore novels but it slipped my mind. We're keeping an eye on Green's place, but so far it's a whole lotta nada.

"You must have some good stories," I say, thinking maybe I have my own floating trashy novel right here.

"Yep," Cane says and leaves it at that. He's nice enough but not the greatest converser I've ever met. Typical old school strong silent type, I guess. I am too actually, but not when I'm bored.

"It's weird, right?" I try. "The whole thing with the dead girls..."

"It's weird alright," he says with a smile.

"Real...weird."

"Yep."

This night's gonna suck.

* * *

It's getting towards three. Big Cane's halfway through his wrinkled pack of unfiltered Delinquents and I'm three Malagueñas deep when he sits up suddenly and grimaces out the window. "I think we onto something," he says with genuine excitement.

"What you see?" I make my way towards where his huge shiny form is crouching against the wall.

"Girls. Dead ones. Three of 'em. 12 o'clock."

Three glowing shrouds are creeping along the block towards Green's building. They're all done up in full party girl regalia, heels, jewelry, makeup—the works.

"Where's the fourth?"

Cane shrugs.

"What you wanna do?"

"Wait."

I guess that's how you get to be the best in the business. The girls hover anxiously around the stoop. After a few minutes I realize my body is tense with anticipation and I make a conscious effort to relax myself. That's when Green rounds the corner walking arm in arm with a pretty college-age white girl. "That'd be Jane Albright," Cane whispers. "The current future ex-Mrs. Green. She's a looker, ain't she?"

I suppose so, but she seems pretty plain Jane to me: Your standard sweater and skirt wearing, irritatingly well put together white chick that hordes in slow-mo shopping riots along the trendy avenues. The fourth ghost flurries behind them, waving her long slender arms in a fury.

Usually things are a little more clear cut: The dead are causing problems, stop the problem however I see fit, write up the paperwork so the Council's happy, walk on. Now we got some femicidal rich kid about to be in the act and four furious dead girls trying to get in the way. I don't like it all.

"You think he's gonna kill her?"

Cane really takes the time to ponder that one. "No," he says after some hemming and hawing. "But them ladies do by the look of things." They're causing as much ruckus as they can, spinning themselves into a frenzy but they only manage to send a few plastic bags swirling up into the night around the couple.

"They might be right."

"Nah." A long pause. "I don't think so." Green and his lady friend disappear into the building and I hang somewhere in between making a break for it and just sitting here sweating all night. "It's not his MO." Cane says, finally indicating that there is an actual thought process behind his random word burps.

"What's his MO?"

"Get to know the vic. Treat her nice. Make her fall in love. Kill her slow and eat the pieces."

"Oh."

The four ghosts batter helplessly against the fancy door panes, producing a mild shuddering and not much else.

"Guess that's it for tonight," Cane sighs. "They locked out."

"Listen, Cane, I know we got clear orders, and I know you ain't here to save no living people. And I respect that. But I ain't comfortable sitting here chilling while this chickadee gets ate across the street. Doesn't sit well with me. Maybe it's 'cause I'm half alive. Maybe it makes me soft, but I don't like it."

Again the deep-in-thought. "I hear you, Carlos, I do. But hear me out." I nod at him to continue." They just met. You can tell by how they strolling, the way she touched her hair, the quality of their conversatory gestures. This I am sure of. Only Green's first two kills were strangers; the hooker and the one-nighter. This was his practice, he was finding his legs. After that, each victim had a very distinct, very long term romantic relationship with him. He's gonna kill that woman, and then he's gonna eat her, but he's not gonna do it tonight." I look at him doubtfully but I can't deny the logic he's working with. "I'll wager my badge on it," he adds with finality.

I gotta hand it to the guy, he's not the hardass I took him for.

"Go home, Carlos," Cane says kindly. "Get some sleep. We'll check back in on the situation tomorrow night."

I take a last look at the four shrouds cluttered around the entrance and then glance back at Big Cane. "Alright," I say. "I'll see you tomorrow."

\* \* \*

The riverway is so quiet this time of night. A few home-less guys nap on park benches. Some empty boats glide on the current and the scattered lights of Jersey become the scattered stars above, but not much else moves. And yet, obviously something is very wrong. It's like a frantic voice inside screaming: All is not well! Maybe it's one of those pri-mal, deeply imbedded scent instincts, or something off in the flow of air, the particular pattern of strewn about trash. I can't put it into words, but it's unnerving as shit.

Then my eyes adjust some to the darkness. Maybe it's those horrible looking giants standing silently by the edge of the water. Yes, that'd be it, the source of all this foulness. I hear a sharp hissing beside me and almost curse out loud as I sidestep and draw my blade but no one's around. The towering figures haven't wavered from their dark vigil. My slow, slow heart pounds at a medium jog in my ears.

"Carlos," comes the hiss again. It's definitely Krys's voice, coming from somewhere in the underbrush behind me. I glance back at the giants to make sure they ain't loping towards us and then duck in.

"The fuck is going on?" I demand. This night has me rattled, I can't lie.

"I really don't know," Krys says. For the first time, I'm relieved to see Greta, cocked and ready to blast towering river creature ass into oblivion. "I been here all night and so have they. Haven't moved, just sway a little and occasionally lean over to confer with each other. That's it."

The seven giants waver in the wind on the river bank about fifty feet from our little hideout. They're hunched forward; skinny heads protrude from slumped shoulders. Their disproportionately long arms dangle like dead snakes on either side of their slender bodies. Worst of all, though, the damn things anathematize light. Most afterlifers glow, the giants are like walking black holes, barely visible against the foggy night sky. It's usually a sign of something very old or very cursed. Or both.

"Can you pick up what they saying?"

"It's an old dialect," Krys whispers. "Old, like, pre-written word old."

"Shit."

"But to really make out individual words Imma haveta get closer. I was just sitting here psyching myself up for it when you showed up. Wanna come?"

"Nope."

"What happened to Mr. Legendary Badass?"

"I gave him the night off."

"Carlos..."

"Krys, I got here by being crafty, not reckless."

She ponders this a moment or two, irritated that I've disrupted her suicide mission. I'm about to spew some reconciliatory shit about dying for something worthwhile when Krys shrugs and slips out of the bush towards the river. She commando-creeps from bench to bench along the walking path, expertly shifting her weight beneath Greta so it doesn't swing out of control. It'd be impressive to watch if I wasn't panicking.

By the time I inch-by-inch my way out of the bush, cringing at every rustle, Krys's crouching behind a trashcan about five feet from the giants. Blade out, I limp-sprint silently across the path, cursing under my breath. We're both panting heavily when I settle in with my back against the trashcan. Now I can smell the bastardos—it's a heavy, putrid combination of rotting flesh and...cologne. Cologne? The fuck...

"Fixation," whispers Krys, seeing my confusion. "It's one of those extra intense, 'the ladies will eat you up' type of scents."

I wave my hands in 'what-the-fuck' circles.

"Your guess as good as mine," Krys shrugs.

A low mournful murmur unrolls in the quiet night air. It can only be described as the sound of many old men gurgling.

"I cut all my Ancient Languages classes," I say. "What they talkin' 'bout?"

"From what I can tell..." Krys squints up her face, "They're waiting for something. Something about a prophecy."

"Awesome. Let's blast 'em."

"What happened to 'you wanna get a sense of what's going on first,' professor?" She does a pretty good whispered impression of me, actually.

"We did that. They're waiting for something. They're religious fanatics. Now we know. Make a diary entry and blast away."

"Shhhh."

They're gurgling again—death's off key didgeridoo—but this time a high whine screeches over the top. Krys sits up, cocking an ear, eyes shut tight behind those little glasses. "They're excited. Whatever it is's supposed to come over the river. A god of some kind, a demon god. Something like that."

"Sounds bad."

"They're frantic over it."

"They don't look frantic."

All of the sudden everything gets real quiet. The Hudson laps peacefully against the shore. Late night traffic trundles along the West Side Highway. I try not to breathe, expecting at any moment a huge dead hand to swipe at me from out of the sky. My blade is ready. Krys's hands wrap firmly around her cannon. I try to imagine what combat would be like with these towering ghosts and my new bazooka-toting teenage friend, but I'm coming up blank. Swipe at the legs and stay the fuck out the line of fire, I guess.

As quickly as the silence set in, the monsters jump back into a frenzied jarble. I hear them moving now, their long legs striding in anxious circles just a few feet away from us. Krys and I exchange nervous glances. And then, just like that, they take off, all seven scattering in different directions towards the city. The foul stench of death plus mack daddy washes over us in a thick wind and dissipates.

"That...was...awesome," Krys pants from the throes of adolescent exhilaration. That was not awesome at all, but I nod wearily anyway. I'm still trying to figure out why all this has me so shook when my new friend decides she wants to head to El Mar and meet the rest of the gang. Imminent danger has blessed Krys with a fierce case of the heebie-jeebies. I shrug off my own weird bout of shakiness and decide I can roll with that. We gather our things and head towards Brooklyn.

\* \* \*

"See, that's what I'm talking about," Riley's saying when I return to the backroom with a tray of drinks. "That's some private school shit."

"What's that?" I pass out the goods: Mojitos for me, Jimmy, Gordo and Cyrus, beers for Riley and Krys.

"Your new protégé here," Riley says. Krys is glaring across the table at him. "She's trying to tell me that just 'cause a dude dress up like a female, don't make him gay."

"Don't," says Krys. "Most cross-dressers straight. Just like most pedophiles."

"Why you gotta take it there? And what about all those priests?"

"The high profile ones gay, no doubt. But I'm saying, they make it look like they all gay. All the freaks and fuckups, right? It's a public image thing. The straight ones never get that kinda publicity."

"And I'm saying, that's some true Walnut Heights Country Day shit."

"What, having an opinion 'bout something?" Jimmy cuts in.

"Oh, don't you start, kid."

Everyone else at the table is busy finding something else to look at. "Riley," Krys says, "for all you know you lived your whole damn life in a mansion, okay?"

I'm about to step in when Riley stands up suddenly. "The fuck is that?" He's pointing at Krys's leg.

"'s my sidearm," she says, squinting at him suspiciously.

"Word?" He's across the room in an instant, peering over her shoulder at the sizable Glock strapped to Krys's left thigh. "So the rumors are true. Ghost killin' guns. Damn. Did you see this, Carlos? The new girl making us look like some prehistoric old fogies with sharpened sticks. No offense, Cyrus."

You gotta hand it to Riley, he can suck the tension out of a room as quickly as he can stuff it back in. "That's nothing," I tell him, "you should see the damn missile launcher she carries on assignments."

"Say what?" He looks at Krys with utter disbelief. "Why you get to walk around fully loaded, young lady?"

"I'm part of their pilot program," she says. "Actually, I am their pilot program. They tried an experimental projectile weapons course on my academy class and no one else could handle it. I came through flying colors and ever since they been sending me out into the field with whatever new shit they come up with."

Riley and Cyrus exchange a series of astonished glances. "Superb," Cyrus says quietly.

Riley stretches a frigid, glowing arm across my shoulder. "You've done well, Carlos. Even if she did go to some artsy-ass suburban school. 'Bout time some of our people be gun-totin' psycho nerds too." Krys looks like she's somewhere between flattered and irritated.

"Listen," I say, "I'm glad you're all happy now that we have a fully armed teenager on our side, but we got some shit to figure out. Jimmy, you find anything out with that fancy computer of yours?"

Jimmy frowns. "Not much, Carlos. The Green situation comes up pretty much as Botus laid it out to you: A few mysterious deaths around him, nothing nailable though. The guy's whole internet presence is locked up tight, purely presentation, but I did hack into a few of his bank accounts and... Well, it's all pretty boring really."

"Thank you for sparing us the details."

"One of the ghost chicks is probably Imelda McKinney, a party girl that disappeared about nine years ago from a Chicago suburb. Caused quite a hubub at the time, but Green had no ties to her. That was the one night stand, I think; he apparently managed never to be seen with her the night she died. Another one is Kristen Mellonhurst, who he partnered with for several years. Raised a few eyebrows when she went missing but the guy, like I said, is ironclad protected in that whatever the fuck force-field them rich dudes manage to cloak themselves in. They barely bat an eye at the dude, officially."

"So little has changed," Cyrus says, shaking his head. "So much and so little."

"What 'bout my giants?" Krys asks.

Jimmy makes a helpless face at us. "I mean...giants pop up all over history, guys. You don't even want to know some of the sites that were showing up in this search, trust me."

"I do," Riley says.

"Best I can figure, there's a few semi-reliable sources talking 'bout an ancient race of giants running around, fucking shit up with the other humans. Then they pulled one of those mysterious species-wide disappearing acts and shazammed themselves out the scene. Never to be heard from again. That's really all I got."

"It's feasible these dudes are the phantom remains of whatever race that was," I say, but it's not really fitting together for me.

"Let's say that's what they are," Krys says, spinning her chair around and straddling it. "And they disappeared themselves on purpose, planning to come back. Let's say that's where the prophecy comes in."

"They didn't say what the prophecy was?" Cyrus asks.

"Not that I heard," Krys says. "But let's imagine it was a pact, more so than a prophecy. A pact with this demon they waiting for."

"It's a good story, even if it's utter nonsense," Cyrus muses.

"And in this pact-slash-prophecy, right? There's a piece missing. Something's incomplete. And for whatever reason, fill in the blank, they think it's coming. Whatever it is that's supposed to happen, it's about to. Maybe they don't even know."

Everyone nods thoughtfully.

"Time is it?" Jimmy asks.

"Damn near dawn," I say. "Let's wrap this up. Tonight we split up, I'll..."

"I'ma go with Krys," Riley says. "Wanna see those babies in action."

"Alright, Riley and Krys take the Hudson and me and Jimmy'll keep stakin' out Green with Big Cane. Gordo..." Gordo's passed out in his chair, his massive body heaving up and down. He's smiling, probably dreaming of some hot Cubana offering him a lifetime supply of Malagueñas. "Gordo'll go with you guys. I'll lend him my phone so he can call Jimmy if anything pops off."

The night had been a warm one, but the coming dawn brings a frosty breeze in from the bay. We say our goodbyes and scatter out into the backstreets of Brooklyn.

<u>3</u>

Big Cane is an erratic dude. Maybe it's Jimmy being around, an unusual addition to our hunting party that Cane took with characteristic cool breeze grace. Either way, now the old ghost won't shut the fuck up. I'm actually yearning for the peaceful boredom of last night. "Yeah, that was a time alright," Cane drawls on, I've lost track about what. "That was back when the Council was first training soulcatcher primes. Before that it was just like some loose scattered shit, just here and there. We were ragtag. Got away with all kindsa bullshit, Jimmy, lemme tell you. Oh, we had our fun."

"I bet," Jimmy says for like the fourteen-thousandth time.

"I remember one time, man, there was this Asian ghost that would not, just would not leave this old man alone." The ghost was Korean, the old guy turned out to be half Korean for some reason, the ghost was his ancestor, blah blah blah. Heard this story sooo many times already and it wasn't that good the first time. "Turned out—"

"Guys guys guys!" I say in an excited hush. "I think I see something." They hustle over to the window and peer out expectantly. I didn't see shit really, but it should buy me a few minutes of peace and quiet. "Guess not," I shrug.

"Where was I?"

"The Korean ghost," Jimmy says.

Damn.

* * *

The ladies show up around midnight, all four of them this time. They're spinning in their usual furious whirlwinds. Green and his girlfriend come strolling around the corner like high school sweethearts, him carrying her books, both radiant with that new relationship excitement.

One of the ghosts detaches herself from the rest. I'm guessing it's Imelda from all her regalia and accoutrements, but who can tell? She throws herself at Green and this time he steps suddenly backward, waving his hands. She must've gotten stronger overnight. Green looks around, his face wide open with terror. Then his eyes narrow and I'm suddenly quite sure this isn't the first time the ghosts have bothered him. He can't see them, but he seems to understand what's going on. He grabs his date's slender wrist and marches her into the building, slamming the door behind him before any of the ghosts can slip inside.

"What's going on?" Jimmy says.

"He got wise to his stalkers," Cane grumbles, rising and going for his blade. "Now we have a situation."

"Stay close," I tell Jimmy. "I'm really not sure how this gonna go."

* * *

We're crossing the street, brushing past the screaming ghosts and entering the lobby. Big Cane nods at me that he's gonna stay behind with the ladies. I push random apart-ment buttons until a lady's voice answers groggily.

"Ambulance, ma'am," I say, "we need you to let us in the building." The door buzzer groans and we charge through the ornate, marble-floored lobby and up five flights of stairs to Green's slightly open door. I draw my blade out from its sheath, but I still have no idea whether or not I'm ready to use it on a living person, even if it's a woman-eating psycho-path. The only noise is the building humming its nonchalant building song and late night cars passing on the street below.

"You wanna go in?" Jimmy asks. His tall, slender frame is tensed for action.

"Not at all," I say. "But we can't exactly walk away."

"Nope."

I enter blade first, move silent as a shadow down the narrow corridor. Jimmy creeps a little less quietly behind me. I hear the struggling before we round the corner: A woman's high pitched scream, the dull thrashing of bodies against each other, the rustle of clothes. I'm about to rush in when a tinny hip-hop beat erupts behind me. I whirl around to find Jimmy fumbling with his damn phone. It shimmies in his hands, oomp-oomp-clacking away and then a staticky voice declares himself to be *the riot, the riot, the motha-fucking riot*. Before I can spin back around, Green is on me, that hairy pale arm tight on my throat, the other clasping my blade hand. He heaves forward and we both stumble into a tangle of limbs on the floor. I'm still trying to catch my breath when he scatters up, landing a few kidney shots on the way, and lunges for Jimmy. That cellphone-on-mute curse-out I'd been saving for my protégé evaporates beneath a surge of terror. I must protect the boy. All those moral questions I'd worried about become suddenly petty.

*Yes, I'm the riot, son / I am the king a chaos come*, Jimmy's phone blathers on. Flooded with that enraged righteousness,

I find my footing and am just rising when something heavy and wet clocks me across the face. The bastard hit me, I think in a boiling flurry. Then I look up. Green is standing in front of Jimmy with his back to me, but something's wrong. I can see more of Jimmy than I should be able to. Ah, yes: Green's head is gone. It starts to sink in. That hairy mess leaning on my shoe, the dark red lake spreading across the hardwood floor. Green's body finally collapses as the world speeds back up to its normal rhythm. I steady myself with one hand against the wall and gingerly lift my foot; the head rolls sideways, landing with a tiny splish in the muck. I look at Jimmy's wide, wide eyes. He's got the newly bloodied short sword in one hand and the still rapping mobile in the other. *I am riot, the riot, the motha...*

"Hello," Jimmy says, raising the phone up to his ear. He looks a fucking mess but definitely isn't the blithering disaster I feared he'd be. Not yet anyway. "Hi, Gordo." His eyes are a million miles away. I'm sure Gordo can hear it in his voice.

"Is a bad time?" mechanical-sounding Gordo says on the other end.

Then Jane Albright comes shivering around the corner and lets out a horrific scream. "Lemme call you back," Jimmy says.

* * *

If anyone's standing on 71st Street between Broadway and the West Side Highway and they happen to have heightened spiritual vision, this is what they would see: A freakishly tall, skinny-ass, dark skinned Puerto Rican kid with thick glasses and baggy clothes; another Puerto Rican, strangely off-color and moving astoundingly fast given his gimpy leg; a humongoid ghost detective, complete with Stetson hat and leather jacket; a dead housewife; a dead sex worker and two dead party girls; all of them rushing along through the streets towards the river.

"Gordo said," Jimmy pants as he strides along beside me, "the giants was acting crazy, getting all riled up." *Pant, pant, pant.* "Says they started right before he called."

"Krys ready to move on them?"

"Didn't say."

"How you feel?"

Jimmy considers for a minute. "Pretty alright, actually, considering."

But I know that's 'cause we still in the thick of it. Trauma waits for shit to slow down before it really settles in.

Cane floats up alongside us, listening somberly. He'd been impressively relaxed about the whole beheading thing. Once the dead chicks mellowed, he simply put out a telepathic message to the Council to get some cleanup folks over to Green's apartment ASAP and then said, "Now what?"

I told him about Krys's river situation and he said, "Oh, she's a buddy of mine from the field. We been through some shit together." And that was that.

* * *

"What the hell are we doing again?" one of the dead exes, Imelda, asks as we cross the highway.

"First, we were just getting out of there quick," I tell her. "But now we're helping out a friend who's got a situation by the river."

"A situation involving giant demons," Jimmy adds.

The exes all perk up. "Giant demons with beady red eyes?"

"Reeking of rot and fancy cologne?"

"That'd be them," I say.

"I'm out," says the housewife ghost. One of the party girls floats off with her.

"I'm in," Imelda says. "Those the bastards that got this whole mess started."

"How so?"

"That's how we all came together, one night last week, we were each chased by one of those giants until we ended up right in front of Green's house. Then we got to talking and put all the pieces together. Figured we might as well make some trouble for him since we all found each other."

"Strange..."

The sex worker, Terry, drifts up beside Imelda. "Count me in too. Let's fuck up some river giants."

We creep along the walking path, a quaint little shrubbery-lined number that meanders beside the rocky shoreline, until I recognize Krys's hideout from the night before. It's a little more cramped now that Riley and Gordo are squeezed in, but we clear some room and peer out towards the river.

"Where the giants?" Jimmy asks after we introduce everyone to Big Cane, Terry and Imelda.

"They're running," Krys says.

"Running like jogging?" I say.

Riley chuckles but it sounds forced. He's nervous. "Running like rioting. These mo'fos just busted out in a frenzy, man. Here come one."

It's a rush of death-cologne first, then I see that towering emptiness come thundering down the path, arms and legs swinging like a marathon runner. Its warble's louder and more frantic than last night, and that shrill whine slices into my ears.

"Jesus Fucking Christ," Terry says. We all nod in solemn agreement.

The giant stops directly in front of us, its long body heaving up and down breathlessly, and looks out into the darkness over the river. A moment passes, and then the thing lifts its arms to the sky and lets out a blood curdling scream.

Is it afraid? Excited? The scream fills the air like a poisonous gas. Pretty soon, the stench becomes unbearable too; the other giants are coming.

\* \* \*

"What you wanna do, Krys?" I ask. "This is your job, you're the boss."

She's been quiet up 'til now, watching, plotting. I can tell she's putting all that rattled terror away for later, just like they trained her to do at the Soulcatcher Academy.

"I wanna wait," she says coolly. "Just a little longer." All seven giants are huddled by the edge of the water now, trading whines and gurgles. "Just a little longer."

Then it happens: An eerie light emerges upriver from us. It's just a dim glow at first, but as it gets closer it glares into our retinas, making little color splotches dance across the darkness. The giants are electrified, they begin trembling and chortling, swinging their long fingered hands in circles at each other.

"It's a person," Gordo says. "It's a man." Indeed, the glow has paused over the water in front of its welcome party and we can now see a trembling human form immersed in the blinding rays. He doesn't have a head.

"It's Green!" Big Cane yells. All the giants turn at the same time. Seven pairs of beady red eyes ogle our little shrub hideaway. The tallest one takes a step towards us.

"Oh hell no," Krys says, mounting Greta on her shoulder and clicking off her safety. "Hell no." No one has a chance to say anything. The world becomes a shuddering jumble, my legs give out, and a milky burst of smoke fills the air around us. There's a raspy shriek, like God's hocking a loogie. Jimmy falls against me and we both go down hard into the bushes. I can't see. I can't hear. I think I could move if Jimmy'd get his Kareem Abdul-Jabbar ass off me.

"The fuck?" a woman's voice yells. From the ground not far from me, Riley's laughing. I manage to untangle myself and peer out of the bushes. Green's still there, his luminous glow dangling eerily over the river like some corny Halloween decoration. The giants, though, are in disarray. It must've been a direct hit. Three of them lay shattered along the shore, their crumpled, dismembered bodies eeking out some unfathomable foulness into the soil. The surviving four are dazed, two sitting on their asses shaking their heads, one leaning up against a tree and one stumbling in dizzy circles. I don't think they'll stay that way long.

"Everyone alright?" I yell. In the clearing smoke I can make out Jimmy and Riley, each with one of Gordo's hands in theirs, trying to help him hoist his fat ass into a standing position. It's not going well. Imelda has retreated to a safe distance and is staring blankly, looking ready to bolt at any second. Big Cane appears dazed but otherwise ready to move, and Terry, Jimmy and Krys are standing at the edge of the bushes, looking at me expectantly.

"Let's do this," Krys says, setting Gerta down and drawing her sidearm. Behind her, I see the giants rising and dusting themselves off. They take a few cautious steps towards us and then break into a run. I believe in moments like these that if I'm not on automatic pilot I would be in fetal position, puking, so I click that little switch in my head and draw my sword. One of the things is closing on me; I sidestep and slash out, a little more wildly than I would've liked, but I still manage to clip off one of its feet. The giant stumbles past onto its knees and twists itself around, arms swatting out at me.

That horrible smell fills the air, floods my nostrils and corrupts my organs. The rot has entered me; it's wearing me down from the inside out. I jump backwards, trip slightly and recover just in time to swipe at one of those long wandering arms. Jimmy's on the thing now, cutting wild slashes in the air with his shortblade. An ear shattering squeal rings out as he chops into its shoulder.

My vision's blurring, but I can make out Big Cane wrapped in a death embrace with one of the giants, his face strained with exhaustion. Riley's egging him on, and Terry is beside them, trying not to get stepped on and taking little swipes with the dagger Cane leant her. A little further off, Krys is chasing her mark, screaming profanities and trying to get a clean shot at it.

The fourth giant has broken from the fray, though, and is wading into the black waters towards Green's dangling phantom. The god he'd been waiting for, I suppose. "You alright?" I yell to Jimmy. He's walking slow, vicious circles around the wounded giant, dodging the thrashing limbs and landing more than his fair share of cuts.

"Do what you do, C, I got this." I turn towards the river, thinking of how proud I am of Jimmy, and break into a run. The murky water rushes up against me and I realize just how fast winter's approaching. Up ahead, the towering wraith is a hideous void, standing in stark contrast to its shimmering god. Or whatever the fuck Green is to them. This'll take some checking up on when it's all over.

Waist-deep in frigid, stinky river water, I pause to catch my breath. That's when I hear the sound: It's the same mournful gargle, but there's something different. The giant's shoulders are heaving up and down, its emaciated head hanging forward, an empty sack. It's crying.

A gunshot shatters the air behind me. Krys has made her move. When I look back, she's pointing the gun at the ground. Another shot rings out and the thing beneath her writhes and then is still.

Green's glow is waning. His headless body claws helplessly at the night sky, the final grasps of a drowning man.

"It's over," Krys says behind me. I'm not sure if she's talking to me or the giant, but either way it's comforting to hear. The giant turns towards us, head hung low, twitchy red eyes blinking back tears. "Your fucked-up god is useless to you."

The giant tenses, warbles hotly over the water at us, but you can see it knows the jig is up. "Go," Krys says. "Get out of here. Never come back." It nods, gargles a few more times and then turns and limps deeper and deeper into the river until it's just a dark splotch and then nothing at all.

\* \* \*

"It was the head."

"Ain't that what I been saying all along?" Riley demands. He's gotten himself good and twisted, we all have actually, and it makes each sentence he says come out on a sloppy wave of laughter. "It's all about head."

Krys has already gotten good at brushing off Riley's jackassery. "I mean without his head, Green was no good to the giants. It's part of their whole system."

"And the cologne?"

"The cologne was like an offering. They knew Green was a mack daddy, thought his spirit'd somehow be attracted to it. They'd been waiting for him for centuries, him being the right reincarnation that is, and when everything was in place they got impatient. Wanted to hurry things along. That's why they linked up Terry and Imelda here, as well as his other two victims." Imelda and Terry nod somberly and clink beer bottles with each other. "He wanted them to off Green, you know, do that ghost kill move..."

"The thing where they, like, plastic-wrap your face 'til you suffocate?" Jimmy says.

"Exactly, which would..."

"Leave the body intact!" Jimmy yells.

"Exactly."

"How'd you figure this shit out?" Riley's definitely impressed.

"I listened to them. On the second day of the vigil they were more talkative."

"Just like Cane," I say. Cane chortles good naturedly.

Krys looks like she's got tolerance for about one more interruption before she goes for the guns. "Anyway, they got into it a little more. But the bit about the head I figured out after Green showed up without one and they got all in a tizzy."

"That was quite a stroke of luck," Cyrus muses with a smile.

"Not at all," Jimmy says with a straight face. "I did it on purpose."

Krys rolls her eyes. "Whatever, playa. It's just a good thing you decided to use your ghost blade, otherwise the cut wouldn'ta carried over into the afterlife. It was a nice slice, let's leave it at that." She swats at him, her chill glow against his warm flesh, and I wonder fleetingly what the chances are for coupling between the living and dead. It's too bad it'd never work in the long run; they're both tremendous spirits and both, in their own way, large and in charge.

"Lissen," Riley says. "I thought on it and Cane can roll with us, he definitely did good out there and being that he a legend and all." Big Cane smiles and nods his big head approvingly. "But he gotta be a sidekick." Big Cane stops smiling. "I'm deadass, people. That's the rule. Sicka white dudes being all primary in shit. He can be the sidekick or the nosey neighbor. That's it."

"Riley, you're stupid," Imelda says.

"And if someone gotta get killed off early in a situation, it's gotta be Big Cane."

Everyone looks at the old detective. "I can work with that," he grins. The room erupts in ruckus laughter and toasts.

Outside, the year's first layer of frost lays its icy blanket over the sleeping city.

# VICTORY MUSIC

One of my favorite moments ever was when the boy called me an Arab and you said, "She's Sikh, fucknut" and then when he said "Oh, like hide and go—" you broke his nose. I heard music playing, I swear to God, and it was victory music, your music: A dusty, unxflinching beat, lowdown and grinding. It didn't matter that my family's not even technically Sikh anymore since my parents went born-again and I'm just whatever. I smiled for days after that moment, Krys. Days.

But so much has happened since then, so much gone wrong.

After that day I found you on the hill at the edge of campus. There's a fence that cuts right through the summit of the hill and the other side is all wilderness and you and MagD would sit against that fence and watch everybody and murmur quietly. Used to want to hang with you guys so bad before you stood up for me and I finally got the guts to walk up there and just say Hey. And then it was us three, and MagD used to *hate* it when we called her that but she probably loved it too, and wherever she is now she probably introduces herself that way, with that big toothy grin on her that looks perfect and so out of place on her serious face.

Anyway, now you're dead.

Is what they told me. That you died. I'm not trying to rub it in: I need to say it again and again so it feels true finally, because it's been months and I still don't believe it. In part because you were SO alive, so flesh and blood, and the thought of you not is just…it doesn't fit. But mostly I don't believe it because I still feel you, my friend, all around me. And anyway, that's what I'm getting at, I wanted to tell you that you've saved my life at least twice. And once was after you died.

* * *

It's been two days and seventeen hours since I told my parents that I'm not a girl. I'm in Boston, on the bridge out-side of Harvard Square actually, so right on the borderline between Boston and Cambridge. I'm alone and it's gray gray and cold, "cold as all the fucks" like you used to say, and my bones clacked against each other with the frostiness. I'm still 9 feet tall practically and only like 100 lbs so you can imag-ine, when the wind picks up I'm just like a big stupid piece of Sikh spaghetti. Or ex-Sikh spaghetti. Whatever, I exagger-ate but yeah, the music was not victory music, it was a dirge. Probably in one of the modes, mixolydian or something, the rearranged howl of a lonely monk, sprinkled across the piano keys while morose string instruments drone behind it and an occasional deep ol' bass drum booms. That was the music and there was no stopping it, because it was rain-ing as if to piss me off more. Just drizzling, but still: I look up at the sky and say "Seriously?" It's strange to hear the sound of my own voice after so much not speaking. The sky doesn't answer back, it just keeps raining.

Sixty-five hours earlier and 300 miles away, my dad sent the twins to bed with a growl and then said to me, "What do you mean you're not a girl?" He really meant it genuinely that first time, like he was really surprised. And I was like, "I mean what I said: I'm not a girl."

My mom just frowned at me.

"But what do you *mean?*" Papa said as if emphasizing a different word would somehow get him a different answer, an answer that made sense.

I mean—I started to say, but he cut me off: "I mean, *what* do you mean?"

"I mean…"

"Your name is Wendy."

As if that settled it.

I told him I knew what my name was, but my name didn't make me a girl.

"But you *are* a girl!" Papa exclaimed, almost laughing now with exasperation.

"I'm not." Think it made it worse that I said it calmly, you know? Made Papa feel like he had to up his explosiveness to bring some sense of urgency to the conversation. Mom let out a sob and we both looked at her for a second. I held back the urge to apologize.

"Are you trying to say," a haughty laugh now from Papa, "that you are a boy, *Wendy?*"

"No."

His palms slapped against his bald head so hard I almost laughed. "Gah!"

"Papa, I'm…look, I don't mean to confuse you. If you'd let me explain…"

"Explain what!" An eruption, not a question. "What's to explain! You say you're not a girl. You have breasts, sort of…"

"Mohan!" My mom gasped. She never uses his first name, so you know she was upset. He shot her a look, one of his sharp ones and she went back to sobbing without so much as a glance at me.

Anyway, if you've never had your dad make a rude remark about how small your breasts are, Krys, you're missing out on some true fun, lemme tell you. I didn't answer; really I was doing everything in my power not to curse him out right then and there. Maybe you wanna know why? You were always the queen of holy curse outs, it's one of the things I love…loved about you. No. I still love that about you. You being gone doesn't make the love past tense. I didn't curse him out because I wanted to do this right, even if no one else was. And because I'm seventeen and have no job and no money and I thought maybe, maybe if I do this right we could have a sensible conversation after everyone gets the bullshit off their chests and then we can work something out, not be such monsters to each other. And then maybe I could still be his daughter/son/whatever when it's all over.

Obviously that's now how things went because here I am. I suppressed the curse out; didn't say anything in fact. I closed my eyes for a sec and the music was sharp and jabby, horror movie music, dissonant and vast and full of clustery notes ambushing each other, sitting too close together and attacking, falling back and attacking and I opened my eyes and my dad was damn near foaming at the mouth.

"You have a…you have a…" Mom put her hand on his and he just looked away, rubbing what might've been tears from his eyes.

"Can I just explain?" I said when his breathing slowed back down.

But he shook his head. "No," he said. "You can go."

And I did.

\* \* \*

On the Chinatown Bus I didn't cry but I did think about how you reacted when I told you. You just listened. It was before you were sick—before you knew you were sick—and I remember your face in the sunlight, the sunlight having its way with your perfect brown skin and little beads of sweat were sliding down your scalp because it was a perfect summer day and you just listened. I waited 'til MagD had left, because I love her but she doesn't have the capacity to hold other people's shit like you do, she's not there. And I said everything, everything that was in me that had never come out except on pieces of paper that got shredded and burnt to ashes immediately after the words were down.

You nodded when I was done. That nod was the only moment in the whole time that made me want to break down and cry but I didn't. I didn't. There was silence then between us and the music was a beat and a bassline and steady synthesizers. Your theme music—it was cool like you, sweet and easy breezy.

After you nodded and we both thought for a while and the music trailed off and then started up again and people on the lawn below us mingled and fussed and then finally you said: "So you're both and neither."

Not a question; an agreement.

I nodded.

"Cool."

· That was the first time you saved my life.

* * *

Now, here on this bridge over the Charles, dark thoughts overtake me, but I don't cry. I drift to sleep, and when I wake I know something foul is coming: The night is serene but the music is sinister, creeping, uncouth. I wait for it. Doze again and when I wake there's a boy sitting next to me. I don't know how he got there; even though I was nodding I'm sure he didn't just walk up. I'm a light sleeper and I'm terrified—a passing rat woke me earlier. This boy is almost as tall as me. He's pale pallid pale and his straight light brown hair hangs down half-mooning his face. He's looking at me, not smiling. It's not threatening, his presence, but when I close my eyes real quick to check? There's no music. None.

We just stare at each other for a few solid seconds, and it's pleasant in that we don't have to speak. There's no stupid small talk to fill in the gaps. The silence is our friend. But then the boy vanishes. He's just gone. I hold my breath, thinking maybe I'm dreaming but I know I'm not. I wait, breath still held. When he reappears he's in the same spot, same position, staring at me.

And still no music.

"Are you a ghost?" I say.

"No."

His mouth only tilts upwards at the far edge, a hint of a smile, smug yet somehow defeated. I break his glare and look back at the river. He keeps looking at me.

"My name is Niles."

"Ok."

"Finney."

"That's supposed to mean something to me?"

"No. It's just my name." He reaches a pale hand towards me and I flinch a little before I realize he means for me to shake it. "You don't have to," he says, frowning.

"It's fine." I take his hand in mine and it's really there.

"You can call me Wes."

"That your name?"

"It's what you can call me."

"Ok."

He doesn't ask if I'm a boy or a girl, doesn't probe 'bout why I'm on the streets, doesn't want to know where I'm from. It's refreshing. So I ask the questions.

"Why did you just disappear?"

He shrugs. "'Cuz I can. It's what I do." A moment passes, then he turns to me and smiles with his whole mouth, shows his teeth even and if he wasn't such a wisp of a boy it might be threatening. But maybe in a cute way, if I was into that kind of thing. "You can do it too. Wanna learn?"

I do want to disappear. It's all I've wanted to do since... since forever maybe. Just not be: unravel myself from everyone else's consciousness and be gone. But without dying. Sounds delicious. And Niles Finney can do it whenever he wants. It hardly seems fair.

"I guess," I say.

"Oh, it's cool. I don't have to teach you. I'm not even sure if you could anyway, not everyone can do it. It's pretty hard. Which is cool cuz otherwise any idiot could do it and then it'd be no fun."

"I said yes!" Comes out shriller than I'd meant it too, but what are you gonna do?

"No, you said you guessed."

"I know, fine, but I meant yes. I just...I've never seen anyone disappear before."

"Exactly!" Then, as if to prove his point, Niles is gone again and it's only the night sky where he'd been before and the scattered lights of Cambridge crowding the edge of the Charles.

"Come back," I say quietly.

He's smiling broadly when he reappears. "I never left."

"Alright, hot shot, what's the big secret?"

Niles inches closer to me and I realize he has no smell. "You're already most of the way there."

"Oh?"

"Yes. That's why I sat beside you." His voice has an antiquated lilt to it. Almost sounds British but no—it's paper-thin though, and crisp. "Because I saw it in you."

"Saw what?" Am I flattered? I am. Something special inside of me, someone who sees it. Yes.

"*It.*" A whisper. "It's like an emptiness. A nothing. But it's beautiful. It carries you; it's a power. They tell you it's weakness but it's strength. It's how I do what I do."

I just stare at him for a minute. It's a minute that hangs in the balance. He may be batshit. But then, I'm the one seeing disappearing boys. I may be batshit. Something about what he says is true though. It's unavoidable. There is something different inside of me. Something besides being a boy and a girl and neither. Maybe that something is what kept me alive all this time, kept me from shattering. An emptiness that sustains. "What's the other part?"

"What?"

"The other part. You said I'm most of the way there. What's the last piece?"

"Oh." He rests his head against my shoulder. He's breathing softly against me. Night birds circle over the Charles, their dark bodies against the darker sky. "It's a word."

"What word?"

"A magic one. But I can't tell you until you're sure you want the power." I almost say I am, right then and there but I hold off. "Because once I say it, you can't unknow it. It's part of you. There's no turning back." He's fading again, fading and falling asleep. "It's up to you," he mumbles into my shoulder.

I can tell something about Niles Finney: He wants me to say yes. He doesn't want to show it, can't, but he wants it. And that makes me want it more. I could solve two problems: End my loneliness and his with one simple move. And I'd be powerful. I slide down a little on the bench and rest the back of my neck against it, my long legs splayed out in front of me.

Maybe I fall asleep too.

Surely this is when you arrive. You hover around me like some beautiful Casper, your spikey hair bouncing and translucent in the night, your smile wide. When I wake up again the first flutters of dawn streak the edge of the sky and the river's still a dark nothingness beneath us and Niles

Finny is still on my shoulder. I feel his body rise and fall with each breath. But when I look down, it's just me. He's still vanished. I close my eyes. I ask you for help.

And I'm not ready for the image that comes to me: it's my dad. It's not his hardened face, the creased eyebrows and forced frown; this is my dad at the bottom of his well of sorrow. It was just a moment he showed it to me, when we were arguing that last time. It was when he wiped what may or may not have been a tear from his eye. His face is wide open, his sadness right at the surface and it's because he knew he was about to never see me again. Mom was crying openly by this time. I only saw her heaving up and down out of the corner of my eye because if I looked her dead on, I would've broke. Then she looks at me and I expect rage or disappointment but there's only love in her face. Only love and then it's the twins; they're watching me go, crying and now, finally, thoroughly, I'm crying, sobbing actually—not the restrained hiccups of someone trying not to cry but honest, low, wails, and I'm not mad and I don't feel guilty, I'm just sad sad sad for the loss of my family—maybe it's for now and maybe it's forever, but I miss them and I still can't go back and I know they miss me too. So I let it surge out of me, finally, that sadness, and when my sobbing slows and I open my eyes, I hear the beat drop.

The music is tentative at first, a low and steady drum, a few cautious clacks and cymbal flourishes. Then it becomes brave: the bass kicks in, bursts of horns shouting and disappearing. I've made my decision, so I look down at where Niles was to tell him and he's gone. I mean, gone-gone not just disappeared-gone. Must've skulked off during my emotional deluge, seen that there was something else there that carries me, even more powerful than the emptiness.

I'm not going home and I won't disappear. A steady organ

spins beneath it all and then the cool, static-laced laughter of an electric guitar. It's the music of victory again, Krys, but it's not yours this time, it's something brand new. It's me. My music: timid at first and then ferocious, brave. It is the rest of my life.

# LOVE IS A FUCKING RIVER

I'm crying when the call comes in that changes my life. Crying on the inside, of course, because I am, after all, a man. I suppose this little surge of emotion is a good thing, because I'd been pretty sure my heart was dead for the past couple days. On Monday, Vanessa packed up the last of her dainty girl things from my place—not that she lived there but you know, practically—and the apartment just felt really totally fucking empty without her panties and makeup scattered around. Felt like I was living inside the heart of the loneliest person in the world, and that was me. Then I just felt nothing, and that was even worse. So I picked up an extra driving shift and there I am, sitting outside my own building actually, and sniffling slightly, when they call me for a pickup around the corner.

I wipe my eyes, because sometimes when you cry on the inside a little bit gets out, and start heading over. There's this song on the radio, the reason I was feeling extra upset actually. It's a bachata track that's pretty hot these days—some fucking crybaby love story, whatever—but there's a part where he tells his guitar to cry for him, *llora guitarra, llora,* he says. Every time they play it on la mega, which is like every ten seconds of course, it reminds me of this time when Vanessa came over all upset because this piece of shit named Devin she used to deal with finally offed himself. She just bawled in my arms for what seemed like hours and that little frail body of hers kept shuddering and heaving and I thought she might just crumble like a little crispy leaf at any second, but she seemed so strong to me in that very moment, too, because what man, for all our strength and awesomeness, can really be *that* vulnerable? You know? What man can really be strong enough to fall apart? It touched me, it really did. When she was done crying she fell asleep, which is probably just as well because otherwise I might've tried to get some and that probably would've tipped off a fight and it really wasn't the time for all that.

Anyway, that song's playing, but I turn it off as I roll up on the pickup spot and there's this fine, fine black lady standing next to a fat old guy. When I say fine, I mean truly a sudden and unflinching gift to a man's eyes. This man, anyway. She's wearing a short trench coat and has a cap on, like a slick little cap tilted to the side, and it's inconceivable that she put any thought whatsoever into angling it right, because her whole way of being is just too smooth for all of that. The fat guy, on the other hand, is kind of a rumbling disaster and when he gets in I actually worry that my car will need some realignment work. I'm not trying to be offensive or nothing, but the guy is immense. Very the fuck like a whale.

I put an arm across the top of the seat and crane my head back to them, trying not to swallow the girl whole with my hungry eyes, and I ask 'em where they're going. I say it in English, because I don't like to assume anyone speaks Spanish. They turn to each other and seem to have a whole conversation just in the tiniest creases of their faces, which gives me a second to take in the ol' girl in her entirety and let me tell you: *Yes.*

Then she looks at me. I meet her eyes and she says, "Te necesitamos la noche entera," which, if the large dude wasn't sitting there I might've taken to be a come on. She doesn't smile when she says it. Her face reveals nothing, in fact, but any time someone tells you they need you for the entirety of the night, well... I wrestle down all the snarky, flirtatious things I want to say back and just nod as smoothly as I can. *Hecho.*

Then the big guy gives me an address in the Stuy and says it's stop number one; they have to pick up someone before they go where they're going. They confer quietly in the back the whole way and I do everything in my power not to keep looking in the rearview to see if maybe, maybe she's looking at me. She's not though; she's either fully concentrating on whatever secretness she's got with the big guy or she's looking out the window with an expression of either sorrow, dread or longing. Who can really tell? She's not happy. I want to ask what's wrong but I don't. I want to tell her about my dogs; I have five, and they're all small and they do drive me crazy with their bullshit, but I love the little motherfuckers. It's a cold-hearted chick that isn't impressed by a muscular man like myself who also loves his dogs. Not that that's why I have them, I really do love them, except possibly Albertino, who really can be a fucking asshole sometimes with his whining.

Turns out to be a dude we picking up, tall and oddly colored, almost gray, but he's not a white dude. Puerto Rican if I had to guess. He slides in beside the lady, nods at me and then the fat guy says, "Carlos, this is Janey, my son's fiancé." And I almost curse out loud but don't. "Janey, this is my good friend and associate, Carlos." Carlos looks like he has to work extra hard to dig up a smile for her, but when he does it's a real one and he offers his hand. When they shake, a certain chill passes over her; not like she's afraid or disdainful, just that she understands something. Her eyes look into his with a question and he nods eversoslightly in response.

Maybe I should be scared. Probably. You hear stories, of

course: Taxi drivers disappearing. Found naked by the side of the road, covered in bitemarks or dressed only in tires and babbling boberias like some asshole in a nursing home. But anyway, I'm not scared. Janey's fine, of course, but that's neither here nor there. Plus, she's already hooked up with Baby Fat. It might be because, for all their weirdness, this strange trio still seems oddly... How do I say it? *Simpático.* There's a warmth to them that emanates out more powerfully than their sad gazes and hushed conspiring. Also, I realize that this is the first time I've gone more than ten minutes without thinking about Vanessa since she left.

When I ask where to next, Carlos looks me dead in the eye and gives me my own address. I try not to flinch or make it obvious that I'm flummoxed but it seems like the guy can see through whatever bullshit mask I put up. He doesn't smile or grimace, just stays dead neutral and holds my gaze for a few seconds, apparently delving into my most fucked up childhood memories, maybe figuring out all my dogs' names, I don't know. I finally turn around slowly and start driving back toward Bushwick.

They're conspiring again, but Carlos doesn't seem to give a fuck if I hear or not. "It's confirmed, Gordo?" Not a very creative nickname, but oh well. The big guy nods, frowning. "And she's the source?" He indicates Janey.

"My great aunt," Janey says without disguising her irritation at being talked about as if she's not there.

"Right," Carlos says. "What'd she say?"

"Ah, you have a great-aunt," Gordo cuts in. "I hadn't realized that's who came to you about this." This seems to carry untold realms of fascination for him, I can only imagine why. I guess if I was his age I'd get gagigidy about a girl like Janey having a great-aunt too.

"I told you that when I first called, Gordo." And then to Carlos. "She said it's this viejito on the floor above her."

That would be Juan-José I'm guessing. And CiCi must

be Janey's great aunt. Interesting. Carlos doesn't look convinced though. "And she's sure? Does she know what she's talking about?"

"Listen, cowboy," Janey's eyes roll all the way back in her head. It's sexy as fuck. "You don't know a damn thing 'bout this lady, so I'll just let that skeptical smirk of your slide for this very moment." Janey pauses and takes a deep breath. I hope she's not flirting with him. "Yes," calmer now. "CiCi knows what she's talking about. Very much so. You don't have to believe me, but trust that when you see this viejito, he will be what you are looking for."

"Okay." Carlos sits back in the seat, apparently satisfied.

Janey directs her sad face out the window and the window shines it back to her, dark and beautiful and barely there against the Brooklyn night. I just drive.

\* \* \*

When Vanessa left me this last time, it was because I could never measure up to a dead man. I'm okay with that. Devin sounded like a passive-aggressive disaster of a human being anyway and, he was, after all, dead. But when she was leaving, she actually said "Fuck you and fuck your dogs too" like that crazy heffa from the Wizard of Oz. Anyway, I don't know how someone's heart can be so shriveled and demented that they could wish malice on five dogs as wonderful as mine, but then again, the world is full of Saddam Husseins and George Bushes, so who's to say?

Can't imagine a woman like Janey ever harboring such pointless aggression. Anger, yes. Rage even. That stunning, justified rage. But that kind of hatred? I think not. But what do I know?

"Aquí," Gordo mutters as we pull up to my building.

I nod.

"Listen," Carlos says, sounding like he's striving for

reasonableness. "I believe what you say about your tía, Janey. I didn't mean to come across like that. It's just that..." He has her attention. Even big Gordo tunes into the gravity in Carlos's voice. "This *thing*, this...entity: It's not like most. I don't know how familiar you are with," he shoots a weary glance in my direction, "this topic, but this particular one is...more powerful. Especially when combined with a living form."

Okay, I don't care if you're Cuban, Dominican, Boricua or straight Southern Black—dig deep enough, we all got brujos in the family tree somewhere. It's a fact of life. I'ma not even get into mine; I tended not to pay her much mind to be honest, but I know enough to know the difference between a charlatan, someone who is just batshit crazy, and someone that knows what the fuck they're dealing in. I'm not even saying I believe in ghosts or nothin'. I'm just saying, Carlos is not playing around. None of 'em are. And whatever entity shit he's talking about? It's real. On some level. I know because when he speaks on it I feel all the hairs on my arm stand at attention and all my insides seem to cringe at the same time.

Janey's got a determined face on, but when she says "Okay," there's a shiver in her voice. Gordo just nods.

"So why don't you..." Carlos starts to say to Janey.

"No." She cuts him off. "I'm coming in with you." It's obviously not up for debate.

Carlos sees it as clearly as I do, so he just sighs and gets out of the cab. "Keep it running," he says with a certain gruff resignation in his voice.

The three of them head up the front steps and into my apartment building and I just sit there staring at the door, feeling oddly giddy and terrified for a few minutes. Then the giddiness goes away and I admit it: I get caught up with all kinds of phantom imaginings. I'm actually pretty well put together, physically. Buff, I'd even say. Much more so since things started getting rocky with Vanessa, because when shit's not right in life, I work out. When I'm confused, I work out. If I can't make heads or tails of a situation, if the words I need to express myself aren't there, if my thoughts are one big tangle of shit? Find me at the gym. There, at least I can make sense of something, feel my body grow, struggle and triumph. Something.

It was a pretty bad breakup, to be honest with you, so I'm huge.

But huge doesn't count much when you're fighting off "entities" like the one Carlos described. I don't know much about it, but I know things like that don't give two fucks how much you can bench-press. And you know, spiritually, I keep my dashboard saints and talk to them when I need parking or the strength not to call Vanessa, but otherwise? Church, only very occasionally.

So when the door of my building swings suddenly open it scares the ever-loving shit out of me. There's a figure standing there, all shadowy and backlit by the rude fluorescents in the lobby. And here I am feeling about as unprepared for this as anything I've ever faced in my life, and Vanessa's angry mug is still dancing around in my mind, telling me I ain't shit. And right about now, she's right: I really ain't shit at all. I'm just some overlarge asshole in a Crown Vic. The figure in the doorway stands there for a few minutes and the whole world around us goes perfectly still, like even the trees don't want to move for fear it'll notice them and hurl some infernal wrath their way. So nothing moves, and then it takes a step forward and everything's swishing and swaying and alive in the night. Trash clutters down the street and leaves are whipping around. Am I making this up? The mind can play some foul and fucked-up tricks on a person, yes, but I swear by the lives of my five that the wind picked up strong right as it started moving, whereas just seconds before the world was cloaked in stillness. The thing, shadow, creature, form—whatever it is—it steps very slowly down each stair. And each movement is jerky, like it's some tin windup toy gone rusty over the years. It's tall and skinny and lurches towards me in uneven spurts, like it might collapse at any given moment into a sorry pile of skin and bones. And I pray it will, but I know it won't. It's got the fury of intention behind each clunky move; it's not going anywhere.

I wonder, just before it steps into the pool of streetlight beside my cab, where Janey, Carlos, and Gordo are and why they let this entity get away so it could come kill me. I hope Janey's alright. Then I think how amazing it is that I just used what might be one of my last thoughts to worry about a woman I haven't spoken more than five words to, and not the woman I spent the last three years of my life loving. I'm thinking how odd that is when the thing creaks forward into the light and I see its face and I almost scream because it is Juan-José, the old guy from the eighteenth floor who lost his mind. But it's also not.

First of all, Juanjo is always hunched over and he holds his arms and fingers all shriveled up into his body like dead branches. This thing, this *entity*, it stands perfectly erect and its arms dangle at its sides. And then there's the eyes. Juan-José's were pretty dull, like he couldn't be bothered to focus on anything. Nothing dramatic, just your average old guy blurriness. But the eyes that look back at me from the passenger window—because now the thing has creased itself at the waist the better to glare in at me—those eyes are sharp, and they seem to even vibrate slightly and the pupils are teeny tiny like a methadonians'—tiny and sharp and fixed right on my face. And when it smiles, everything inside me says to peel off as fast as I can, and be gone.

Well, not everything apparently, because that's not what I do. I think about Janey again, and what it'd be like if she came out and found me gone, and this thing here instead, and what she—any of them—would do. They asked me to stay, to leave it running even, and so that's what I do. And then the entity opens the damn passenger door, which I could've sworn I'd locked and sits down and says in a voice crawling with worms, "*Drive,*" and so that's what I do.

* * *

Something smells and obviously, it's not me. I'm damn near metrosexual about my personal hygiene, especially on the fragrancy tip. That is to say, I generally smell impeccable; swoonworthy even. Not to brag. But the harshness invading my nostrils right now is another thing altogether. An evil thing. It reminds me of the time Cespedes killed a mouse and hid it under the fridge and I had to track the stench to the little crimpled corpse. It's a wretchedness that enters me like a poisonous gas and I can almost feel it clouding up my airway, corroding the tiny vesicles in my lungs. Or whatever it is that's in my lungs. If I breathe too deeply, I'll probably die, so I just take shallow gasps of air.

"*Take a right,*" it says and I do. It directs me north, north and further north until all the quiet little midnight blocks have turned into factories and then it tells me to pull over in a gravelly area surrounded by rusted out industrial skeletons. I'm sweating. Maybe because I know I'm about to die a gruesome, supernatural death at the hands of my geriatric neighbor. My mind races through possibilities: Beg, make a break for it, fake a seizure. But all the mini-movies that play out afterwards are stupid and end with me dying anyway.

There's an awkward pause. Absurdly, my mind still fills with thoughts of this strange and amazing new woman, Janey. What does she do in her spare time? Who are these comrades of hers? Is she possibly wondering about me, right at this very moment? Then the thing breaks into my reverie by croaking, "*Vanessa.*" I damn near fall out of the car in surprise. I turn and face it full on for the first time and I see the old man and something else very hideous lurking in the air all around him, something writhing and dying and salivating all over his empty form. For a second my thoughts are all confusion and then it clicks into place. Nothing that happened tonight was an accident at all.

"Devin," I whisper.

It looks up, heaving rattly, mucous-filled breaths, and nods.

"It's not like that anymore," I say. "We ain't a thing anymore." I'm kinda improvising, but it also happens to be true and I pray that Devin's dead ass can see that through my fear. I've been in this situation before. Okay, no, I've never been in *this* situation before, but I've talked down more than a few angry exes actually, but usually I'm the one with the upper hand. "She left me. She..." as I'm speaking I realize I really don't care. In some perverse way, I'm happy. She left me. And she took all her crap baggage with her.

Well, almost all of it.

*"Out,"* the thing belches. When I don't move, the air gets heavy around me and I have to yawn to unpop my ears. I just look straight ahead because if I look it in that decrepit face again I'll probably turn to dust. A cold, cold hand reaches slowly out, grazes my cheek and then slithers down to my neck. First I'm breathing way too fast and then not at all. I pull and pull for oxygen but it's like there's nowhere for it to go; my lungs have closed up shop and shut down. I feel my eyes get wide, all the vessels in my face seem like they're about to explode and I imagine blood streaming from my ears, my nose, my fucking soul.

And then it's gone, whatever it was and I'm sucking in desperate mountains of air, wrapping my whole mouth around that sweet empty savior and coughing and blubbering and carrying on. When I recover myself some, Devin-entity says, *"Now, out!"* and I stumble out of the cab.

We pass through a hole in a fence, walk along beneath giant shadows of cranes and scaffoldings, breach another fence and come out on a rocky embankment by the water. Trucks thunder along the expressway a little further down the creek. Queens is sparkling back at us from the far shore, a world away from this horror show that is my life. I wonder briefly if I could make it across but then I remember all the filth and pollution that they've dumped in these blue-green waters and I think about all the mutant diseases I'd probably get and I opt to try my chances with the demon-Devin-thing. And then the demon-Devin-thing shoves me hard and I trip forward and land face first in the shallow rocky river edge, scratching my arm and bruising my face.

I roll over just as it lurches on top of me. It's doing something down around my abdomen, but I can't tell what, just see its arms reach down there and feel a sharp cut and then pressure. For a few seconds the sheer terror renders me useless. I just thrash and flail. Water gushes into my open mouth and I vomit it back up and gasp for air. Then I realize I can breathe. I don't know why—maybe it's growing weaker somehow, but whatever it was doing to me in the car isn't happening right now. Once I clear all the mutant river water out of my airway I take a deep breath and come back to myself.

I'm a fighter. My whole body is a well-tuned machine that is capable of total destruction. Of course, I've never employed it that way before, but I know my way around the boxing ring. And maybe this is some horrific demon of my ex's ex working me over right now, but it's inside a mortal shell—an old frail-ass one at that—and I certainly don't plan to go out without doing some damage. I swing my brollic arm, catching the thing across the face. It's not the strongest hit in the world; I'm still getting my bearings and I only clip it its cheek and brush along the nose. But the follow-up hit finds its mark and the old man's body goes slack. I heave him off me and pin him down in the shallow water, landing a few more cracks across his face to give me some time to get my bearings.

It's amazing, not to care. I wish I knew how it happened so I could reproduce that thing again and again. It's not even in a cruel way, simply that the horror of this poor fool being haunted all the way into the afterlife by that ridiculous woman... They made each other miserable in life and now he's come back to make me miserable too? Absurd. I'm almost smiling at it all when Devin drives an old, frigid hand into my neck and closes off my airway again. I look down, shocked back into the moment, and see only rage in those eyes glaring back at me. Watch my hands snake around the old man's neck, all folds of skin and goiter collapsing beneath my fingers. Watch my muscles strain to close off the airway even as my own vision blurs.

Janey. The river is rushing around us: Me, this empty old body and Devin's hideous ghost. Janey. Her face glistening out of the night, reflected in my backseat window. She's no one to me really, a ghost. It hasn't been Janey trying to reach me telepathically all this time, it's been me; my own heart. I swipe those old arms away from my neck. My heart is still alive. Those flashes of Janey are like tiny distress signals. That flush of freedom; letting go of Vanessa. I'm still alive. I'm free.

The airway is collapsing in my grasp. The old man's dead eyes grow even deader as he gasps and sputters beneath me. My stomach is still burning from whatever fuckery Devin's ghost did down there. It's getting worse actually, but I can't worry with that right now: I have to survive. Because even after that world-shaking shattered feeling, and even after that grave silence that's been haunting the inside of my chest since shit with Vanessa went sour—I still have a heart. It's got nothing to do with Vanessa or Janey. I'm alive and capable of love, and love is a fucking river. It's never ending and it flows through us, all around us, keeps us alive and decadent, fierce from struggle and genuine in our vulnerability.

I look down, see this poor old man dying beneath me. I throw myself off him. What have I become? My arms cradle his frail body and I heave him onto the rocky shore. I'm trying to think what the fuck to do next when I remember there's something terribly wrong with my stomach. Before I can figure out what, I'm sitting down hard and trying to keep the world from carouseling so fast. When I put my fingers there they don't touch skin but instead something wet and gooey like pasta. Guts. I'm wide open.

Then I see Janey, only this time it's really the flesh and blood beautiful Night Queen of Brooklyn, fitzing along the shore like some motherfucking pixie to the rescue. At least, I think she's real this time. My body wants me to collapse. I feel the weight of unconsciousness tugging at me like the edge of a sleepless night, but more than anything I want to see what Janey will do next, so I blink away the drowsiness and wave at her. Carlos comes next and I can hear Gordo struggling with the fence not far away.

Janey stops in her tracks, taking in the carnage. The old man is bleeding too. I hadn't noticed it, but he has an identical slice to mine, right along his gut. Nothing dangling out though. I wonder if I'm going to die, if I look stupid or heroic, why there's no pain, just an odd throbbing that takes over my whole being. My pulse. The river flowing from my heart. I hope it doesn't stop.

Carlos seems to know exactly what's going on. "It's still in the old guy," he says to Janey. "See if he has a pulse." Janey reaches down to the old guy's neck while Carlos crouches beside me.

"How you feel?" Carlos says in a surprisingly gentle voice.

"Not too good," I admit. "A little nauseous. No pain though!" I manage a smile.

"What happened?" Pleasantries over. Business.

"He...It brought me here and tried to drown me in the river. I got the upper hand, though."

Carlos frowns. "Did it fight back, once you got the upper hand?"

"Yes." But then I think about it. How easily I had swiped its grasp from my neck, how its whole being seemed to collapse after I pinned it. "Not really, actually. Kinda deflated in fact."

"That's because it was trying to transfer into you. That slit." Carlos nods down at my hands, which are still holding my guts in. "It's an entrance point. The ghost wanted you to kill its horse so it could enter into you."

"You mean if I'da killed the old guy..."

"You'd be a walking nightmare. And a much bigger problem for us to deal with than Juan-José."

"Pulse," Janey reports. "But only barely. It's thready."

"Step away, Janey," Carlos says. "It was lurking in that old man for a while, gathering strength and waiting for the right moment. I'm sure we rustled it up ahead of whatever demonic schedule it was keeping when we came hunting. And now it's looking for a body."

"It's looking..." I manage to whisper. "...for my ex."

Carlos stands and unsheathes what looks like a samurai sword from his cane. "Well," he says like this shit happens all the time. "She's not here."

That's when things start getting hazy. Carlos makes some vague explanation-slash-apology about what's about to go down, but I can't make out all the words. Then Carlos does something with his sword to the old man. Janey stands there watching; doesn't even flinch. The air gets nasty thick again and I think my head might explode. A few more sword swipes happen, the thickness gets worse until every cell inside me is screaming for it to stop and then it does stop and the sense of imminent universe collapse dissipates. The world is very peaceful again. The breeze is gentle.

We're stumbling back through the dark lot. Carlos and Janey are on either side of me, helping me along. I'm still holding my guts in but I'm pretty sure I'm going to make it. Carlos says he's going back for the body and Gordo mentions something about an ambulance coming, and yes, I'm quite sure I will make it through this alive. And when I wake, I will remember the river, the one that's always been there, flowing out of my heart and through my veins, keeping me alive; keeping us all alive.

# FORGIVE ME MY TANGENTS

I love the night.

Feels like it was built for me: A canopy of stars stretched over my head, and they're vibrating so hard I can feel 'em even through all these layers of concrete. There's three floors above mine. Maritza lives one level up with the memories of her bobofied father who used to always declare his love to me. There's a young couple of indeterminate race above her, not even sure if they know, and then an empty apartment. Then comes the rooftop and then the sky, the sky, the sky and then stars. Hundreds of thousands of them, all bouncing light back and forth and spinning in their crazy long-dead so alive cycles, just like us.

My thoughts loosen like they can't in the daytime and I just sit in the middle of my living room and let them go. They bounce easily through general topics, memories, occasional hopes, fears and fantasies. Sometimes I wonder, sometimes longingly, what it must be like for those folks that lay down every night beside the same person—those who have a vessel in the form of a partner into whom they can unload all those reams and reams of raw mind material. Quickly though, my thoughts keep moving, an unceasing caravan through the night.

My computer is on. I have one of those screensavers that's

all the blinking lights of the city. It sits beside the window and outside the lights of Manhattan sparkle with all their splendor, so the silly screensaver is like a joke beside it. A chiste.

Joke is okay as far as words go. It's curt and to the point, but chiste is something else altogether. It brings the bestial ferocity of the *che* followed by the childlike *ee* and closes out with a resounding *eh*, which doesn't carry an accent but might as well—it's a power sound. So chiste is playful and ferocious power. Which is about right, I'd say. The adjective form, chistoso, takes it one step further, adding the Spanish word for bear at the end. Surely the Wise Masters of Language weren't intentional about such a homonym, but still, there it is.

Forgive me my tangents. It's been suggested by more than one of my astrologically-inclined lovers that I'm a Gemini and since I don't remember my birthday I usually just pick a day in the May-June transition and take myself out to dinner at the spot around the corner.

Anyway, they're probably right. I'm more than a century old but in my heart of hearts, I'm still that little girl skipping back and forth through the trees behind our little house on the edge of the cloud forest. Every tiny thing held its own sense of wonder, deserved a good solid stare from my wide eyes and I thought I could spend hours looking at each leaf of each tangled vine until a bird would fly by and I'd have to go chase it to see where it went. I thought at the time the world was putting on a show for me, displaying its finest shapes and colors like a proud lover showing off, but I later realized we were looking at each other. The Living Earth wanted to watch me, bask in my wide-open amazement. She put her finest on display so she could see me gasp with delight. A child's excitement is its own force of nature.

Ugh, see how I do? Here I was trying to tell you about the chistoso screensaver and you got me talking childhood memories. I can't stand myself sometimes. Especially at night.

The point is, the computer is on and all at once just like that, *pum*! A little noise erupts out of it, like a digital rock plunking into a digital lake and I swear I nearly fell out of my chair with shock. What in the name of all that is holy could that be? It is, after all, almost three o'clock in the morning and I'm used to being perfectly alone with my many thoughts.

I advance on the thing like it's a wild beast. All those ones and zeros there's no telling what it could be up to. I push the spacebar and the screen comes to life and there's a little box on it. The box says:

LAMUSICA718: *hello?*

My computer is speaking to me! Then I remember that Janey had been over a few days ago and fixed me up on some kind of social something or other. A *chat*. And this must be said chat. And it's chatting. But who LAMUSICA718 might be is a mystery.

The computer burps again and more words appear.

*1*

*2*

*3? 123...*

*Hello hello!*

*Hola!*

I watch in wonder as a little stream of letters flows by.

*bsiurghspr oiushg;s*

*sg h;hsgs*

*test 1 2 3*

*yo soy un hombre sincero*

I know that song! I sit down and tap out carefully:

*de donde crece la palma.* Then I press the RETURN key like Janey showed me. It appears on the little window beside the screen name we picked for me, SIEMPRECICI. A moment passes.

*You exist! Im sorry didn't mean 2 trouble u so late was just trying out this thing + i saw u were online*

I actually chuckle at this point, because the whole situation has simply become so absurd I don't know what else to do.

*are you Cicatriz Teresa Cortázar?*

Nobody calls me Cicatriz! It's a weird name to most people. They say, what kind of a name is *Scar* for a woman? And they have a point. I used to say the same thing until I got used to it, and realized, a scar isn't about the injury, it's about the healing. Still, I don't tell many people my real name.

*People just call me CiCi. But yes.*

A pause.

*Ok.*

I stare at the screen.

*CiCi.*

I do believe this gentleman is flirting with me. Perhaps inadvertently. If it is a gentleman at all. Could be a twelve-year-old girl for all I know. This cyber-thing will take some getting used to.

*What's your name? And how do you know mine?*

A little interrogative perhaps, but I am a lady, and I have a right to know.

*They call me Gordo.*

My eyebrows rise all the way up to the top of my head.

*My future daughter in law Janey signed me up to this thing.*

I burst out laughing and when I stop there's a profound silence left in the room and I can hear my heart beating in my ears. Janey. I met her fiancé once. Nice boy. A little serious perhaps, but he is excessively handsome and they had a certain quiet fire between them that couldn't be missed. And this is his father. Fascinating.

*Janey gave me your screen name and said i should "friend" you. I told her I didn't even know u so how could I do this thing but she said it was ok thats how things work now.*

Now I'm giggling and cringing at the same time. And I'm not entirely sure why.

*I see,* I type, just to not leave him hanging.

*she said also that you wanted to learn about music and because I am a music teacher to the little kids at the school on halsey and I still sometimes perform at small bars around the neighborhood perhaps I could tell u some thing about it?*

Lies! Janey is telling him lies about me! I know plenty about music, in fact I have studied with several masters, and I have no need to learn any more from some random fat guy online. Ridiculous.

*how interesting,* I type. *I would be curious to hear what you have to say about music, Señor Gordo.*

That's not a lie. Technically, I would be curious. Perhaps I'm flirting.

*Very good. I am glad I could be of help to you, Señora CiCi. When is a good time for us to commence?*

I smile. Janey is a devious and beautiful soul. I wonder about that swirl of potential rising inside her. She reminds me of myself when I was about twelve decades younger. I wrap the thought up and pocket it for later. There are more pressing things at hand.

I look back at Gordo's question and then, very slowly and deliberately, I type: *Late, late at night.*

# PHANTOM OVERLOAD

I'm late to a meeting with The New York Council of the Dead so I swing by my favorite Dominican spot for a ferocious coffee. It's kind of on the way, but mostly I do it to bother my icy, irritating superiors. I'll roll up twenty minutes in, smug, caffeinated and palpably disinterested. I linger even longer than I have to, partially because I'm in a good mood but mostly because the counter honey's strapless shirt keeps slipping up like a curtain from her paunchy little tummy. Every time it happens my meeting with the Council becomes less and less important.

The spot's called EL MAR. It's one of those over-decorated 24-hour joints that always has dim lights and a disco ball. Corny papier-mâché coral reefs dangle off all the walls and there's usually a lively crowd of stubby little middle age couples and taxi drivers.

"My friend Gordo's playing here Friday," I say, aiming for casual chitchat but achieving only uninvited randomness. The counter honey raises two well-threaded eyebrows and pouts her lips—which I roughly translate to mean *"Whoopdeedoo, jackass."* But it's spring outside, a warm and breezy afternoon, and my good mood has granted me temporary invincibility. Besides, I like a girl that can say a lot without even opening her mouth. "The big Cuban guy?" I offer. "I've never seen him play before but I hear it's amazing."

She softens some, leans back against the liquor cabinet and exhales. "Gordo's a friend of my tío. He alright." The shadow of a smile is fluttering around her face, threatening to show up at any moment. I try not to stare. "Brings a weirdo crowd though," she adds.

Here's the part where I'm supposed to hand her the dollar, letting the touch linger just a fleeting moment longer than it has to so my fingers can tell her fingers about all the rambunctious lovemaking I have planned for us. But my skin is inhumanly cold; my pulse a mere whisper. I am barely alive at all, a botched resurrection, trapped in perpetual ambiguity with not even so much as a flicker of what life was like before my violent death. Surely, whatever flutterings of passion trickle through my veins wouldn't make the jump from one body to the next. Plus I'd probably ick her out. I put the money on the counter and walk out the door.

* * *

The New York Council of the Dead holds court in a warehouse in the industrial wastelands of Sunset Park, Brooklyn. The outside is nondescript: Another towering, dull monstrosity clustered between the highway and the harbor. Inside, a whole restless bureaucracy of afterlife turns eternal circles like a cursed carnival ride. Mostly dead though I may be, it's here that I always remember how alive I really am. Everyone else in the place is a shroud, a shimmering, translucent version of the person they once were. The glowing shadows spin and buzz about their business in the misty air around me. After a few years of showing up here every couple weeks for a new assignment, the presence of this walking anomaly doesn't even warrant a sidewise glance.

I stroll through chilly little crowds of ghosts and into

the back offices. I'm a good half-hour late and still murkily ecstatic from the nascent spring and my non-conversation with Bonita Applebum. Unfortunately, they seem to have been waiting up for me.

Chairman Botus's hulking form rises like a burst of steam from behind his magnificent desk. He's the only one of the seven Council Chairmen that anyone's ever seen; the rest lurk in some secret lair, supposedly for security purposes. "Ah, Carlos, wonderful you're here!" Something is definitely very wrong—the Chairman is never happy to see anybody. Botus smiling means someone, somewhere is suffering. I grunt unintelligibly and sip at my lukewarm coffee. There's two other ghosts in the room: A tall, impish character that I figure for some kind of personal assistant or secretary and a very sullen looking Mexican.

"Carlos," Botus grins, "this is Silvan García, spokesman for our friends out in the Remote District 17." The Mexican squints suspiciously at me, nodding a slight acknowledgment. His carefully trimmed goatee accentuates a severe frown. "Silvan, Agent Delacruz here is our leading soul-catcher prime. An investigator of the highest spiritual order. He's done terrific work in the Hispanic communities."

I don't believe in spirit guides, but if I had one it just curled up and died. Nothing marginalizes marginalized people like a dead white guy talking sympathetically.

Plus he's managed to deflate my rare bout of perkiness. The secretary, apparently unworthy of any introduction, just stares at me.

"It seems Mr. García's community is experiencing some, er, turmoil," Botus grins hideously down at Silvan. "Is that the word you would use, Sil? Turmoil? Anyway, in short, they're in Phantom Overload and need our," another smirking pause, false searching for the right word, "assistance."

It's a tense moment. The Remote Districts are a few scattered neighbor-hoods around New York that unanimously reject any interference from the all powerful Council. Instead, they deal with their own dead however they see fit. I believe 17 is the strip of East New York surrounding the above ground train tracks on Fulton Street, but either way, for them to ask help from the COD means something's really messed up over there. Unfortunately, I haven't peeked at my terminology manual, well, ever, so I just nod my head with concern and mutter, "Phantom Overload, mmm."

The meeting wraps up quickly after that: Many nods and smiles from Botus and grimaces from Silvan García.

"The fuck is Phantom Overload?" I say once the curt spokesman has floated briskly away. Shockingly, Botus's smile hasn't evaporated along with his guest. He appears to be genuinely happy. It's a terrifying thought.

"Oh, Carlos Carlos Carlos," he mutters, letting his long cloudy form recline luxuriously behind his desk. "You're weird and of questionable allegiance, but you're the best we got and I like you."

"You're sinister and untrustworthy," I say, "and I can't stand to be around you. What's Phantom Overload?"

"It means our good friends at RD 17 can't handle their business. No surprise there of course. Seems they have a bus that makes a routine drive through the area picking up souls, collecting the dead, you know—it's all very quaint."

"Until?"

"Until the motherfucker disappears!" Botus lets out a belly laugh.

"The ghost bus disappeared?"

"Can you imagine the irony? Is there anywhere Mexicans *don't* go stuffed into buses? Man!"

I have this blade that I carry concealed inside my walking stick. It's specially designed and spiritually charged to obliterate even the toughest afterlifer. In moments like these that I have to work very hard not to use it.

"Anyway," Botus continues once he's collected himself,

"yeah, the ghost bus gone and disappeared, or ain't show-ing up for whatever reason and so yeah, of course," he rolls his eyes and makes an exaggerated shoulder shrug, "they're gonna go into Overload. Phoebus, tell him what Overload is."

The slender secretary ghost, who had become so incon-sequential that I'd actually forgotten he was there, suddenly leaps into action. "It means, sirs, that the souls are all hang-ing around and can't be carted off to the Underworld and instead congeal and cause havoc and generally make nui-sances of themselves. The situation can be exacerbated by high murder or infant mortality rates and can reach a criti-cal point in as few as 72 hours."

"Critical point?"

"Would be classified as an utterly overwhelming level of chaos derived from the overcrowding and massive spiritual collisions."

"A fucking disaster," Botus puts in. "A Mexican cluster-fuck of the highest order. Trust me. You don't wanna see it. It'd be like 9/11 for the dead, but worse. Or like that other thing that happened, the one with the levees and whatever."

"So they sent an emissary?"

"To beg for help. Cocksuckers refuse and refuse and refuse assistance from the Council for decades. *No, it'll compromise our autonomy! It'll create dependency on the COD.* Blah blah blah. You know the whine. What can you do? Wait around 'til some shit pops off they can't handle. Fine. Here we are. Took a little longer than expected, but no matter. We'll move ahead as planned."

"As planned?"

"Like I said, we all knew this was gonna happen. It was only a matter of when. So did we have a plan in place for when the inevitable occurred? Of course we did, Carlos, that's what the COD does: It prepares. That's how these things work. Stay ahead of the game and you rule the planet.

Come unprepared and the world will fuck your face and shit in your soul."

"Is that what it says on your gravestone?"

Botus chuckles mildly and I start getting antsy.

"So you want me to..."

"Set up in RD 17 and lay some preliminary groundwork for an incoming squadron of soulcatchers. It's gonna be a hazy mess in there, kid, and I'd like things to be a little ready for our boys when they show up. Minimize damages, if you know what I mean. You start tomorrow. Phoebus here will be your partner."

*My what?* I gape at Botus for a full three seconds before recovering. "My what?"

But the matter's closed. The Chairman has already immersed himself in some other paperwork and Phoebus is hovering eagerly beside me.

* * *

I'm heading back towards Bushwick, running through all the reasons why the Phoebus thing is a wack disaster. Number one on the list is Jimmy. Jimmy's a high school kid, my friend Victor's cousin. A freakish incident with a granny and some soul-eating porcelain dolls a couple months back left him able to see afterlifers. He's not half-dead like me but he's definitely another uneasy interloper between two worlds and I've taken him under my wing to thank him for making my unusual status that much less lonely.

But with winky little Phoebus tagging along, I'll have to explain why I'm bringing a live teenager around in flagrant disregard for the most basic Council protocol: Stay the fuck away from the living.

Whatever, I'll figure it out.

I find Jimmy playing checkers on a little sidestreet off Myrtle Ave. Even sitting down, the kid towers over the table and has to squint through his librarian/Nation of Islam glasses to see the board. He's playing against Gordo, a great big Cubano cat who's down with the living, the dead and probably a whole slew of saints and demons no one's even heard of yet. Says it has something to do with the music he writes. He plays a mean game of checkers too, and from the look of it he's hammering Jimmy something fierce.

"If this were a real game, like chess," Jimmy is saying when I walk up, "you'd be on the floor beggin' me for mercy."

Gordo is tapping away on a cell phone, which is a startling new addition for him. Whatever it is he's doing must be fascinating, because his eyes are wide and he's grinning like a school kid. When Jimmy prods him, Gordo looks up and triple jumps across the board.

"How is it," I say, pulling up a chair, "that you can be such a freaking wizard at a game as complex as chess and get your ass handed to you in a glorified Connect-4?"

"Who asked you?"

I gank one of Gordo's Malagueñas and light it up. "I need you both tomorrow." Gordo raises an eyebrow but keeps his concentration on the board.

"What you got?" Jimmy asks.

I explain more-or-less the situation, minus the part where I had to ask what Phantom Overload is.

Gordo's looking interested when I finish. "This ghost bus—she just disappeared? She estopped coming completely?"

"Apparently. Maybe it's on strike. The little irate Mexican Silvan said he'd try to arrange a meeting for us tomorrow with the ghost bus driver but it wasn't a guarantee."

"Silvan García?" Gordo says. "He's Ecuadorian."

Figures my oversized living friend would know more about my assignment than I do. "Either way," I say, "he's already given me the dirty eye 'cause Botus did his poor Hispanic communities routine and now I look like Malinche again."

Gordo lets out a long sigh. "One day, Carlos, I am going to kill your boss." It's not an idle threat but he'll probably have to wait in line.

"Who's Malinche?" Jimmy asks.

"The chick that helped a couple white guys on horses take down the whole Aztec empire," I say. Jimmy looks crestfallen. "Or got kidnapped and forced into being a historical scapegoat, more than likely."

Gordo looks very sad all the sudden. "It is always easier to blame one of our own."

"Oh and there's more," I say. "They stuck me with a partner. Some doofy little guy named Phoebe or something."

"Phoebe's a girl's name," Jimmy informs me.

"Either way, I want you to tag along. Should be an interesting mess. We'll work it out with the partner. Gordo, can you mingle around Fulton while we meet with Silvan, see what you can find out?"

Gordo nods and then jumps Jimmy's last two checkers.

"Fuckassshit."

Gordo just chuckles: "Should've stuck with basketball."

\* \* \*

"Who's that?" Phoebus wants to know when I show up to meet him with Jimmy in tow. It's the beginning of a beautiful breezy autumn night. The whole world seems to be milling pleasantly about under the Fulton Street train tracks. It's gametime and gossip hour outside the bakeries, dollar stores and beauty salons of East New York. I'm in another weirdly chipper mood but I don't let it show; instead I get up in Phoebus's face.

"Listen, partner," I say real slow and menacing, "I'm glad you have the protocol book memorized and got good grades in the academy, but now you're in the streets and it's a different game." Okay, I got the speech from a cop flick I was watching the night before, but it translates pretty well. "Now we gonna play by my rules. Got it?"

"Got it," Phoebus mumbles. "But who's that?"

"That's Jimmy," I say. "He's my trainee. And he's coming with us."

"Nice to meet you," Jimmy says, smiling down at Phoebus.

"He can see me?" The new guy is scandalized.

I'm about to spit out some other slick line I had memorized when I notice it: With the coming dusk, the ghosts have floated gradually out into the streets and there's hundreds and hundreds of them. More ghosts than people. Phantom Overload. What's more, they're bustling about and interacting with the living like it's just the way things are supposed to be. I'm rendered speechless for a few seconds. It's disturbing but strangely beautiful too. My first instinct is to leave Phoebus and Jimmy behind and go for a jaunty stroll down a street where for once, the two disparate halves of me happily cohabitate.

"This is all highly irregular," Phoebus sputters. I can tell from Jimmy's awed face he's as entranced as I am. But there's business to be taken care of. Several battalions of soulcatchers are gearing themselves up and will soon be on the way to wreak havoc on this quiet intermingling. And we still have no idea what's going on.

"Phoebe," I say.

"Phoebus."

"Phoebus, keep an eye on things over here. I'm going to meet Silvan and the bus driver at the abandoned lot."

"We're not—uh—we're not supposed to split up."

"And yet: Off I go."

"Oh."

I almost feel bad, but then I remember that Phoebus is just a feeble extension of Botus. Sympathy dissolves into disdain. Much better. Jimmy and I walk off towards the lot.

* * *

"Turns out you're not Mexican," I tell Silvan when we reach the top of the trash-strewn hill where he's waiting for us. "You're Ecuadorian."

"I know," says Silvan. "But you fucking Dominicans can't tell the difference."

"I'm fucking Puerto Rican."

"I know that too."

So a little Latin-to-Latin humor is not the way to start things out. Live and learn. The busdriver and Jimmy are looking uncomfortably back and forth between me and Silvan.

"Um—con permiso," The busdriver ventures timidly. He's a tall, round ghost with big bulgy eyes and three days of stubble. His beat up old van idles a few feet away. "You think we could get down to business? I can't stay long."

"I'll be brief," I say. "I don't know what the problem is, sir—"

"Esteban Morales, from Michoacán." The bus driver's wide eyes dance across the abandoned lot like shivering searchlights.

"Señor Morales, The New York Council of the Dead has been anxious for any excuse to kick some Remote District ass. Now, I for one, don't want that to happen, and I don't think Mr. Silvan here does either, ornery bastard though he might be, but believe me when I tell you they are on their way and it won't be pretty. So, Esteban, please, tell us what it will take to get you to start collecting the dead again."

"No," Esteban says. "No se puede."

"What do you mean, no se puede?"

"It means it can't be done," Silvan says.

"I know that," I growl. "I mean why not?"

"It's that the dead won't let me take them because they

aren't from my jurisdiction. They're not from here. They're our people but they're from faraway."

Immigrant dead? That in its own right isn't so unusual—when you die and get carted off you can turn up any damn place or nowhere at all. Thing is, it's really not up to you and folks certainly don't go moving from place to place in packs. You're basically stay in whatever city or township you pop up in. At least, in the States that how it works...

"It seems," Silvan says, "that several communities around Latin America have figured out how to travel in the afterlife."

"And they've come to be with their families?" Jimmy blurts out. "That's sweet!"

"It is sweet," Silvan nods, "but unfortunately it is also an untenable situation. Resources are running dry. Over-crowding has become the constant state. We are quickly approaching critical point."

All this terminology is getting on my nerves. I'm about to say something slick about it when I notice a rustling motion at the foot of our trashy hill. A crowd of ghosts is waiting down there, glaring icily towards us. Their wraith clouds wave gently like drying laundry in the evening breeze. They look pissed.

"We're not leaving," a tall gangly ghost calls out from the crowd. "Never leaving. Not by force and not by choice. And not in the damn bus."

Esteban takes his cue and makes himself scarce. The ghost bus leaves a puff of exhaust behind as it sputters off into the night. Jimmy is suddenly very anxious. I can feel his jitters sparkling around him like eager fireflies. The crowd of ghosts hovers up the hill.

I take a step towards them. "Look, I'm from the Council but I hear where you're coming from. I don't want this to get messy."

"Then get out of here, güey, and take your Council goons. We've come this far to be with our families. We're not going nowhere." A general hoorah goes up. As the ghost mob starts to clutter closer around us I notice most of them are carrying chains and clubs.

"The Council goons are coming regardless of what I tell them to do," I say. As if to prove my point, the mournful battle howl of the approaching soulcatchers rings out in the night air. It's not a comforting sound. "They wanted an excuse to get in this place and you've all given them one. I know you want to be with your people, but all you're doing is putting the ones you love in danger."

"You really believe that mierda, compadre?" the tall gangly one demands. He steps a few feet out of the crowd. He has a scraggily black beard and eyes that keep rolling in different directions. An epic adventure is scrawled in tatts over his translucent skin. Jimmy takes a step behind me, but surely his skinny-ass moose head is poking out well above mine.

"We are happy here!" gangly says, to more uproarious applause.

"Tell 'em, Moco! ¡Dile la verdad!" someone yells. "¡Sí se puede!"

"No," I say. "No se puede. Something must not've been working out because..." I have to stop mid-sentence. My mind is suddenly too busy working things out to bother making my mouth move. "Silvan!" I say quietly. "Jimmy, where's Silvan?"

"Dunno, Carlos."

I whirl around but the slippery instigator has vanished. And here I was thinking I was the Malinche.

"Your representative is the one you need to talk to, people," I announce. "García went to the Council begging for help. Probably received a pretty payoff from it too. The wheels are in motion now though, there's no stopping it. You have to clear out."

"We'll crush the Council!" Moco yells, his eyes boggling wildly. Another hoorah goes up.

It's getting to be time to leave. I back up a few steps to position myself behind a rusted-out refrigerator. At the edge of the field I see my new partner Phoebus at the head of a group of armored soulcatchers. He looks different, Phoebus. His whole demeanor has changed—he's floating upright instead of in the usual cowering posture. Also, he's yelling out orders. But I don't even get a chance to think it all through because then Moco spots the soldiers.

"¡Compadres!" he hollers. "Let's kill the insolent pigfuckers!" Doesn't take much poetry to rile up a bloodthirsty crowd. The angry ghosts rush towards the edge of the lot, chains and clubs swinging wildly above their heads. At a command from the newly non-doofy Phoebus, the soulcatchers jump into a defensive position: A solid wall of impenetrable supernatural armor. It looks fierce, but some of those boys are pissing themselves with fear. The mob moves as one—they surge suddenly up into the air above the lot and come crashing down on the heads of the waiting soulcatchers like a damn tsunami wave.

You can see right off the bat it's not going well for the COD boys. Armed with the superior numbers, the fury of the righteous and those nasty clubs and chains, the mob is laying a solid beating on the dozen or so soulcatchers. Three fellows in straw hats have cornered a soldier and are laying into him with their clubs—I hear him screaming in agony as the blows pierce through his armor and shred his translucent cloud. Moco storms through the melee, his chain whipping in a vicious circle above his head. The thrill of victory is in his stride, a casual overconfidence that I know well.

"What you wanna do?" Jimmy says behind me.

"This whole damn situation is starting to feel like one big setup, kid."

"Silvan?"

"Definitely in on it, somehow. I don't like it. Feel like a damn pawn and I'm not even sure whose."

"Can we go?"

I realize Jimmy's trembling. It wasn't so long ago he was having his living soul torn out by those American Girl dolls, so I can see where he'd be a little hesitant about the vicious battle raging a few feet away. "You go head, kid. I have to see this one through."

"'salright," he says, fixing his mouth into a determined frown. "You stay I stay." Not bad. "You got a plan?"

"Nope. Gotta see what happens next."

\* \* \*

The fighting has scattered out into the streets now and it sends a vicious whirlwind of combat swirling beneath the tracks. The few living folks walking by recognize something wrong and take cover in shops and behind cars. Seems the soulcatchers have rallied some: They've slashed a few mob members into tattered ghost shards that lie motionless on the pavement. Suddenly Phoebus rears up above the fighting. I'm still stunned by his transformation from dweeb to superghost. "If you won't heed the Council," he calls out over the din of battle, "perhaps you haven't fully understood what is at risk to you and your loved ones." Jeering and shouts from the crowd as a few objects fly up towards him. Undeterred, my deceptive partner nods at four of his men and they immediately detach from their adversaries and bee-line it into one of the storefront churches.

"Stop them!" Moco hollers. But the soulcatchers have already returned out onto the street, each wrapped around a living, breathing, screaming person. The fighting, the yelling, the sound of weapons tearing into dead flesh: Everything stops. The angry mob is suddenly very quiet as they turn and stare at the hos-tages—two middle aged women, a guy in his twenties and a fourteen year old girl...

"That's my granddaughter!" an aging guajiro ghost yells, throwing down his club and stepping forward.

"And my nephew, Alex!" calls out another.

"¡Mi hija!" screams a middle-aged ghost as she rushes forward.

"I thought the COD wasn't supposed to fuck with the living!" Jimmy whispers.

"They're—we're not." I realize now I'm trembling. For all the chaos, everything's still feeling like it's playing out according to some heinous plan. "Someone high up must've given them the authority to..." Nothing is what it seems. I already knew that but apparenly I have to learn again and again. I'm getting ready to hole up for an extended hostage negotiation when the four soulcatchers wrap their arms around their hostages' faces like cellophane. I think the crowd is just too stunned to react in time: After a few seconds of squirming each living human goes limp and then sprawls out lifelessly on the pavement.

The crowd surges forward en masse, toppling the four soul-catchers and instantly tearing two of them to shreds. I hear Jimmy throwing up behind me. In the chaos of it all though, I notice the remaining COD soldiers jump into motion and sprint away from the fray. "Now that you see what we will do to your beloved families," Phoebus yells at the crowd, "maybe you'll rethink sticking around. We're pulling back, but not for long. Regroup yourselves and come to your senses, rebels!" The soulcatchers pour out of the shops and salons, each wrapped around a struggling human, and fall back towards the abandoned lot that Jimmy and I are hiding in.

"Get out of here, now!" I whispershout at Jimmy, who's trying to spit the last bits of vomit out of his mouth. He stands but just stares past me, eyes wide. "Go!" I say. "Not the time to be all heroic, kid, just get out!" He's still not moving, just staring. Finally, I turn around to see what he's looking at.

"They've got Gordo," he says. And it's true.

* * *

The Council soulcatchers are all in a tizzy as they retreat up the hill towards us. They're young, barely older than Jimmy, and by the look of their crisp, unstained uniforms and shiny helmets, brand new recruits. A few of them are injured, limbs hanging useless at their sides. Whatever plan is in place, these kids were clearly kept far out of the loop. Gordo walks calmly along with his fatigued captor. He's trying to appear unimpressed but is probably terrified. Or maybe I'm projecting.

I grab Jimmy roughly around the neck and throw him on the ground as they walk up. A couple of the boys I've seen before come running up to me. "Where you been, Carlos?" a kid named Dennis asks.

"Yes, Agent Delacruz," Phoebus says, eyeing Jimmy. "Where have you been?"

"Infiltrated the rebel mob," I say. "And I took a hostage of my own while I was at it."

"We're not really gonna kill these ones too, are we?" Dennis says. You can hear a quiver of fear in his voice. A few of the hostages are sobbing.

"We can't!" another one yells. "The mob'll tear us to pieces! This is crazy!"

"Everyone shut up," Phoebus snaps. "You're soldiers, soulcatchers. You will not show fear. You will not retreat or give up, ever. Understand?"

"But you knew they would rush in on our guys when you had them kill those hostages, didn't you?" Dennis demands. "You did that on purpose."

"It's not for you to question my decisions," Phoebus says. He's seething with restrained rage. "Now, everyone fall into line and shut up." There's a few murmurs of frustration and the soldiers fall into a tense kind of quiet. Shouldn't take much to rile 'em back up though.

"I heard the mob is planning an ambush," I say. "There was a few lurking around here I had to deal with before you guys showed up, but a couple got away. They're probably crawling all over this place by now."

"Oh shit oh shit oh shit," one of the soulcatchers starts chanting.

"What's the matter, Tyler?"

"I thought I saw something move over there by that old car!"

"Where?"

"By the car, asshole, by the fucking car!"

"Wait!" I yell pointing at some random spot in the dark lot. "What's that over there?" Everyone turns and gapes into the emptiness.

"This is fucked up," someone says.

"Calm down!" Phoebus yells. "Everyone calm the fuck down!" I suppress a chuckle.

"Listen," I say. "I have orders from Botus. Everyone is to remain here with the prisoners. Phoebus and I are gonna go politick with the rebels and see what we can work out to end this mess peacefully." A general murmur of approval rises from the soldiers.

"Now now," Phoebus stutters, "let's not be rash. Let the fools have a moment to discuss..."

"Every moment more we give them is a moment they have to plan another attack," I say. "Rebels love ambushes."

"He's right!" Tyler declares. "Go now!"

"It's true," says Dennis. "Wrap this shit up quick."

I start walking down the hill. "You coming?" I can feel Phoebus's furious glare on the back of my head as I hobble down the hill on my cane. He growls and then floats after me, frowning.

"How quickly your young friend went from student to hostage," Phoebus muses when we round a corner onto a quiet residential block. By way of an answer I pull the blade out of my cane and swipe at him. He hurls himself away just a split second too late and I hack a sliver of cold cloud off him. Before I can swing again, he's on me, icy hands wrapped around my neck, cool breath on my face. I push forward against him, throwing us into a brick wall. Phoebus loosens his grip just long enough for me to shove him off and stumble backwards a few steps. I raise my blade. "Alright, Phoebus—or should I say Chairman Phoebus?"

He pulls his own blade out and grunts with irritation.

"You can act, I'll give you that," I say. "Definitely had me convinced you were just a sniveling little new guy. But why bother? You could've just waltzed in as is and torn shit up."

"But you see, we don't trust you, Carlos." His voice seethes with hatred. "We wanted to see what you'd do. Keep an eye on you. For the plan to proceed, it had to be kept completely secret."

"Even from the youngins you got doing the dirty work."

He lunges forward, blade first, and I parry off the attack and sidestep out of the way. The Chairman is panting heavily now.

"What I want to know," he says, "is are you just a renegade dickhead or are you working for someone?"

"Too many questions," I say, making like I'm going to swipe at him again. When he goes to block I stab forward instead, catching him right in the core of his long silvery body. Chairman Phoebus howls and stumbles, forcing the blade deeper into himself and pinning us both back against the brick wall. Higher ups are usually crap at one-on-one combat.

"You can't...kill me," he gasps and for a second I'm afraid he might mean that literally. Did the bastard figure out some slick supernatural way not to die again? But then he finishes his thought: "...I'm a Chairman..."

"Guess now there's only six," I say, pulling out my blade. He's oozing out all over, his flickering corpse now a dead weight draped over me. Don't know if I'll ever be able to shower enough to get that feeling away. I heave him off me as his whole body sheds itself into a mess of tattered ghost flesh.

The angry mob has transformed itself into a confused support group when I find them huddled in a storefront church. A few of the ghosts are sobbing inconsolably while others pat them on their heaving backs. Moco is walking in anxious circles, trying to rile folks up again.

"Listen up," I say, walking into the dusty church, "we can end this now. It's only gonna get worse if we don't." I send Moco a piercing stare, which isn't easy the way his damn eyes keep boggling, but he seems to take my point and stays quiet. "I can tell you that any battle that comes after this won't go well for you, and it'll go even worse for your loved ones. It's not a threat—I didn't know it was going to go down like that tonight, and I'm sorry it did." Ghosts are looking up at me with sorrow and fear in their eyes. "I know you just came here to be with your families, to carry on in an afterlife that's harmonious with the living. And believe me," I had been in let's-clean-this-mess-up mode but I'm suddenly choking over my words, "I want as much as any of you to see that happen, here in New York." They believe me. Even I believe me. I guess it's 'cause it's true, but still— I'm startled. "But it's not time yet. There's more work to be done. Foundations to be laid. I dealt with the dickhead that ordered your living relatives to be murdered." A cautious hurrah rises from the mourning ghosts, startling me again. "But I'm going to have to say that you did it so I can keep working things from the inside." That seems to be alright with everyone.

"You can't stay here in RD 17 though, you have to scatter." More nods and whispers. "Moco and I are going to go back to the Council soulcatchers and work out the arrangements."

\* \* \*

"What do you mean they killed Phoebus?" Botus is livid, which means somewhere an angel is getting head. "I don't understand. Which one of them? We have to exact revenge!"

"Well, that won't actually be so easy. He was kind of torn up in the mob, it wasn't like one or the other. And they're all gone now anyway. Scattered."

"What do you mean they're all gone?"

"Isn't that what we wanted?" I'm trying so hard not to smile that it actually hurts. "Phantom Overload no more. Situation remedied. Voilà. A few of them lit out for Mexico I think. Shame about Phoebe though."

"I don't understand," Botus says again.

I light a Malagueña and exhale thick plumes of smoke into his office. "My full report's on your desk, sir. Just had one more question."

Botus barely looks up. "Eh?"

"Where might I find Silvan García?"

\* \* \*

It's another beautiful afternoon. My mark is hovering in a quiet reverie on the walking path that winds alongside the Belt Parkway, not far from the Verazzano Bridge to Staten Island. Perhaps he's contemplating the sun sparkling on the water or the way the lapping of waves contrasts with the rushing traffic. Either way, he's about to get sliced.

I come up quietly, trying but failing, always failing, not to look too sketchy. Standing by a tree on this unusually warm late-autumn day with my long trench coat and walking stick. There's something definitely off about that guy, the joggers are thinking, where's his spandex and toothy grin? Why no headband or fanny pack?

I'm just biding my time, waiting for a break in the constant stream of exercise dorks so I can make my move. When it comes I take one step forward before a thick, warm hand wraps around my arm. It's Gordo, looking cheery as always but a little worse the wear after his harrowing hostage experience. I already apologized too many times to him for that and he's already swatted away each one jauntily, so I just nod at him. "What are you doing here, papa?"

"I am estopping you."

"What you mean?"

"Not this one. This one is not for you."

"Gordo, if it wasn't for this asshole..."

"Yo sé lo que hizo. And it doesn't matter." His hand is extremely strong and me tussling with a fat old guy would not be a good look right now. "It's not right and you know it's not right."

I'm about to argue with him when I realize he has a point. Ending García gets us nowhere and risks blowing my cover. It was Botus, after all, that told me where to find him. The trail would lead right back to me. All I'm left with is 'but I want to' and that's obviously not going to get me anywhere. "It is always easier," Gordo says, "to blame one of our own."

I shrug my acceptance and Gordo cautiously releases his hold on my arm. We turn together, away from the water, away from Silvan and my useless vengeance schemes, and begin walking back into Brooklyn. "You are coming tonight?" Gordo wants to know.

"Wouldn't miss it."

\* \* \*

Six mojitos deep, I stumble towards the counter honey. Around me, the living and the dead are bopping up and down together to the sacred and sexy rhythms coming from Gordo's motley crew of musicians. Even a few of the soul-catchers showed up, including Dennis and Tyler, which I found kinda touching once I was drunk enough not to be eeked out by it. Moco is dancing up a storm towards the front, apparently in a world all to himself. The music is pounding and relentlessly beautiful. It strips us, if only for this night, of all inhibitions and traumas.

The counter honey's making eyes at me. I think. She's smiling even. Maybe at me. I'm not so sloppy yet, just have a little extra swing to me. I've been watching her and she's not fazed by the ghosts. The bar must be its own little Remote District—outside the Council's grasp, free of the fears and taboos of the living.

"What's your name?" I say, careful not to slur.

"Melissa." It's a little plain for how pretty she is, but I don't mind.

"It's a little plain for how pretty you are." Oops. She looks me dead in the eye and then laughs.

"You don't like to touch people?" she says, still burrowing her gaze right through me. "We're Latin, man. We touch. Get with it."

"I know, I know," I say, putting a hand to my face. "It's that, I'm...I'm like them." I nod at the ceiling, where a few adolescent ghosts are grinding their crotches into each other in anxious imitation of adulthood.

"What, a horny teenager?"

"No!" Ah, she's laughing again. She also touches her hair, which my best friend Riley once told me means she wants me to eat her ass. I manage to keep that insight to myself though. "No, I'm partially slightly dead. I died. But I came back."

"Ah." She nods knowledgably, like customers tell her that all the time. "That's cool."

It is? I mean, I knew it was, to me anyway, and to my dead friends, and to Jimmy, who's gawking at me rudely from a few barstools away, and of course...the others like me. But I never thought it was alright to someone like Melissa. "I don't know who I was before I died. Or how old I am." It's been a year since I've felt the tender touch of a lover. A year since Sasha walked away and almost nine months since she came back and I walked away, vowing to forget, forget, forever forget. Closed my heart up like a house after a hurricane, nailed planks over the windows, spray-painted warnings on the door. Perhaps it's time I let some sunlight seep back in.

I put my hand on the bar and squint up at nothing in particular, trying to look thoughtful.

Melissa reaches over, in this room full of stunning music and the pulsating, celebrating bodies of the living and the dead, and puts her hand on mine.

# ABOUT THE AUTHOR

Daniel José Older is the New York Times bestselling author of Salsa Nocturna, the Bone Street Rumba urban fantasy series from Penguin's Roc Books and the Young Adult novel *Shadowshaper* (Scholastic, 2015), a New York Times Notable Book of 2015, which won the International Latino Book Award and was shortlisted for the Kirkus Prize in Young Readers' Literature, the Andre Norton Award, the Locus, the Mythopoeic Award, and named one of Esquire's 80 Books Every Person Should Read. He co-edited the Locus and World Fantasy nominated anthology *Long Hidden: Speculative Fiction from the Margins of History*. His short stories and essays have appeared in the Guardian, NPR, *Tor.com*, *Salon*, *BuzzFeed*, and the anthologies *The Fire This Time and Mothership: Tales Of Afrofuturism And Beyond*, among others. Daniel has guest edited at *Fireside Fiction*, *Catapult*, *Crossed Genres*, and *Fantasy Magazine*, and served as a judge for the Scholastic Art and Writing Awards, the Burt Award for Young Adult Caribbean Literature, and the PEN Center USA Literary Award. He holds a Master of Fine Arts from Antioch University and has taught at Voices at VONA, Mile High MFA Program, Vermont College of Fine Arts Writing For Children and Young Adults MFA Program, Boricua College, St John's University, and Rikers

Island among other sites. You can find his thoughts on writing, read dispatches from his decade-long career as an NYC paramedic and hear his music at http://danieljoseolder.net, on youtube and @djolder on twitter.